The Case of Mr. Wonderful

A Richard Sherlock Whodunit

By
Jim Stevens

Creative Inc. Publishing

The final approval of this literary material is granted by the author.

First Printing

All the characters appearing in this work are fictitious. Any resemblance to real persons, living or dead, is purely coincidental.

ISBN: 978-1-942424-00-0

This book is dedicated to

Otis Criblecoblis

The Richard Sherlock Whodunit Series

The Case of the Not-So-Fair Trader (Book 1)

The Case of Moomah's Moolah (Book 2)

The Case of Tiffany's Epiphany (Book 3)

The Case of Mr. Wonderful (Book 4)

The Case of the Woebegone Widow (Book 5)

The Case of the Missing Milk Money (Book 6)

The Case of the Dearly Departed (Book 7)

The Case of the Comatose CEO (Book 8)

Also by Jim Stevens:

WHUPPED

WHUPPED TOO

Hell No, We Won't Go,

A Novel of Peace, Love, War, and Football

CHAPTER 1

"Kill or be killed." He pauses. "It's that simple."

This guy is serious.

"Look around you. To your left, to your right, forward and back, these are your enemies. They want what you want. They want what you have. They want to see you destroyed.

"Strike first. Strike fast. Destroy them before they destroy you. You are at war, and the war never ends. A new battle is waged each day. You must stay mean. Stay hungry. Stay in the fight until you achieve your ultimate victory."

He takes a breather, walking back and forth, staring into the eyes of the assembled—not merely looking at them, but looking through them. I certainly hope he doesn't get to me.

"You may already be, or are about to become, commissioned officers in the art of war. You must learn to study the landscape, consider the construction, and be creative in the design of your particular battle plan, which will lead you to success. You must see what others do not see. You must find positives where others see faults. You must do more than your competitors.

"Fellow warriors, be cunning in your plan of attack. Be clear and forthright in leading your troops, the people behind you, to carry out the orders you have given. You are the general, so act like the general."

He stops in front of this little guy in the front row. The guy's name badge might as well read: Caspar Milquetoast.

"You!"

"Yes, sir!"

"Are you strong?"

"Yes, sir."

"Are you capable?"

"Yes, sir."

"Are you going to rise above the mediocre competition, flex your muscles, and reveal you are a force to be reckoned with, and no one will stand in the way of you achieving your goal?"

"Yes, sir!"

People stand stock still, at attention, hanging on every word. And I'm one of them. This guy is amazing.

He moves on and stops right in front of me. We're nose to nose. Every eye in the room is upon us.

"You!"

"Yes, sir," I answer.

"I can't hear you."

"Yes, sir," I scream.

"Are you willing to do what it takes?"

"Yes, sir."

"Are you willing to go the extra mile?"

"Yes, sir."

"What is your name?" he asks.

"Richard Sherlock."

"Are you, Richard Sherlock, willing to sell your soul to the devil if he is willing to pay your price?"

"Yes, sir."

"And it is not just about winning and losing, is it Mr. Sherlock?"

"No, sir."

"It is about mentally breaking your adversary, so that the next time you come up against him in battle, in a bidding war, or negotiating a settlement, your opponent will be so overwhelmed by your force of absolute power, he will wither and crumble beneath you."

"Yes, sir."

"I have one last question for you, Mr. Richard Sherlock."

There is not a sound in the room. No one moves. Not one twitch, sneeze or sniffle. There is nothing in the world that can disrupt this man's total mastery over the people before him.

Except...

"Oh, Mr. Sherlock."

The words ring out like the final buzzer at a basketball game. These three words are the bane of my existence, the shackles to my soul, and the albatross around my neck.

Our guru is stunned into silence.

I turn to see my protégée coming down the aisle. "Tiffany, not now," I plead to no avail.

Tiffany comes right between the two of us. "Oh, Mr. Sherlock. You got to come right away! Daddy's got a big case for us to investigate."

"Who are you?" the leader of our session bellows out like the Man Behind the Curtain.

"Tiffany Richmond, detective in training. Who are you?"

"Charles B. Closer, the king of the real estate seminar. I am to real estate what Patton was to the infantry, Attila to the Huns, and Buddha to the Buddhists."

"Well, no offense, Mister, but I don't know them, I don't know you, and we got to go," Tiffany tells him. "It was nice meeting you."

"Tiffany, please, can't it wait?"

"No. When Daddy says 'jump' Mr. Sherlock, you got to say 'which way?' You know the drill."

Unfortunately, she's right. I have no choice.

Tiffany waves to all in the auditorium and says, "Ta-ta," as she pulls me up the aisle like a second grader on his way to the principal's office.

***

My name is Richard Sherlock. I spent nineteen years in the Chicago Police Department, sixteen as a detective. I got kicked off the force due to a very uncharacteristic temper tantrum. I took a swing at my superior's face and made a solid connection. I lost my position and my pension, and couldn't find another job. I ended up as an on-call investigator for the Richmond Insurance Company, where I'm forced to investigate settlement frauds, suspected frauds, or any settlements that can be proven fraudulent.

I hate my job.

I'm also a divorced dad of two girls, twelve and fourteen. I have a bad back, no savings, and an ex-wife who hates me. I live in a crummy, one-bedroom apartment. I'm a lousy dresser, can't find a steady girlfriend, and I drive a 1992 Toyota Tercel. Could life get any more pathetic? Yes, my new career in real estate has hardly gotten off on the right foot.

A major portion of my job with the insurance agency is mentoring (aka babysitting) the twenty-something, spoiled heiress of the Richmond fortune, Tiffany Richmond. On the surface Tiffany is a vapid, spoiled-rotten, rich, self-centered, egotistical girl who will never experience an "I can't afford it" moment in her life. Deep down, Tiffany is a vapid, spoiled-rotten, rich, self-centered, egotistical girl with a good heart. I've found in life if you have one of those, all other frailties diminish. Plus, my kids think the world of her. I suspect they like her more than they like me. I really can't blame them.

***

"What are you doing here, Mr. Sherlock?" Tiffany asks on the way to her car.

"I'm learning how to sell real estate."

"King Kong Closer looked like a real weirdo to me."

"He's famous for instilling salesmanship and confidence in new real estate salespeople."

"It sounded like he was giving a pep talk before a game of Mortal Kombat."

"Tiffany, I'm getting into a business where I can make some real money."

"Oh, Mr. Sherlock..."

"I took the real estate exam last week, and once I get my license I'm off to the races."

"Mr. Sherlock, we don't have time for the turf club right now," Tiffany tells me. "One of Daddy's biggest clients has put in a claim for six million dollars. And you know how Daddy hates that."

Oh, jeesh.

"Daddy says the guy got swindled, and we have to find the swindler doing the swindling."

"Do I have to?"

"Of course you do. It'll be fun."

Tiffany's new Lexus 450 is parked at a meter blinking *Expired*, but there's no ticket on her windshield. As we approach the car, I see a blue, plastic hanger with a white wheelchair symbol, hooked onto her rear-view mirror.

"When did you become crippled, Tiffany?"

"I'm not crippled; I'm perfect."

"Then why do you have a handicap sticker?"

We climb in the car. She's driving.

"Daddy got tired of paying my parking tickets, so he got me one of these."

"That's not fair, Tiffany."

"What's not fair is they don't work if you park in somebody's driveway," Tiffany says. "You would think the parking gods would have the common sense to allow people who can't walk to park in a driveway."

"But you're not crippled."

"That's not the point, Mr. Sherlock."

Why do I bother?

Tiffany fires the Lexus up and zips into traffic like a cop heading out to catch a speeder.

"Where are we going?" I ask.

"To see the victim. You always told me 'the longest journey starts with the first source.'"

"I never said that."

"Well, you said something like it."

Ten minutes later, Tiffany parks in a handicapped space in the basement parking lot of the Willis Tower in the South Loop. The Willis Tower was once the Sears Tower when Sears was known as the "World's Biggest Store," but Sears got their retailing butt kicked by K-Mart—who later got their retail butt kicked by Walmart—and had to move to the suburbs. The building became the Willis Tower. Willis is an insurance company based in London. The Sears/Willis Tower was billed for years as "The World's Tallest Building," but has fallen to a lousy tenth in the category, just like Sears has fallen in the retail rankings. Talk about similar falls from grace, nobody ever brags about being the "Tenth Tallest Building in the World" or the "Tenth Biggest Store."

We take the elevator up 104 of the 108 stories and step out into the offices of the SSS Financial Corporation. I can almost taste the money when my feet hit the plush carpeting. The place exudes wealth. Original oils on the walls, sculptures on the glass tables, and furniture so perfect I'm afraid to sit down.

"You like this, Tiffany?"

"Not too shabby," Tiffany remarks at the lobby area, "but if it were me, I'd feng my shui a little more."

As we approach the mahogany reception desk, I ask, "Who are we here to see?"

"Sterling S. Sheckle, who else?" Tiffany says.

I suddenly feel like a swine in a sea of pearls.

Sterling S. Sheckle is one of the richest men in the universe. He owns hundreds of companies, millions of acres of land, and enough buildings to populate his own metropolis. His yearly gross is greater than the GNP of Finland. In the 1990s, he cornered the copper market and made billions. In 2006, everyone thought he was crazy when he cashed out of his real estate holdings, but the same experts changed their minds when the crash hit in 2007. A year later, Sterling bought the properties back at reduced prices and has made mucho more millions during the current real estate revival. I hope I can do the same, although on a much smaller scale. I'll be thrilled if I can make enough real estate commissions to get out of my crummy apartment.

Sterling, the businessman, is somewhat of a man of mystery. He's not a Howard Hughes recluse, but he keeps his business life to himself.

He never gives interviews, has only a handful of friends, and seldom has his picture taken. You never hear the Sheckle name when his company is making a play for another company who might not want to be played. Sterling S. Sheckle is recognized as one of the biggest wheels when it comes to wheeling and dealing. He keeps his family under a veil of security, probably for their own safety. He lives in a two-story penthouse atop a forty-story building on "The Block" portion of Lake Shore Drive. He doesn't drive his own car; he has people for that. His employees must sign a stack of release forms before joining his firm, everything from non-compete to "I'll never tell." I wouldn't be surprised if they are asked to sign the forms with their own blood.

The public Sterling Sheckle is a much different persona. Sterling is known to bequeath portions of his fortune to some very lucky charities. A chunk of his charitable change goes to big established charities, but nobody cares about these because lots of rich people give to these charities. What gets the play, and makes Sheckle different, is his unique manner of dropping cash into the hands of the needy nonprofits, new research labs, and the latest potential medical breakthroughs. Without any warning or prior contact, a number of individuals, do-gooder groups, and charitable organizations have gone to their mailboxes to find an envelope with a sizable check inside. Boom, there it is—money from heaven, theirs to keep with few, if any, strings attached.

It is little wonder why Sterling S. Sheckle is better known around Chicagoland as Mr. Wonderful.

His charity, known as the SSS Fund, has no address, phone number, email, or perch for a carrier pigeon to land. He probably does this to keep every Tom, Dick, and Harry from hounding him relentlessly for a hundred grand of his mad money. It is rumored that he has given away millions upon millions of dollars to needy charities near and far. Maybe, when I'm in his office, it would be a good time to ask if the Richard Sherlock Charity for the Eradication of Richard Sherlock's Credit Card Debt can be added to his giveaway list.

Tiffany introduces us to the receptionist, and we're told to take a seat.

"Alpaca," Tiffany says.

"Al, who?"

"Alpaca, Mr. Sherlock," Tiffany says. "You're sitting on alpaca."

I thought I was on a couch. "How do you know its alpaca, Tiffany?"

"I've been blessed with sensors all over my body that can detect fine fabric."

"Lucky you."

"You'd be surprised how often it comes in handy."

"Yes, I would be."

A gorgeous woman, impeccably dressed, comes down the hall and greets us. "Miss Richmond, Mr. Sherlock?"

We stand. Tiffany moves to the woman, ogles her like a fashion critic, and asks, "Vera Wang?"

"Yes," the woman answers proudly.

"May I?" Tiffany asks, and before waiting for her answer, gently squeezes the sleeve material on the woman's dress. "Thai silk from Bangkok."

The woman nods, as if to say, "Correct."

"That's what I would have said, too," I say in mock modesty.

The woman smiles; she has perfect teeth.

We are escorted through hallways of offices and cubicles to the far corner of the floor. It's about a two-block walk. Another woman, as gorgeous and as well dressed as the first, meets us. Tiffany doesn't press test her outfit.

"One minute, please," she says, removing the phone headset she's wearing.

We wait patiently.

The woman rises, opens one of two massive double doors, steps inside, closes the door behind her, and comes right back out. "He'll see you now."

This should be interesting.

The door opens. Tiffany goes first. I follow. The door behind us closes automatically. I look up, and about forty feet away, across Persian rugs on a teak floor, is a man sitting behind a massive desk, almost empty, except for a phone console with enough lines blinking to light up the White House Christmas tree. The instant he lays his eyes upon us, he stands up, slams his fist down hard on his desk, and screams out his question of the day, "Where's my money?"

This is hardly the Mr. Wonderful I expected.

The office is quite spectacular. Two couches, high-back chairs, a conference table that seats twelve, and floor-to-ceiling windows on two sides of the room. The view on a clear day must be all the way to Detroit, but who'd ever want to look at Detroit? As I quickly take it all in, I notice something missing.

No wonder Sterling S. Sheckle is camera shy; the guy's a shrimp. Standing, he's my size when I'm sitting down.

"I want my money. You tell that no good, tighter than a miser-on-a-budget Richmond, whose been sticking me for years with inflated premiums, it's his turn to shell out the gelt."

"That's what we're here to discuss, Mr. Sheckle," Tiffany tells the man as we approach his desk.

"Who are you?"

"Tiffany Richmond; that no good miser is my daddy."

"Good, then you can write me a check. Make it out to Cash for six million."

I don't have fabric sensors built into my DNA, but my eyesight is still pretty good. Sterling wears a blue suit with wide stripes, the kind Al Capone wore before he was shipped off to Alcatraz. His belt tightens a few inches above his navel, and his white shirt with a frayed collar billows out at the belt line like frosting hanging over the edge of a cupcake. The tie he's wearing makes my ties look fashionable. I notice a hearing aid in one ear. He wears a pair of thick, half-frame reading glasses low on the bridge of his bulbous nose. Another pair of regular-sized eyeglasses rests on the desk blotter. He's at least seventy years old, although he looks a day or two past eighty. He has more hair in his ears and nose than on his head. If this guy weighs more than 125 pounds soaking wet, I'd be surprised.

"Oh, Mr. Sheckle," Tiffany says to the man. "Nobody writes checks anymore. We use smartphones."

"I want my money, and I don't care how I get it."

"This is Mr. Sherlock, he's going to find your money," Tiffany tells him.

I am?

"How about if you pay me the six million, then whatever he finds, you can keep?" Sheckle asks.

"No," Tiffany says. "I don't think my daddy would be too wild about that idea."

I put out my hand. "Hi."

We shake. His hand is the size of Tom Thumb's.

"Do you have any idea of where the money you lost went?" I ask a standard question from the list of the most popular detective questions.

"If I knew where I lost it, I'd have already found it."

"Was it stolen?"

"Of course it was stolen."

"Who stole it?"

"A thief."

This is going well.

"When?"

"I don't know."

"How?"

"I don't know that either."

I'm down to the bottom on the detective question list. "Why?"

"Why do you think? It's six million dollars!" he wails at me.

Good answer.

"You must have a head of security for your firm?" I continue doing my job.

"Of course I have a head of security."

"What's his name?"

"Head of Security. The woman outside will give you his name and extension."

Interesting nomenclatures for his employees.

"But the money didn't come out of the company," he tells me.

"Then where did it come out of?"

"My checking account."

"You have six million dollars in your checking account?" I ask, wondering if I heard this wrong.

"I used to," he yells back at me.

"Six million bucks?" I'm stunned.

Tiffany notices my absolute disbelief. "What's so weird about that?"

"Last time I looked, I had sixty-two dollars in mine, Tiffany."

"Tsk, tsk, Mr. Sherlock."

"I want my money!"

"Yes, Mr. Sheckle." I try to calm him down.

Sterling probably realized the six mil was missing when his statement was "off a bit" at the end of the month.

"You don't mind if I talk to your accounting people or anybody else at the firm?"

"Talk to anybody you want, as long as I get my money!"

"No problem, Mr. Sheckle," Tiffany assures him. "When Mr. Sherlock's on the case, the case gets it on."

Yet another phrase I never uttered.

"I don't care what you have to do, or how you got to do it, but get my money back or pull out your checkbook and start writing." Sterling slams his fist down on the desk to make his point clear.

"Yes, sir, Mr. Sheckle, we're on it like salt on a margarita," Tiffany assures him.

Sheckle points to the door. "Now, get out of here so I can make some more money."

We walk to the elevators without assistance. Tiffany is itching to start talking, but I won't let her within the confines of the company. When we get to the elevator lobby area, we wait with three other people. Tiffany can't hold out any longer. "I can't believe it; Sterling dresses worse than you."

Two of our fellow waiting riders laugh.

"Tiffany, shush!"

We step into the elevator with the other people. Tiffany can't stop. "I can hardly imagine what he wears to the company Christmas party."

I cut her off. "Tiffany, do you realize we're going down faster in this elevator than we would if we were falling off the top of the building?"

"What does that have to do with the case?"

"Nothing. That's why I brought it up."

I allow our fellow riders to exit first after the car lands gently on Mother Earth. "Tiffany, never talk in an elevator."

"Why not?"

"Because you never know who's listening," I inform her. "Loose lips sink ships."

"What difference could it make? We're not at the yacht club, Mr. Sherlock."

Why do I bother?

We take another elevator down to Tiffany's car.

"Okay, Tiffany, what did you learn?"

"Learn about what?"

"The case, the crime, the victim, everything?" I ask, as we get into her car.

"Well, I don't think Mr. Sheckle got rich by being fashionable."

Not what I expected, but it's at least something. "Did you notice anything odd about the office?"

She thinks it over. "No."

"You didn't notice anything missing?"

"Missing from where?"

"His desk."

"On the top of his desk?" Tiffany attempts to narrow down the search.

I shake my head in frustration.

"Am I getting warm?"

"Tiffany..."

"The game isn't as much fun if you don't tell me when I'm getting warmer."

"Okay, you're getting warmer."

She thinks it over and says, "Would I be getting warmer if I said what was missing was on the left or right side of the desk?"

"You want me to just tell you?"

"Yes."

"There was no computer screen or terminal anywhere in the room."

"You're right. That's what I would have said, if I would have thought of it."

"There's not a CEO in America without at least two monitors staring at him all day. Sterling has none." I pause for her to, hopefully, take this fact in. "And did you notice how every phone line he had never quit blinking?"

"Yes."

"Really?"

"Well, once you mentioned it," Tiffany says, "I remember it distinctly."

"What does that tell you?"

"He'd rather talk than Twitter."

"Close enough."

Tiffany beams after scoring so well on the test, at least in her mind.

"Let's go."

"Where to first, Mr. Sherlock?"

"My apartment."

"I hate your apartment. Why are we going there?"

"So I can get my car."

"I hate your car even worse," Tiffany says. "Why do you need your car?"

"Because I got to pick up the girls. Tuesday is my kid day."

CHAPTER 2

Kelly's middle school and Care's grammar school are adjacent to one another. In the morning for the drop-off, the one lane street bordering both schools is one way going south. You drive in, drop off, and loop around to exit. In the afternoon for the pick-up, the direction is reversed. You loop first, drive north, pick up, and go on your way. There is one crossing guard, dressed in an orange windbreaker, equipped with an oversized stop sign, and holding a whistle between her incisors. The kids refer to her as Tessie, the Traffic Terminator. Tessie's job is to halt the cars for walkers, as well as keep the line moving so that the moms won't age dramatically during the process. I find it quite intriguing that the system works well for the morning drop-off, but is fraught with problems during the afternoon pick-up. After serious study, I've concluded the reason for this phenomenon is that in the mornings the mothers all hold a latte in one hand, a cell phone in the other, and scream at their kids in the back seat. They sip, talk, and yell simultaneously. Their adrenaline level, at a daytime peak due to the over-caffeinated beverage, keeps the line moving at an astonishing speed. When the oversized SUVs and banged up minivans do come to a stop, the kids either bolt from the cars like escaping POWs or are thrown from the vehicles physically by mom.

The afternoon pick-up is a much different scenario. This is because one person can totally screw up the works for everyone. Let me give you an example how, and at the same time reveal one of the worst pick-up traffic offenders, my daughter Kelly.

I enter into the line like all good parents at the school at 3 p.m., make the loop, and see my youngest daughter, Care, standing on the grammar school sidewalk. At the sight of my Toyota, she unslings her backpack, walks quickly to the car, opens the door, tosses in the backpack, and sits herself down in the front passenger seat. "Hi, Care," I always say. "What did you learn today in school?"

"Nothing," she answers as her door closes and the Toyota moves. "Can we go to McDonald's for a snack?"

"No," I answer for the millionth time.

We proceed approximately 100 yards north to the middle school where kids also line the sidewalk waiting for their family car. My oldest daughter, Kelly, is in the middle of the throng. She's chatting, waving, snapping cell phone pictures, texting, and doing everything except looking for my Toyota. I have to stop the car, which stops the line, which angers the cars behind, and horns start to blare. Today, Kelly is chatting up a boy whose braces throw off the sun's reflection and almost blind me.

"Kelly, hurry up," I scream over the honking horns.

Kelly doesn't respond. She's way too busy yuk-yukking to care about the hundred cars lined up not moving behind me or that Tessie the Terminator is on her way over to thump my hood with the butt of her stop sign.

"Kelly!"

She finally turns toward my voice, gives me her *how can you embarrass me so much* look, and slunks her way over to the car no faster than a sick snail going uphill. Finally, she climbs into the back seat of the car.

"What is your problem, Dad?"

"When you do that, Kelly, you hold up the whole line," Care tells her sister.

"Shut up."

"Don't tell your sister to 'shut up,' Kelly," I tell her.

The Toyota moves and the horns cease.

"She started it," Kelly says to me.

"Care's right," I defend my youngest. "When you're not ready, the whole line has to stop, and everybody gets mad. Didn't you hear the horns honking?"

"No."

"What are you, deaf?" Care asks.

"I was busy."

"Doing what?"

"Talking to my new boyfriend, Cameron," Kelly answers.

I hit the brakes. The car clunks to a stop. The kids almost get a case of whiplash. I turn around and scream, "Your what?"

Kelly answers, but I can't hear because of the ensuing horn cacophony, the screeching of SUV tires behind me, and Tessie the Terminator whacking the side of the car with her stop sign, screaming, "Keep the line moving!"

"What did you say?"

"Boyfriend."

"What?"

"We're dating," Kelly repeats as I get the Toyota back in gear.

"No, you're not."

"Yes, we are."

"Who said you could date?" I ask.

"Dad," Kelly tells me, "I'm old enough to start dating."

"You're fourteen."

"I'm almost fifteen."

"No, you're not, you're fourteen."

"You have nine months before your next birthday, Kelly." One daughter is on my side for a change.

"But I'm mature for my age."

"No, you're not."

"Yes, I am. All the girls in my class say I am," Kelly continues her argument.

"How would they know? They're fourteen, too," I counter.

We're out of the school zone and on the highway-like road going west from the school.

"Where are we going, Dad?" Care asks.

"Kelly has to go to her orthodontist and get her braces tightened."

"Can we go to McDonald's on the way?"

"No."

"I'm starting to date, Dad," my oldest informs me.

"No, you're not," I inform her.

"I have to."

"No, you don't. You have plenty of time before you start dating."

"It's the natural order of things," Kelly says.

"No, it's not."

"Yes, it is. It's been that way for generations," Kelly explains.

"Where do you come up with this stuff, Kelly?" I incredulously ask.

"It's time, Dad."

"Okay, Kelly, why is it time?"

"Because I've become a woman."

Thank God, I'm in the right hand lane, because the Toyota jolts onto the gravel shoulder, swerves a few times, and kicks up a few thousand pebbles before skidding to a stop on the side of the road. "What?" I scream back at her.

"Last Saturday, I became a woman."

I'm in shock. "How?"

"You want me to explain it to you, Dad?" Kelly asks. "It was embarrassing enough explaining it to Care."

"I already knew when you told me; I was just testing you," Care shoots back.

"You're only fourteen, Kelly."

"Dad, I'm going on fifteen."

"You're too young for all this to start happening."

"Dad, I can already feel my breasts getting ready to burgeon out of my chest."

"Burgeon?" Am I really hearing this?"

"You don't have any breasts," Care tells her.

"But I will," Kelly snaps at her sister. "And they're going to be C cups."

"Don't say that," I plead.

"That's why I have to start dating. There's no time to lose in finding Mr. Right."

I'm sweating. This is all too much for my mind to process. I thought I had a few more years before this happened. Kelly's already a handful. Now, with her hormones going bonkers, she'll be an unholy terror. My life is going to be a hotter living hell than the living hell I'm already living in. Oh God, where was my Y chromosome that weekend away in the Wisconsin Dells?

"Kelly, we're going to table the dating discussion until later."

"Why?"

"Because this much information, this soon, this fast, is way too much for my brain to handle at one time."

"There's really not much to discuss, as far as I'm concerned," Kelly says, "except I'm going to need a lot more clothes for all the new and exciting places I'll be going."

This isn't happening. It's all a bad dream. I'm going to wake up any minute, and Kelly is going to ask me if I'll buy her first Barbie doll. And I'll have to tell her no because Barbie is an unrealistic rendition of the normal teenage girl, which can negatively skew her view of herself.

Kelly asks, "Do you think I should put on my Facebook page that I've become a woman?"

"No!"

When my breathing returns to normal, I get back on the road.

"Dad, I'm really hungry," Care tells me. "Can we stop at McDonald's so I have something in my stomach while Kelly's getting her dumb braces screwed on tighter?"

"How many times have I told you? The food at McDonald's is a death sentence, Care."

"But it tastes good."

"That's because they put chemical flavor enhancers in it to disguise the taste of the awful, so-called meat they're selling."

"I'm hungry."

"How about if we stop for some fruit?" I suggest.

"Gross," Kelly gives her vote on the topic.

"Bananas are one of the best foods you can eat if you have a growing body, Kelly." I'm not sure about this, but it does make sense.

"They are?" Kelly asks and puffs up her non-existent chest.

"How about if we compromise and stop for a Fruit Roll-Up?" Care asks.

I give up. "All right, I'll stop, but only one snack for each of you."

"I'll have two bananas," Kelly says.

***

While in the orthodontist's chair, Kelly exchanges her red braces for silver. Instead of having a mouth that looks like a red sky in the morning, hers now resembles new bars on a jail cell.

We don't get to the apartment until close to six. I broil chicken breasts for dinner and serve them with salad, fresh green beans, and rice. They hate it. I tell them children are starving in other parts of the world, and they should be thankful they get to eat such healthy, nutritious food. Each offers to wrap up what's left on their plates, and send it to wherever starving kids don't have good taste buds.

After dinner, I confiscate their cell phones and tell them to start their homework. This is my latest good-parenting idea. I believe all distractions should be kept to an absolute minimum during homework time so nothing is in the way of expanding their brainpower.

They don't agree.

"Dad, you can't do that," Kelly says. "What if Cameron calls?"

"You'll call him back."

"What if something really important happens that we have to know about?" Care, who has switched back to the enemy side for this debate, asks.

"Like what?"

"Like somebody found a mistake in the textbook, and I have to know about it so I don't learn stuff the wrong way, screw up my education, flunk my SATs, and not be able to get into a good college," Care argues.

"We'll take our chances with that one."

"Dad, I'll die without my phone," Kelly takes it to the extreme.

"No, you won't."

"Yes, I will. I can feel my chest tightening up." Kelly grips her front. "A heart attack could be on the way."

I should tell her it's her "burgeoning breasts," but I hold my tongue.

"We didn't do anything wrong, Dad. Why are you punishing us?" Care asks.

"I'm not punishing you. I'm doing what every good parent should do."

"Torture us? Take us away from our friends, ruin our social lives, and take me away from the boy I love?"

"Kelly, you can't use your phone while you're in class, so what's the difference not using it during homework?" I do my best to make them understand.

"You're not our teacher, Dad, you aren't credentialed."

Where does she come up with this stuff?

"How about this, Dad?" Care asks. "We can have our phones, but we won't talk on them?"

"No texting either," I add, ruining Care's end run around the problem.

"Shoot."

"You know if you spent this time doing your homework instead of arguing, you probably would be done by now."

I take the phones and leave the room. End of discussion.

Forty-five minutes later, they emerge from my bedroom, retrieve their phones, and go into a ten-minute texting frenzy worthy of a Western Union Teletype operator's competition. Technology, isn't it wonderful?

"Kelly, can I talk to you for a second?"

"Do I get to listen?" Care asks.

"No," I tell my youngest. Although, if I did allow her to listen, I probably would avoid having the same conversation with her in a few years. "Go take your shower."

Kelly reluctantly follows me into the front room.

"Could you turn off your phone, Kelly?"

"Dad..."

"Please."

She pretends to turn off her phone, but I see she merely switches it to *Vibrate*. We sit on the couch.

"Kelly, about this dating thing..."

"Dad."

"Kelly, you are only fourteen; you have plenty of time in your life to start dating."

"My other friends are dating."

"I don't care what your friends are doing. I care what you're doing."

"Mom doesn't have a problem with it."

"I haven't spoken with your mother about this, but I assure you it is on my list."

A list that will never be completed. Her mother and I seldom speak, and when we do, it is always the same conversation:

"I need more money."

"So do I," I tell her.

"I need it now," she always tells me.

"So do I."

This goes round and round until I pay her more money. Then she reverts to sending me notes via the kids on everything from changes in schedules—always hers—money for school, money for clothes, and money for their pet—a horse that eats constantly. The topic we never discuss is: What's best for the kids.

"Kelly, listen..."

"Dad, you don't trust me," Kelly says. "That's the problem."

"No, it's not."

"You don't trust my judgment in men."

"No, that's not it either."

"You don't think I'm mature enough to find the right guy to date."

"No, Kelly." I pause and then explain, "I know I have a very intelligent daughter who wouldn't be dumb enough to go out with a boy who would be stupid enough to put the hit on my daughter in the front seat of a car when I'm sitting in the back."

"That's not funny."

"You're too young, Kelly. It's that simple. Wait six months, and we'll discuss this again."

"Six months! That's forever. All the good guys will be taken by then."

"Trust me, there will always be enough guys to go around."

She folds her arms, gives me her *stare.* "You're being mean to me."

"No, I'm not. I'm being your father."

"You're ruining my life, stunting my emotional growth, and keeping me away from the boy I love."

"Kelly, you're fourteen."

"And already a woman."

"Kelly, forget it. No dating. You can wait six months. You are not ready. End of conversation."

"You're not being fair. You hate me, and you're destroying my life." She's squeezing her phone so tight, all four G's might explode.

"Sorry."

She runs out of the room and into the bedroom, slamming the door behind her.

The remainder of the evening is uneventful, thank God.

They both climb into my bed. I kiss Care goodnight, but Kelly buries her head under her pillow. I make sure their cell phones are off before I shut the door for the night.

"Good night. I love you."

The next morning, Kelly won't speak to me. At the school, Cameron waits for Kelly on the middle school sidewalk. She bolts out of the car to greet him faster than Halley's Comet.

When I drop Care off 100 yards down the road, I tell her, "Love ya, Care. And don't forget, *learn something new every day*."

"Yeah, right Dad."

CHAPTER 3

To save what's left of the tread on the Toyota's tires, I take the 'L' downtown to meet Tiffany at the Willis Tower at 10 a.m. At 10:30, still no Tiffany. I call her on my cell phone.

"Tiffany, where are you? We're late."

"I'll be there in a minute, Mr. Sherlock," she snaps back.

She shows up at 11:05.

"Tiffany..."

She has a latte in one hand and her phone in the other as she looks at her Tag Heuer watch. "What's the big deal?"

"You're an hour late."

"Mr. Sherlock, an hour is early for me being late."

Why do I bother?

On the way to the elevator, she sips via one hand and texts with the other.

"You can text with one hand?" I'm amazed.

"Of course, can't everybody?"

"No."

"Sorry, forgot who I was talking to."

I have a problem when it comes to technology. For some reason, I have a mental block in the understanding of anything to do with the modern age of communication. The malady probably comes from the belief I have that as humans we should speak to one another face to face or, at the least, mouth to ear, instead of tapping letters on tiny keyboards, leaving voicemail messages, or misspelling emails back and forth. Call me a cretin, call me a caveman, call me a curmudgeon, but I hate technology.

We only go up ninety-seven stories this trip.

"Richard Sherlock, to see the head of security," I announce to the receptionist on the floor.

"Leslie?"

"I wasn't given his name, just Head of Security," I explain.

"Leslie Ambrose."

As the nice lady makes the connection on her phone panel, Tiffany whispers, "His parents named him Leslie? I bet they wanted a girl."

If I am ever asked to describe a computer geek to someone who has lived his whole life under a rock in Mongolia, all I would have to do is pull out a picture of Leslie Ambrose: A short, skinny, spectacled, spaced-out, steely-eyed guy with a pocket protector on his chest and a headset buried in his unruly hair.

"Mr. Ambrose, I'm Richard Sherlock, and this is my assistant, Tiffany," I hand him my business card.

"Yo," he says as we shake hands.

As Tiffany puts out her manicured paw, she asks, "Do you have any sisters?"

"No." He answers in absolute wonder.

"I didn't think so," Tiffany says.

"We're here to discuss a missing six million dollars from Mr. Sheckle," I jump in to quickly change the topic.

"I didn't take it."

"I didn't say you did."

He leads us onto a floor filled with identical grey cubicles lined up in rows like bunk beds in an overcrowded prison. "You think he was hacked?" Leslie asks.

"From what I'm told about the case, it seems logical."

"Chinese," Leslie says.

"Chinese, what?" I ask.

"Chinese, Chinese."

"Are we ordering takeout?" Tiffany asks.

"No, Chinese hackers," Leslie answers.

"Are those like chicken wings?" Tiffany asks, even more confused.

"Hackers, people who break into your computer, hackers," Leslie explains.

"They didn't sound very appetizing," Tiffany concludes.

Leslie leads us down the outer row of cubicles, each one as boring and nondescript as the last. "Hack, hack, hack, it's all the Chinese have to do all day. They'd hack into Poverty.com if they thought there was something there to steal."

"Do they ever succeed?"

"If they weren't succeeding somewhere, I doubt if they'd keep doing it," Leslie says.

"What do you do to keep the wolf at bay?" I ask.

"We have firewalls on our firewalls, we change passwords more often than we change socks, and we recode our information constantly."

"Why don't you have something on there that hacks them back when they try to hack you?" Tiffany asks a very good question.

"By law, we can't; it's illegal."

"But I bet you do it anyway," Tiffany says, which is exactly what I was thinking. Thinking like Tiffany is scary.

We enter Leslie's office, which is across from the last cubicle in the row. At first glance, it looks more like a dumping ground for massive terminals, but on closer inspection, I see each monitor is tracking away like an air traffic controller's console, except one with a movie poster-like screen that says *League of Legends*.

"Have the police been called?" I ask.

"No."

"Why not?"

"Can you imagine a Chicago cop sitting here with his gun and his gut both out trying to put computer cuffs on a bad guy?"

"You know," I tell him, "I used to be one of those cops."

"Yo."

Onto the next topic. "Do you also protect Mr. Sheckle's personal accounts?" I ask.

"We do, but not to the extent we protect the financial accounts."

"Could they go through you to get to them?" I ask.

"Impossible."

"Could they go through them to get to you?"

"Improbable."

"Could they ever go through the two of you and come out the other side?" Tiffany adds one last question to the mix.

"I would doubt it."

"Mr. Ambrose, why doesn't Mr. Sheckle have a computer on his desk?" I ask.

"He doesn't want one."

"Isn't a computer a necessary weapon in the daily battles of business?"

"For most, I'd say 'yes,'" Leslie says, "but Mr. Sheckle lives by his own rules in his own world. He doesn't believe in conducting business via technology."

"Neither does he," Tiffany points at me. "Mr. Sherlock is to technology what a Nehru jacket is to fashion."

"Would it be possible for one of my technology people to come in here some day?" I'm thinking of having Herman stop by for a visit. "And maybe hang out and take it all in?"

"That would be akin to a programmer with an empty database being allowed to come in here with a list of passwords in his cloud drive to access our binary codes."

I hesitate before asking, "So, is that a 'No'?"

"Yes."

Tiffany taps me on my arm. "I knew that."

"What would you suggest I do, Mr. Ambrose?" I ask.

Leslie shrugs his shoulders.

"If the six million was hacked out of his account, there has to be some way of tracing it, and it's my job to figure out how," I tell him.

"Good luck."

"Will you help?"

"No." Leslie is emphatic in his refusal.

"Why not?"

"I'm busy."

An alarm goes off. One of the monitors in the office starts doing electronic gymnastics, and an Asian techie the size of the Little Emperor runs into the room like a fireman into a burning building. His eyes almost come out of their sockets when he sees Tiffany. Leslie has to slap him to get his attention back. "What?"

"Hack attack!"

The man, joined by Leslie, sits at the console and logs in.

"This one's as Chinese as chicken chow mein," the Asian tech says.

"Go into stage three, intercept, hyper mode," Leslie sounds like Captain Kirk on the Enterprise.

The men are striking their keyboards with fingers of fury, faster than nervous stenographers on speed.

"Hack 'em back," Tiffany screams out, turning into a rabid fan as she watches the action.

The Asian man looks up at Tiffany with eyes the size of moon pies.

"And put enough MSG in it to give 'em a panic attack," she orders.

***

Next stop is seven floors up.

"Did you bring the six million with you?"

"No."

"Is the check in the mail?"

"No."

"Are you transferring the funds electronically?"

"No."

"Then what are you doing here?"

"We had a little time before lunch and thought we'd stop by and put a face to the name," Tiffany answers, which I am thankful for since my "No" wouldn't have worked for his last question.

C. Franklin Witherington is the CFO of the SSS Financial Corporation and has been obviously schooled by Sterling S. Sheckle. "He wants his money." He even utters the words with the same inflection as his boss.

"And I'm here to find it."

"Well, I don't have it," CFO CFW tells me.

"Would you mind if we started at the beginning?" I ask.

CFW harrumphs.

"Mr. Sherlock always says 'the longest journey starts with your first leg,'" Tiffany explains poorly, "or something along those travel lines."

"What exactly does SSS do?"

"We are a conglomerate which finds undervalued companies, buys them for cash, turns them around, and either sells, splits them up, or holds them until the time to sell is right."

"How many does SSS own?"

"What time is it?" Witherington answers sarcastically.

"Quarter to lunch," Tiffany answers.

"What he means, Tiffany, is the number of companies SSS owns changes constantly."

"Oh, I thought he was hungry."

"This is a multi-billion dollar corporation, is it not?"

"Multi, multi."

"So, six million dollars slipping through the cracks isn't all that improbable?"

"We employ a financial staff of one hundred. I have accountants upon accountants, accounting for accountants. In my three years working for Mr. Sheckle, we have never misplaced a dime."

He must check the couch cushions on a weekly basis.

I consider asking CFO CFW if he'd take a look at my financial situation and give me a few tips but decide this may not be the best time. "So, where did the money disappear from?"

"His personal account."

"You don't account for his personal account?"

"Not on a daily basis."

"Then how did you discover it was missing?"

"Audit."

"You audited Mr. Sheckle's personal account?" I ask.

"Yes."

"Why? Isn't that crossing the line in the ledger sheet?"

Witherington doesn't appreciate my line of questioning. "It became necessary."

"What did you do when you found out he had six million dollars in his checking account?"

"Nothing."

Why am I the only one who finds six million in a checking account a little odd? I pull out my pocket checkbook, and flash it at the CFO. "Does Mr. Sheckle have one this size, or does he have a bigger one?"

"I don't know, I've never asked."

"So," I say, "you went to balance his checking account, it came up six million short?"

He's looking at me like I'm an idiot when it comes to accounting. "We went back two years, charted every payment, every deposit, every fee, and came up six million in the red."

"I'd say that would certainly fall into the *bad day* category for most people. You think he was hacked?"

"I don't. Others do."

"What do you think happened?"

"It was that idiot, Chester."

"Chester?"

"His personal accountant."

"Chester, first name or last name."

"I don't know, ask Chester."

"Who is he?"

"A negative adjustment on the ledger of life," he scowls as the words come out of his mouth. Mr. C. Franklin Witherington is not the man a fledgling comedian wants in the audience on open mic night.

"So, what are you going to do?"

"Me," he says, "nothing."

"You're going to let the six million fly away like geese in the winter?"

"No, the insurance will cover the loss."

"I wouldn't be too sure about that," Tiffany says. "My daddy and six million aren't easily separated."

"My responsibility is to the corporation, Mr. Sherlock. And it will be in the corporation's best interest to dispose of this problem as soon as possible." Mr. C. Franklin Witherington gives me his *that's enough of this* stare.

"It is my job to investigate and find the funds, Mr. Witherington."

"Get a new job," he advises me.

I should tell him I am and I will soon be able to help him with all his real estate needs, but he impresses me as the type to already have an agent. "I'm working on that." I chuckle a bit. "No pun intended, but I have a case to solve first."

"Mr. Sherlock leaves no leaves turned or stones by the road," Tiffany assures him.

"It would be best for you to write Sheckle a check for six million, Mr. Sherlock," he says smugly, "and end this silliness."

"I would, but I don't have six million in my checking account."

"You?" he turns to Tiffany.

"I don't write checks anymore, and my smartphone is out of juice," Tiffany informs him as she waves her iPhone.

"Thank you very much for your time." We get up to leave.

"Mr. Sheckle wants his money," he reminds me, as if I need reminding. "And he always gets what he wants."

"So do I," Tiffany says.

We're out of there.

In the crowded elevator, Tiffany says, "Wow, two fun guys in a row. The company must only hire people who were beaten as young children."

I wait until we are out of the elevator before I respond. "I agree. Mr. C. Franklin Witherington is hardly a candidate for the Mother Teresa Benevolent Corporate Executive of the Year Award."

"Who's Mother Teresa?"

"She was this nun in India, Tiffany."

"Named Mother? That doesn't make sense, Mr. Sherlock. Nuns can't have kids."

We take another elevator down to where Tiffany *handicapped* parked her Lexus.

"I got a taste for Chinese food," she says, unlocking the doors with her remote.

"Really?"

"I don't know why."

"Chinese food is terrible for you, Tiffany. The sodium and fat content is through the roof," I explain.

"You sure? Most of the Chinamen I see in pictures are little skinny guys."

"Everything is fried in chicken fat."

"I hate fat, Mr. Sherlock. I'll cross the restaurant grouping off my list."

"Good."

"But I'm still hungry, Mr. Sherlock."

"What do you want?"

"I don't know. What do you want?"

"Something simple," I tell her.

"Not me. I hate simple."

We end up in the executive dining room of the Richmond Insurance Corporation, not too shabby.

"Will your dad be joining us?" I ask Tiffany.

"I doubt it. He still has indigestion after hearing he might have to pay out six mil."

"You don't see your dad much, do you, Tiffany?"

"He's pretty busy all the time," she says with a slight negative lilt in her voice. "And when he does see me, he seems to get busier."

"That's too bad."

"I was mostly mom's job when I was growing up."

Tiffany's mother died a few years ago during a botched liposuction surgery when the doctor mistakenly sucked out a kidney.

"Maybe your dad sees so much of your mother in you, it's too painful for him."

"Either that, or I make him nuts," she says.

A waiter approaches. "What can I get for you?" he asks politely.

"We haven't seen a menu," I tell him.

"We don't have menus," he answers, not as polite as before.

"Then what do you have?"

"What do you want?"

Tiffany has a frou-frou salad I can't pronounce, and I have soup, grilled whitefish, veggies, and saffron rice. I should eat this well every day, or at least once more in my lifetime.

"Any thoughts on the case, so far, Tiffany?" I ask as we partake in our repast.

"I'll bet the C's for Charlie," she says.

"What C?"

"The C of C. Freshman Worthington."

"You mean the C of C. Franklin Witherington?"

"Yeah, that guy. He probably doesn't want to take the chance of someone calling him Chuck," she says. "It makes him into a cheap piece of meat."

"He certainly was a bit testy," I say to her.

"He seemed a bit nasty with a snappy streak to me."

"Interesting he and Ambrose won't help us out," I say. "I would think they'd welcome help finding out who lifted the six million."

"Me too."

"It was also pretty obvious C. Franklin didn't think much of the Chester guy."

Tiffany's face lights up, "Maybe Fremulon Washington's C stands for Chester too, and he doesn't want to get mixed up with the other Chester?"

"Why don't you be in charge of following that lead, Tiffany?"

"I'll get right on it, Mr. Sherlock."

The food is fabulous. I ask for another roll to sop up every tasty morsel on my plate.

"What's important, Tiffany," I tell her, "is the CFO didn't appreciate being excluded from Sterling's personal financial matters and the SSS Charitable Foundation."

"It's the difference between having your finger in the pie or your whole mouth, Mr. Sherlock."

"Tiffany, what do you know about Sterling Sheckle?"

"He's rich."

"I know that."

"And he doesn't have any marriageable sons."

"Anything else?"

"What else is there?"

I hate it when someone answers a question with another question.

"Does your dad know Sterling well?" I ask, hoping for a real answer this time.

"Daddy knows his money, but I don't think he knows Sterling. I don't think anybody knows Mr. Sheckle. He's never at our parties, doesn't belong to our clubs, or hangs out where we hang out."

"Do you know why not?" I ask her.

"Probably scared."

"Scared of what? The guy's worth billions."

Tiffany sips her cappuccino and quickly napkins off the froth on her upper lip before speaking. "Mr. Sheckle is like an athlete playing in the World Series of Moneyball. He thinks he can't show his cards or any weakness, or give any hint of what he's up to, because he never knows who he is going to fight with next. He has to win, but even more important, I'll bet he hates to lose."

I am amazed at Tiffany's understanding of the man. "So, it's not really six million dollars he's mad about. It's more someone figured out how to get the best of him, and that's why he's so unfriendly."

"You don't get Sheckle-rich by being friendly, Mr. Sherlock."

"It also proves money can't buy happiness."

"Yes, but it sure can buy you everything you need to go out and look for it."

Lunch is over. It was delicious.

"Where to now, Mr. Sherlock?"

"Well, since Witherington won't let us in the front door, we're going to have to enter through the back."

"What does that mean?"

"It's time to visit Herman McFadden."

"Oh God, that's a fate worse than shopping at a garage sale."

"You don't want to come along?"

"When it comes to Herman the Vermin, include me out, Mr. Sherlock."

CHAPTER 4

Herman McFadden is a cross between Edward Snowden, Warren Buffett, and the loser on the *Biggest Loser.* He's a computer whiz and a financial genius wrapped in three hundred pounds of excess fat. He lives in a two-bedroom apartment on the north side in desperate need of a cleaning lady. He spends the majority of his day in front of a computer, his shower gets little use, he hasn't tucked in his shirt in years, and his only hobby is porn. A few years back, Herman was accused of the murder of a runaway teenager with enough evidence against him to send him to the XXL electric chair. Herman is as disgusting as they come, but he's no murderer. I figured out how he was framed, and he's been beholden to me ever since.

I knock on his door and get ready for a waft of odor to hit me like the tsunami hit northern Japan.

It doesn't happen. Instead of noxious body odor, the scent of lavender fills my nostrils.

"Sherlock, so nice to see you."

"Herman?"

"Come in."

I enter. I can't believe my eyes. "What happened? This place is usually the pit's pits." I stare in wonder. "Now, it's neatnik neat."

"I've turned over a new leaf," he tells me, ushering me inside.

I'd be surprised if Herman can turn over.

"I've lost thirty-four pounds, up to walking all the way around the block, and given up cheese."

"Good for you Herman."

"I hired a service to come in and clean the place. After only one day, they were out of their Hazmat suits."

"What brought this on?"

"Decided it's about time I found a mate," he says. "Need to hear the patter of little Herman Junior feet around the place."

Any offspring of Herman would pound instead of patter. "What are you going to do, go on Match dot com to find her?" I ask.

"No, I tried that once. I'm thinking more along the lines of a Russian bride."

"Best of luck, Herman."

I sit on his clean couch. He sits in the chair facing his computer but swivels around to face me. "What can I do for you?"

"You're not going to complain if I'm over here to ask a favor?"

"No. I've turned over a new leaf."

"Somebody stole six million dollars from Sterling Sheckle, and I have to find out how, who, and get it back."

"Good luck with that."

"Can you do what you do and see what was done?"

"Hack him?"

"So to speak."

"I don't hack anymore, Sherlock. It's part of my new leaf."

"I'm stuck, Herman. The accountants and the security guys won't help, Sheckle's filed a claim against his Richmond policy, and Mr. Richmond will have a coronary if he has to pay out six million."

"I don't know, Sherlock."

"The security guy says 'it was the Chinese,' the CFO blames the personal accountant, and Sheckle hasn't a clue."

"They call the police?" Herman asks.

"No. They said that would be like 'sending an error message' to Microsoft when your computer gets stuck."

Herman contemplates for a few seconds, turns his chair around, and starts tapping computer keys. "SSS owns lots of companies."

"They own half the country," I one-up him.

"They buy and sell all the time. They have to keep their business close to the vest, especially when they're in negotiations."

"I don't think they're too wild about me hanging around."

Herman's fingers are faster on the keyboard than a boogie-woogie pianist. "They got money moving around like a rat stuck in a maze."

"What does that tell you?" I ask.

"The game is afoot, Watson."

"I'm Sherlock."

"Not in this case," Herman says.

"I'm told the money was hacked out of his personal account," I tell the suddenly over-concentrated Herman.

"Six million?"

"Out of his checking account," I say in disbelief. "Who keeps six million dollars in their checking account?"

"Lots of people."

"You're kidding?"

"Everybody needs a little mad money, Sherlock."

Where did I go wrong in life?

Herman continues to concentrate on the pages of data jumping on the screen before him. "I'll see what I can find out. This might be fun."

"Thanks, Herman." I get up to leave. "And I can't tell you how impressed I am with the changes you've made so far in your life."

"Eighty-four pounds to go."

"And Herman, once you're on the way to the altar, you'll want your own place, and I just so happen to be getting my real estate license. Let me help you find the home of your dreams."

"You, in real estate?"

"Sure, why not?"

"There are so many people in real estate in this town, Sherlock, you'll be like one calorie in an extra big serving of pie à la mode."

***

I look everywhere from the Better Business Bureau to the Yellow Pages. I Google, Bing, and Ask.com and get nothing. I search Angie's List to Listomania and come up empty. The SSS Charitable Foundation is so secret, it makes the members of the Skull and Bones Society public knowledge.

I call the SSS corporate office and get put on hold more times than a caller to Richmond Insurance trying to lower his premium. Chester isn't listed on any company roster, employee listing, or the starting lineup of the SSS softball team. Chester is nowhere to be found. He's probably hiding out at the SSS Charitable Foundation.

I call "the woman," as she was referred to by Sterling, and ask, "Could you please help me find Chester."

"Chester, who?"

"Chester from the SSS Charitable Foundation."

"The what?"

"He works for Mr. Sheckle."

"Oh, that Chester."

I didn't expect so many choices. She gives me the number. I call.

"Hello."

"Chester?"

"Yes."

"My name is Richard Sherlock. I'm an investigator with the Richmond Insurance Company."

"How are you, sir?"

"Fine, thank you. And you?"

"Excellent," Chester says.

"I was wondering if my assistant and I could stop by and meet with you today?"

"Concerning?"

"A missing six million of Mr. Sheckle's money."

"Oh," he says, "that would be splendid."

Splendid?

"Whatever time is best for you, sir. I will gladly make myself available."

"Three o'clock?"

"Perfect."

I'm wondering if the entire politeness quotient in the SSS Financial Corporation exists in this one employee.

I call Tiffany. Line's busy. I leave her a message. "Call me."

She texts me back. *What do you want?*

I call her back. Line's busy. I leave the same message.

She texts me back. *What do you want, now?*

I call her back. She doesn't pick up. Third time's the charm, I hope, "Call me."

Tiffany calls me back ten minutes later. "You didn't text me back when I texted you, Mr. Sherlock."

"Well, you didn't call me back when I called you."

"Because I didn't know what you wanted. That's why I texted you."

"But if I would have texted you back, you would have ended up calling me back anyway, so, what's the point of texting?"

"To save our valuable time."

"But all the time you spent texting could have been saved by calling me back, hearing what I had to say, and finishing the entire conversation."

"That's not the way it works anymore, Mr. Sherlock," she schools me. "It starts with a Twitter, goes to a text, and ends with a talk. I call it the three T's of today's telephone talk technology."

"I call it 'Call me back when I call you.'"

"Whatever."

I hate texting. It's nothing more than an excuse not to speak with another person. But to be honest, I can't figure out how it works. My brain just won't work when it comes to texting. Neither will my fingers. I can never seem to hit the right letter with any digit on my hand, and the texts I do send are spelling nightmares. It's like I'm allergic to texting.

Everything I try is a cyberspace thud. I can never remember if I first put in the message or the address. When am I supposed to hit send? What do I set into the settings? What am I transferring when I transfer, and when is it tech-proper to use "BTW," "OMG," and "LOL?" I can never figure out how or when to delete, so I either don't read the message or have a string of messages that are months old. I never know what to do when I run out of room on the little screen. Do I hit send and do another text, and if I do, do I wait until they respond to the incomplete message before I text the rest of it? A lot of the problem may be the phone I bought from the More-For-Less Phone company, which operates out of an old hot dog stand by a guy named Les who is, no doubt, making more and giving me less. All the apps and gadgets on my cheap phone must fight with each other for dominance, and in doing so, screw me up royally. The good news is if texting follows the usual progression of high-tech development, some new device will take its place, and I will never have to figure out what "CRS," "PMP," and Tiffany's favorite, "TTFN" stands for.

"Tiffany, meet me at the elevator of the Monadnock Building at three." I interrupt myself, "No, make that 2:15."

"Okay, text me the address."

Yeah, that's gonna happen.

***

The Monadnock Building is one of Chicago's architectural gems. It was built in the late 1880s by the famous architects Burnham and Root, who based it on designs of the ancient Egyptians. It has bay windows, a copper cornice, and more funky twisted ironwork than a Salvador Dalí rendition of Shirley Temple's curly top.

Tiffany is waiting impatiently when I arrive at ten to three.

"Where have you been Mr. Sherlock? I've been waiting forever."

"How long is forever, Tiffany?"

"Over ten minutes."

"Sorry, but ten minutes would still make you twenty-five minutes late."

"No, ten minutes late," she corrects me. "The first fifteen minutes, *fashionably* late time, doesn't count as being late."

"Thanks, I'll remember that fact next time around."

"What are we doing here?"

"It's Chester time."

The office, six floors up, is the last one on the left side of the hallway. There is no nameplate or company name stenciled on the door. As I push the door open, a little bell attached to the top inside door panel ting-a-lings.

An older man in a perfect-fitting, three-piece tweed suit and a bright red bow tie comes out of the inner office to greet us. "Mr. Sherlock, I presume?"

"Yes. Mr. Chester?"

He puts out his hand to shake. "It's actually Longtooth, Chester Longtooth. With a name like Longtooth, I use Chester as often as possible."

"This is my assistant, Tiffany."

"Pleased to make your acquaintance, Miss."

As they shake hands, Tiffany gets that look on her face again. "Would you mind if I touched your tweed?" she asks.

"Certainly not."

Tiffany squeezes a sleeve but isn't impressed. "This ain't alpaca."

Thankfully, I can tell Chester has no clue what she is talking about.

"You're a tough guy to get in touch with, Mr. Longtooth."

"I can't imagine why. I've been in here for over thirty years. And call me Chester, please."

We are ushered into his corner office with a brass-footed, antique desk, high-backed chairs, and bookshelves, which go to the ceiling. On the far wall, are wall-to-wall file cabinets. In one specific way, his offices match Sterling Sheckle's.

"And how may I be of service to you?" Chester asks as we all sit.

"I am trying to find the six million dollars of Mr. Sheckle's money which has gone missing."

"Yes, horribly unfortunate."

"And I am told it came out of his personal account, which you control."

"As of this point, it does seem to be the case," he says with his hands folded like a churchgoer on the edge of his desk. "I feel awful about it."

"Do you use a smartphone to pay bills?" Tiffany asks.

"No."

"What exactly do you do for Mr. Sheckle?" I ask.

"I'm his personal accountant. I have been for the last thirty-four years."

"Pretty big job doing the books for a guy who makes billions?" I ask.

"It's a lot of zeros."

Something strikes me as odd. "Where's your staff?"

"I don't have one. My wife helps out with the daily ledger and comes in full time in March and April. She had a doctor's appointment this afternoon."

This isn't kosher. "You and your wife handle the entire personal account of one of the richest men on the planet?"

"He is our only client."

"I'm no accountant, Chester, because I have so little to account for, but the machinations of the income of a Sterling Sheckle must be mind-boggling."

"It can be a bit unsettling to the outsider," he says without hesitation. "But, by the time the numbers come to me, they have been massaged to the nth degree. All of the subsidies, government allowances, interest payments, depreciations, and ledger adjustments have all been accounted for."

"You short form him?"

"Ah, no."

My curiosity gets the best of me, and I have to ask, "May I ask what tax bracket a guy like Sheckle would be in?"

"Twenty, twenty-one."

"What? I'm, like, twenty-eight," I tell him.

"Mr. Sheckle's income derives entirely from his capital gains distributions, which are taxed at a much lower rate than the average income earner in America."

"That's not fair," I comment.

"Sounds fair to me," Tiffany voices her financial opinion.

"I don't write the tax laws, I merely follow them," Chester says.

"No offense, Chester, but something is wrong with this picture."

"Mr. Sheckle has an extensive personal portfolio of investments which has to be accounted for, but due to the amount of income he earns, his taxes take on a different aspect. For example, the one hundred thousand in interest payments Mr. Sheckle makes on his personal residence is a tiny drop in the bucket for him to write off."

"I'll be more than happy to buy the bucket if you want to drop some in mine."

"I'm sorry, but that would not be in keeping with the manner in which I file Mr. Sheckle's returns."

Darn.

"So," Tiffany asks, "if you're not sitting around figuring out new write-offs to cheat the government, what do you do all day?"

"I give away his money."

"Chester," I ask, "where do I get in line?"

Chester goes on to tell us the only real write-offs that make a big difference are contributions to charity. It's his job to find the most worthy recipients based on write-off capability. Some charities offer more than others, especially on the basis of paying state taxes. And, unlike other philanthropists, all of Mr. Sheckle's giving comes out of his personal account.

"What about the SSS Charitable Foundation?" I ask.

"It doesn't exist. I don't know how that name ever came about."

"Explains why I couldn't find it."

"If all contributions are made from a personal account, there is no public record, and having no public record allows us the freedom of operating under the radar, which in this day of technology, can be a benefit to someone of Sterling Sheckle's financial stature."

"Gifts are made anonymously?"

"Never."

I sit and think *I got to get on this list.*

"Why the animosity between you and C. Franklin Witherington?" I ask.

"I hold no animosity towards anyone, I assure you." It's easy to see he's not kidding. "How Mr. Witherington may feel about our situation is entirely up to him."

"When we spoke to him, he didn't seem to appreciate being kept out of the loop when it came to Mr. Sheckle's private accounts."

"Again, I have no control over his feelings."

"He's the one who had your work audited?"

"Yes."

"An activity you didn't appreciate?"

"Mr. Witherington and I have different fundamental understandings of accounting standards."

"And his is wrong?" I ask.

"No, different."

"C. Freddy seemed a bit tacky and snappy to me," Tiffany says. "I personally wouldn't want him counting my money."

I ask, "Do you have any idea of how someone was able to get into the account and steal millions?"

He coughs out of embarrassment, no doubt. "No, and if you find out, I'd like to be the first to know."

"Has this ever happened before?"

"Not that I am aware."

I decide to cease my questioning. The man seems sincerely troubled and sorrowful of the situation, and I would feel cruel to continue. "You've been very open and helpful," I say sincerely.

"If there is anything else I can do to help you in your search, please do not hesitate to ask."

"I will. Thank you for your time."

In the elevator, Tiffany asks me, "Do you ever wear tweed?"

I refuse to answer.

"Why are you giving me the silent treatment, Mr. Sherlock?"

I wait for the doors to open and say, "Because I'm trying to teach you to never talk in an elevator."

"How about if I text you, then?"

I return to the silent treatment after that comment.

After we make our way out onto the street, I ask, "All right, Tiffany, what was missing this time?"

"Missing from what?"

"Chester's office."

"There was something missing from Chester's office?" she asks.

"Yes."

"What?"

"Think, Tiffany."

"I hate thinking."

"I'll give you a hint. It's bigger than a bread box."

"What's a breadbox?" she asks.

"A box where you put bread."

"I don't eat a lot of bread, Mr. Sherlock, unless I'm carbo-loading for some reason."

She pauses. "Give me another hint."

"You're supposed to be paying attention wherever we go, Tiffany."

"Why?"

"Because that's what detectives do."

"Now you tell me."

I take a deep breath. "Tiffany, think. What was missing from Chester's office?"

She hesitates. "I can't think right now, Mr. Sherlock. I'm having a brain freeze."

"Think, Tiffany. What was missing from Chester's office?"

She puts her hand to her chin. "Could you give me a hint?"

"No."

"Please?"

"Remember Sheckle's office?" I'm giving her a hint. "What was missing in Chester's...?"

Tiffany perks up and interrupts me. "I know," she says, "a hot secretary in Vera Wang."

"No."

"Two hot secretaries in Vera Wang?" She tries again.

"Tiffany, you have to learn to notice the obvious."

Tiffany puts on her *poor, poor, pitiful Tiffany* look.

I hate that look. I give in. "Chester didn't have a computer on his desk either."

"That's the same answer as before, Mr. Sherlock."

"Exactly."

"Well, that's not fair," Tiffany says. "You gave me a trick question."

CHAPTER 5

I call my girls in the afternoon, as I do every day I don't see them. Care tells me about a classmate vomiting during third period, and the class got to go to the gym and hang out instead of learning about Manifest Destiny. Kelly speaks to me as if our conversation last evening never happened. She tells me about how her love for Cameron is "flowering like an orchid in springtime."

"Where do you come up with this stuff, Kelly?"

"When you are filled with love, Dad, words flow from you like sands through the hourglass."

"You make that up?"

"No, I picked it out from my new phone app, *Lovely Lyrics of Love.* I got it for free for thirty days."

It's always nice to speak from the heart.

I'm glad I'm back on speaking terms with both daughters.

The rest of the evening I sit at my computer. First, I check the status of my real estate exam and am told I am *In Process*. Next, I Google *Sterling Sheckle* and come up with 376 listings. I go through the first ten, learn little or nothing, and get bored. This is what I don't understand about the Internet. Why would anyone slog through 376 pieces of information, the majority of which are totally worthless, to find one or two absurd facts that mention your subject? And 376 is nothing compared to Googling a topic like *bed bugs* or *bad haircuts*, where there are tens of thousands of pieces of information, most of which are a total waste of time. What's the point? It's overkill to the max.

People forget that the reason the computer was invented was to save time. The first computer was used to process payroll checks of employees of large corporations, which was a horribly time-consuming task. So, some guy invented a computer to do it mechanically, which not only saved thousands of hours, but millions of typing ribbons and stenographer's fingernails. Yes, the computer worked writing checks. But fifty years later, we ask ourselves: do we have more time because of our computers? The answer is "No," because we spend so much time at our computers trying to save time.

The phone rings.

"Hello."

"Sherlock."

"Herman."

"You have any money?"

"You've got to be kidding, Herman. I'm so broke, if a burglar broke into my apartment, he'd end up leaving me a couple of bucks."

"Just wondered," he says. "I discovered why SSS didn't go to the police or the FBI when they lost the six million."

"Why?"

"They had a data breach a month ago. Somebody tapped into the credit card system of Bill's One Dollar Bill stores, a chain of ninety-nine cent plus a penny stores SSS owns in the south."

"Who would want the credit card data from people who put a dollar on their credit cards?" I ask.

"That's not the point," Herman says. "They didn't want the publicity."

"How much did they get taken for?"

"Whatever it was, it's a mere drop in the bucket compared to what they're worth."

"I wouldn't mind some of it dropping in my bucket."

"I thought you said you didn't have a bucket, Sherlock."

"I don't."

"Did you meet with his personal accountant?" Herman asks.

"Yes." I go on and relay everything Chester told me about his one and only client and end with, "He spends most of his day giving away Sheckle's money."

"You ask for any?"

"No."

"You should have. If you're going to be in real estate, Sherlock, you got to learn how to ask for money."

"Thanks for the advice."

"What did you think of C. Franklin Witherington?" Herman asks.

"I wouldn't say he was 'my kind of a guy.'"

"Twenty years ago, when he was Chuck Witherington, he got caught cookin' a few books."

"His name is really 'Chuck'?" I'm not going to tell Tiffany.

"The DA at the time couldn't get the charges to stick, so he walked."

"How about since then?"

"He either went legit or he got smarter. I'd bet on the latter."

"Herman, why hasn't your new leaf changed you from glass-half-empty guy to glass-half-full guy?"

"Because I know figures lie, liars figure, and the best liars lay out figures to lie about what other liars can't figure out. Those are the guys who become chief financial officers."

I'm more confused than I was before when I had no idea what I was doing. "You think Witherington could have hacked his own company."

"No."

"I don't think the money was hacked out," Herman says. "After what happened with Bill's Dollar Bills, they went into crisis mode. Let me tell you, it wasn't easy getting what I got."

I have no clue where to begin, so I ask, "What should I do, Herman?"

"I'd work the charity angle."

"You think a charity ripped him off?"

"Probably."

"You need more faith in the common man, Herman."

"Those charity guys give the CFO crooks a run for their money."

"Herman, you put dents into my faith in humanity."

"Most humanity is dented to begin with, Sherlock." And he adds, "Sure you don't have any money?"

"Positive."

"Too bad."

***

I put in a call to Chester first thing the next morning.

"Chester, I'm going to need a list of last year's recipients of Mr. Sheckle's benevolence."

"That's privileged information, Mr. Sherlock."

"Trust me, I can be trusted."

"The list will be ready by ten," Chester says without hesitation.

"Thank you."

Something must be wrong; this guy is too easy. To be honest, I'm not used to working with people who are cordial, helpful, and polite at the same time. After years of dealing with bunco artists, forgers, armed robbers, thieves, and other unsavory characters, it's a little difficult to switch gears.

Less than three minutes after ending Chester's call, my phone rings.

"Hello."

"Is this Richard Sherlock?"

"Yes, it is."

"My name is Al Zazou, I'm the managing director of the Halstead Street office of LPRE, and I see your real estate test scores are in process."

The Lincoln Park Real Estate Company is one of the premier sellers of upscale homes in the city of Chicago. They specialize in multi-million dollar residences. They sell to Arab Sheikhs, captains of industry, and people who have more money than Mafia Dons. If I sold one of those houses, I'd be out of my crummy apartment forever.

"What can I do for you?"

"I'm not sure," he says, "but I'd like to investigate the possibilities." He gives a slight chuckle before continuing. "At LPRE we pride ourselves in having the best agents in the city, and if you have the drive, determination, and desire of becoming one, we'd like to have you on our team."

Wow! This is the best phone call I've received since the night I was called and told I won the Illinois Lottery. The worst call I ever received was when the Lottery called back, and told me I was the wrong Richard Sherlock.

"I would very much appreciate the opportunity of speaking with you, Mr. Zazou."

"Call me Al."

"Al."

"When would be convenient, Mr. Sherlock?"

"I have to be downtown at ten. I could drop by your offices around eleven."

"I'll be waiting," he says. "And remember, Mr. Sherlock, when opportunity knocks, invite it inside."

"Yes, Mr. Zazou, I will."

"Call me Al."

This day is starting off in spectacular fashion.

***

Chester wears a blue wool suit, which Tiffany would fabric fondle in an instant.

"Mr. Sherlock, nice to see you again," he greets me before the bell stops ting-a-linging.

I look around and see we're alone. "Wife not in again?"

"No, not today."

Remembering yesterday's conversation, I ask, "Is she okay?"

"My poor wife has her share of medical maladies, Mr. Sherlock. If she is lucky enough to cure one pain, soon after, two others arrive to take its place," Chester says. "It is no fun getting old."

His revelation is hardly good news for me. My body is going downhill faster than a runaway sled down Mount Everest.

I follow him into his office. He hands me a weighty document, and I do a brief page-through as he explains, "The organizations are listed on the left, dispersal dates in the center, and the approximate amount of each donation is on the right. Each has a contact name, address, and phone number if you care to speak with any of the recipients."

I quit scanning the lines, go right to the bottom of the last page, and remark with absolute awe, "Sheckle gave away eight million dollars last year?"

"Approximately."

"That's a lot of money."

"It is all relative, Mr. Sherlock. And again," he says, "this is privileged information."

"I understand."

A few moments pass before I ask, "Does Mr. Sheckle have a family?"

"Yes," Chester says, "but currently inactive."

I wonder if this means he is free of financial obligations and ruling on the proper age to start dating.

"A very nice wife and two adopted, grown children." Chester fills in the blank.

I bet his two kids have trust funds coming out of their ears.

"Is he currently looking to adopt anymore?" I ask, wondering if he'd want to adopt a middle-aged guy with two kids, one of which has hormones going into overdrive.

"I would doubt it."

It was worth a try. Herman would be proud that I at least asked.

I glance at his ancient desk clock. I don't want to be late. "Thank you very much, Chester, I appreciate your help. I'll be in touch."

"Do you believe you'll find the money, Mr. Sherlock?" Chester asks as I turn to exit.

"I certainly hope so."

"I hope so, too," Chester says with a forlorn, hangdog look on his face, which makes me feel sorry for him. "My entire service over the last forty years will be marked by an untreatable stain, which will be difficult for me to take with me to my grave."

I consider espousing the benefits of cremation but feel this is not the time or place. "I assure you, I will do my best, Chester."

***

Al Zazou has the biggest teeth I have ever seen. When he smiles, which he does constantly, it's like looking at a shiny new grand piano keyboard without the sharps.

"So glad you could come in for a visit, Richard," he says, pumping my hand like he's trying to raise well water.

"Thank you, Mr. Zazou."

"Call me Al."

He leads me into a conference room that is festooned with hundreds of pictures of multi-million dollar homes, each with a LPRE banner across signifying *Sold*.

"Richard, you impress me as the kind of man who knows what he wants out of life."

"I do?" I hesitate, realizing I sound like a hesitant groom. "I mean, I do," I repeat more forcefully.

"What do you want, Richard?"

What I want is to make enough money to get out of my crummy apartment. "Mr. Zazou, I want to be a success," I say instead of the aforementioned immediate truth.

"Call me Al."

"Sorry, Al."

"And how do you expect to achieve your success?"

"I will do what it takes, go the extra mile, and I'll sell my soul to the devil if he is willing to pay my price," I tell him, making a fist to drive my desire home. The $150 I doled out for King Closer's seminar may be the best money I've ever spent.

"That's what I like to hear," he says, flashing his teeth wider than the shark in *Jaws*.

"It's a kill or be killed business," I say. "It's that simple."

"Richard, you are my kind of guy."

"Thanks, Al."

"What we do with our new associates is bring them in and team them up with one of our seasoned professionals. We put you right in the field so you can learn the business and learn the business from the best."

"Sounds like a plan, Al."

"I can't tell you how many agents we have put through our program that have gone on to multi-million dollar careers."

"Great."

"Are you interested?"

"Of course."

"When can you start?"

"I won't get my license until my test scores are in," I tell him.

"A mere formality, Richard," he says. "We want you in here now, in the trenches, so the day you hang up your shingle you can hit the ground running and take off like a rocket."

"Zoom."

Al stands up, thrusts out his hand, and he shakes even harder than before. "Welcome to LPRE, Richard Sherlock."

"Thank you."

"And remember, Richard, you don't just sell houses, you sell yourself."

I'm off to the races.

***

It's after noon, so Tiffany should be out of bed. I call her. She doesn't answer. I leave a message, "Call me."

She texts me back. *What do you want*?

Nope, not this time. I'm going to wait her out.

Fifteen minutes later, she calls. "Mr. Sherlock, you didn't text me back."

"Obviously."

"That's not fair."

"Nobody ever said life had to be fair, Tiffany." I say this, but then consider this comment is usually used with a negative connotation. In Tiffany's case, *life isn't fair* takes on a whole opposite meaning.

"Was'up, Mr. Sherlock?"

"Time to go to work."

"But I haven't had lunch yet."

I was hoping she'd say that.

We meet at the Vegan Vittles Café and Wine Bar thirty minutes later. Tiffany must be awfully hungry to move so quickly. She has the organic beet, flaxseed, wheat germ, dried chickpea, soy pasta salad, and I have a turkey sandwich, a free-range turkey sandwich.

I pull out Chester's list. "We have to start going through this list."

"Why?"

"Because it's the only lead we have."

"Sounds boring, Mr. Sherlock."

"Boring is what detective work is all about, Tiffany."

"Why don't we spend the time we'd spend getting bored and go out and find a more exciting lead?"

"Because it doesn't work that way, Tiffany."

"I'm willing to give it a try."

Why do I bother? "Okay, fine. You go out and find us a new lead while I work the list."

"Are you going to help me?"

"No."

"How am I going to learn if you don't help me, Mr. Sherlock?"

"Trial and error."

"You want me to go to court and make mistakes?"

"No."

"What do you want me to do then?"

Lo and behold, I come up with an idea. "Charities always have big parties to raise money, right?"

"Yes."

"Okay, Tiffany, find us one where we can schmooze with the movers and shakers who shell out the big cash."

"I can do that."

"Good." If nothing else, this should keep her occupied.

"But if I get us invited, you can't go wearing those awful clothes you own. You'll have to buy a new suit."

"I'll let you pick out the fabric."

"I'd love that."

As Tiffany munches through her salad, which looks to me like monkey lunch at the Lincoln Park Zoo, I page through Chester's list. The first few pages are real killers: cancer, muscular dystrophy, heart disease, Parkinson's, malaria—a regular *pick your death wish* section. All of the recipients are large, well-known, and recognized charitable organizations, including the American Cancer Society, Susan G. Komen, Alzheimer's Association, and ALS Association, to name a few. The next section of the list is also disease-related, not killer diseases, but maladies, which make you miserable: psoriasis, angina, sciatica, and arthritis, among others. So far, the subject matter doesn't go well with a turkey sandwich, even a free-range turkey sandwich. Next are the social causes: YMCA, YWCA—I'm glad to see Sheckle isn't sexist—NAACP, Latino Community Organization, Italian American Federation—or racist—amfAR AIDS—or homophobic—Habitat for Humanity, ASPCA, and PETA—and he likes animals, as well as humans. Also included in this section are quasi-religious organizations: Jewish Defense League, Americans for Israel, and Anti-Defamation League; it's obvious on which side of the aisle Sterling worships. And since Sterling is so fair-minded, I wonder if Jews for Jesus will ever make the cut. The final two pages of the report are where it gets interesting. Most of the charities I don't recognize. AEA could stand for the Association for the Eradication of Acne, for all I know. The Homeless Project, Fruit for America, Obesity Busters, Use Used Food, Homeless Helpers, Carpools for Cancer, and about thirty more, all fall into the category of highly suspicious in my book. This tells me exactly where to start my search.

"Aren't you hungry, Mr. Sherlock?"

"Kind of lost my appetite, Tiffany."

"Want some of my salad? The antitoxins can do wonders for your skin tone." Tiffany pushes her plate of nibbled rabbit food in my direction.

"No, thanks. I checked my toxins this morning and I was a quart low."

"Suit yourself, Mr. Sherlock, but you don't know what you're missing." Tiffany pulls the plate back to her, spears what looks like a section of molted snakeskin, and pops it in her mouth. "Yummy."

While she chews, I ask, "You ever give any money away, Tiffany?"

"No, it's not really my thing, Mr. Sherlock. One time I offered half of a Starbucks scone I didn't want any more to a guy with a sign saying, *Will Work for Food*, and he turned his dirty nose up to me and said, 'No thanks, lady.' Wouldn't you know it," Tiffany continues, "I give the guy exactly what he's asking for, without requiring him to do any work, and he disses me."

"The nerve of some starving homeless people," I add an exclamation point to her comment.

"The man should be sent to bed without dinner."

"Does your dad give any money away?" I ask.

"Yes, but he could give more."

"Who gets most of his money?"

"Me."

CHAPTER 6

"He's wonderful."

"Mr. Sheckle?"

"Truly wonderful."

I'm standing in the Use Used Food warehouse on the South Side speaking with Alan Smithy, the president of the nonprofit.

"Mr. Sheckle not only supplied our first van but bought us one more a month later," Alan informs me. "The man is a saint."

"What exactly does Use Used Food do?" I ask.

"After a big party, event, gala, wedding, wherever there is a dinner for hundreds, there is always food left over. You can't have a big party and run out of broccoli, so the chefs always cook way too much. We arrive just after dessert, pick up what's left over, and deliver it to shelters around town, usually before the fingerling potatoes get cold."

"How often do you do this?"

"We average one night a week in the off-season, and three or four nights a week during the holidays."

"So homeless people eat better than me?" I ask.

"A lot of the poor in Chicago are developing some very selective taste buds."

We walk past the panel vans. Smithy opens one and shows me the built in refrigeration unit and warming trays.

"And we owe it all to Mr. Sheckle."

"And how did you go about finding him and asking?"

"We didn't," Alan says. "He found us."

"How?"

"There was an article in a local paper about what we were doing, and a week later we had our first fully equipped van. It was a miracle."

"Have you ever met him?"

"No."

"Was there anything to sign, promise, or swear to before you received the gift?"

"No."

"How much does one of these food trucks cost?" I ask.

"Anywhere between eighty and a hundred grand."

I quickly remember a $300,000 amount across from Use Used Food on the list Chester supplied. "Has he given you any more money?"

"Some."

"When is your next pickup?" I ask.

"Tomorrow night, there is a dinner for two hundred at the Four Seasons. Prime rib, lobster tail, soup, salad, and a veggie—should be a big night for us."

"And where will you be dropping off the leftover food?"

"Hungry?"

I hate it when people discover my ulterior motives. "Just wondered."

"Pacific Garden Mission on South Canal."

If the Mission does takeout, it might be worth it to stop by.

***

"We call him Mr. Wonderful."

"In person?"

"No, never met him."

"Did you find him or did he find you?"

"He found us."

I'm speaking with Sylvania Rayleen Evergreen, the founder, owner, and chief proprietor of the Neighborhood Coalition for a Better Brownsville Neighborhood, the N, C, 4, double-B, N. "And he gave you over two hundred thousand dollars?"

She seems a bit taken aback, me knowing her total. "I'm not sure. I never added it all up," she tells me sheepishly.

"And what has the money gone for?"

"Everythin' from graffiti removal, to tree plantin', to after school programs," she says proudly. "Our next project will be job trainin'."

"I applaud your efforts, Ms. Evergreen," I compliment her. "But, if I may ask, one day you opened your mail and there is a personal check from Mr. Sheckle for thousands of dollars?"

"Hallelujah."

"I bet that was a good day?"

"I thought it was someone playin' wit my mind, until I took it to the bank and they cashed it on the spot," she tells me. "One of the glorioust days of my life."

"And there were no strings attached?"

"What do you mean?" she asks.

"Agreement about how the money would be spent or how you got the money?"

"I'da signed my soul away for dat kinda money."

"And you've received other checks?"

"Yes."

"But on no set schedule or timetable?"

"Every day before openin' the mailbox I be prayin' a little prayer, Mr. Sherlock."

I think this through and conclude I got to get Chester to put me on the list.

"Thank you for your time, Sylvania."

"You're welcome," she says. "And if you ever see Mr. Wonderful, please thank him for me and everybody in the neighborhood."

"I will." I hesitate. "One last question..."

"Yes."

"How did you ever get the name Sylvania?"

"While she was birthin' me, Mama looked up and saw the name shinin' down upon her."

***

There are two thatched huts side by side on forty feet of dusty earth. Three buzzards sit motionless toward the rear, a wooden water bucket is on its side to the right, rags hang listlessly from the limbs of a dead tree, and a plate of what looks like week-old meat sits in the center. The light from above shines down and causes an intense heat that puts my sweat glands into overdrive. There are no colors; everything is a shade of dusty, depressing brown. It is a desolate, sad, and repellant scene.

I stand off to the left, as quiet as a church mouse.

Two four- or five-year-old black children, filthy and barefoot with distended stomachs, walk past me to the middle of the crusty earth. Dirt covers their arms and legs and on their faces, dried mud. What hair they have on their heads is unwashed and matted down. They are almost naked. Only scraps of cloth cover their bodies. They sit across from one another with the disgusting plate of stinky meat between them, I can only hope they don't sample the meal. The two start to sweat profusely.

A few seconds of quiet, and a loud voice bellows out. "Roll tape, speed, and ACTION!"

The two kids crawl around in the dirt for a few minutes and do what kids do, which is poke and prod each other. The buzzards in the background move in the exact same movements. The klieg lights seem to get hotter. A voice is heard from a man behind the cameras.

"All right, queue the flies."

The tops of two wooden boxes slide open, and an uncountable number of black houseflies are released. They immediately buzz around the set trying to get their bearings and look for a place to park. They are drawn to the two kids frolicking in the dirt. This is disgusting.

The two kids do their best to swat them away with jerky hand movements, but find little success. The man who queued the flies is yelling out directions, "Keep swatting, jump around, and let them land on you, keep the buzz up, swarm, swarm."

I'm not sure if he's directing the kids or the flies.

It doesn't take the little buggers long to make a fly-line to the crusty meat, where they land and start in on lunch, laying their larvae, or doing whatever flies do in this situation. The meat is crawling with black insects.

"Now, pick up the meat."

Both kids grab a tasty morsel, causing the flies to go into an angry frenzy. Each kid now has his own black cloud of insect buzz encircling his body as they bring the meat closer to their faces.

"Keep going, you're doing great. Let them crawl on your face for a while."

After about forty seconds, the kids can't take it any longer. They drop the meat, jump up, and go into their own frenetic frenzy to shake the flies off their skin. I can't blame them.

"CUT!"

Three stagehands jump onto the set holding a can of Raid in each hand. They spray like demented crop dusters, atomizing enough DDT-like aerosol into the air to thwart a locust invasion. The flies drop like flies. Another stagehand, with plastic bag in hand, picks up the meat the same way a dog walker picks up poop. The electric buzzards in the background are switched off. Two mothers hesitate until the poison smog lifts, rush onto the set, grab their kids, and begin to heap praise on them: "You were great," "That was marvelous," "What an actor!" They wrap each kid in a blanket, pick them up, and rush them off to the side of the studio where two three-foot-wide tubs are filled with water. Each kid gets dunked, shot with soapy foam, and scrubbed top to bottom. The rags they were wearing in the scene are tossed to the side to be used another day. The prosthetic stomachs, which were glued to their tummies, are released by the soap and water and float to the top of the tub.

The director checks with the three cameramen while the stagehands exchange their Raid cans for flyswatters and go on an expedition to eradicate the flies clever enough to outrun the spray.

"I didn't know Chicago was so close to Equatorial Africa," I say to the director when he finally finds time for me.

"This one is going to make us a ton of money," he says.

"Really?"

"It all comes down to *flies in the eyes*."

Arch Steen is the director, producer, and chief financial fundraiser of the Rescue the Little Ones Foundation. We sit in his editing bay watching the tape of the scene just shot. It's gross.

"Couldn't this be considered child abuse?" I ask, seeing the two kids jumping around the fly-infested set like they were hit with nerve gas.

"They both made fifteen hundred bucks for less than two minutes on camera," Arch says.

I immediately wonder if they ever use white, twelve-to-fourteen-year-old girls for this type of work.

"Both of those kids have worked with us before. If they hated it, they wouldn't come back."

I am a bit fascinated by the footage we're seeing. One camera did a wide shot, one did close-ups, and one did individual shots, all very well done. "What happens next?" I ask.

"We'll find some washed-up actress, pay her a flat fee, and have her read an empathic plea," Arch says. "Put it on TV, the phones will ring off the hook, and the money will pour in."

"How much of the money will actually get to Africa?"

Steen gives me a dirty look. "The percentage of funds to the actual problem is close to 80 percent, which is a hell of a lot better than the Parkinson's, Heart Fund, or even breast cancer."

"Sorry, I didn't mean to be accusatory."

"I know this looks pathetic, but we know what works," he explains. "And nothing raises money like *flies in the eyes*."

We talk for another twenty minutes. Arch pretty much repeats the same litany as the prior charities I visited. He was off on the money, but that didn't seem surprising. I thanked him very much for allowing me to be a different kind of fly on the wall during the filming of his commercial.

***

If you are a viewer of public television, the names John D. and Catherine T. MacArthur are most likely familiar to you. Their foundation, with an endowment of six billion dollars, supports charitable activities the world over. John D. and his wife, Catherine T., started it in 1978 with the money John D. made as the owner of Bankers Life and Casualty Company. I'm not sure if this is true or not, but it is said that John D. ran his insurance business from the back booth of a diner somewhere in Florida. I wonder how good of a tipper he was and if he got to request which entrees would be the *Special of the Day*. Each year, the MacArthur Foundation, which is based in Chicago, awards around twenty-five Genius Grants, to the tune of about $300,000 per grant, to some very lucky individuals. It is very secretive on who gets chosen. There is no formal nomination; any Tom, Dick, or Harry can write the Board of Directors and say, "My cousin is a pretty good guy, really smart, and could really use the cash to study the mating habits of the California snail darter." The winners can use the money for anything they want, no strings attached. Winners have included playwrights, scientists, poets, physicists, doctors, lawyers, Indian chiefs, and professional do-gooders. I should be so lucky.

I mention this because as I sort through the charities on the Sheckle list, there are some similarities with John D. and Catherine T.'s modus operandi. First, there's no rhyme or reason on who gets the money. Second, it's a surprise; the cash just shows up. Third, there really aren't any strings attached. This all leads me to believe a copycat may be in play here. Could Sheckle be mimicking the MacArthur's? And if so, why? There is something weird going on, and it would be best if I found out what. And while I do so, I will also be doing my best to get on either of the lists.

CHAPTER 7

Al Zazou calls first thing Saturday morning.

"Sherlock..."

"Mr. Zazou..."

"Call me Al."

"Al."

"Richard, I'm pairing you up with a true legend in the world of Chicago real estate," he tells me. "She has sold more multi-million-dollar properties than the entire offices of some of our competitors. She's a whirling dervish of salesmanship. Hanging out with her, you'll pick up more by osmosis than most junior agents learn in a year. *Commission* should be this woman's middle name. Does the name Ms. Ramona Missy ring any bells, Richard?"

"No," wouldn't be a good answer. Instead, I say, "*The* Ms. Ramona Missy?"

"The one and only." I'll bet Al's teeth are shimmering in a smile right now.

"I can't wait to meet her."

"She's expecting your call." Al gives me her cell number. "And remember, Richard, you only get one chance to make a good first impression."

Actually, that wouldn't be true if you are a sandcastle artist or posthole digger, but I don't correct him.

"Al, I'll keep it in mind."

"And remember, Richard, nothing in life begins until someone makes a sale."

This isn't true either, but I get what he's talking about. "You got it, Al."

Three seconds after I hang up the phone with Al, it rings again.

"Sherlock..."

"Herman."

"Thanks."

"Thanks for what, Herman?"

"Eighty-seven thousand four hundred thirty-seven dollars and eighty-three cents."

"What?"

"That's how much I made off Sheckle," Herman says, then adds, "So far."

"What are you talking about?"

"I told you there was something funny going on at Sheckle's place. The more I snooped, the more I found."

"You didn't rip him off, did you Herman?"

"No, I just read a few emails, checked a few hundred phone records, saw money moving from one account to another, and put two and two together, then four and four, eight and eight."

"And came up with eighty-seven grand?"

"The power of compounding."

"Herman, if you ripped them off, I have to report it."

"I merely bought a few options, did a few warrants, margined a few shares, leveraged a little money, and took a ride on the elevator when Sheckle pushed the button to go up."

I have no clue what he's talking about. "Herman, speak English."

"Sheckle's made a play to take over a California biotech company that is hot on the trail of a cure for toenail fungus, and I just happened to get in a day before the news broke."

"Is that legal?"

"The boys on Wall Street do it every day."

"But is it legal?"

"Close enough."

"And you made eighty grand?"

"Eighty-seven and change."

"Do I get a cut?" I have to ask.

"No."

"Why not?"

"I asked you if you had any money, and you said you didn't," he says. "You can't make any money unless you spend a little money, Sherlock."

"You didn't tell me what was going on," I argue.

"I couldn't."

"Why not? For that kind of profit I would have mortgaged my soul."

"Can't get much for a soul, Sherlock, especially yours."

"Well, you should have let me in on it, Herman."

"But that would be insider trading, you could go to jail."

"You couldn't?"

"Nobody told me anything," Herman says. "I didn't get any clandestine phone calls, messages in code, or privileged information."

"You hacked into their computers."

"Which you, Detective Richard Sherlock, ex-Chicago PD, asked me to do."

"Herman..."

"Sherlock, you wouldn't have done it anyway. Who are you kidding?"

He's right. I hate my conscience. Every time I've ever been near easy money, it kicks in, and I kick out. If my ship ever comes in, I'll be waiting at the wrong ocean.

"What other great news do you have for me, Herman?"

"This Sheckle guy makes Donald Trump look like a puny piker in pigtails."

Sterling doesn't have enough hair to do a Trump flip, so Herman must be speaking of his methods of doing business. "Really?"

"Ruthless."

"It doesn't make sense."

"This guy would sell his kids into slavery," Herman says, "if he could get a good price."

"So, why don't we hear his name in the same sentence with Bernie Madoff?" I ask.

"Beats me. From what I've found out, Sheckle should have a sentence like Bernie Madoff."

"Such as..."

"He was at the head of the line in the subprime mess, his numbers came up in the Swiss bank sting, and I'll bet he kicks little dogs if they try to pee near his driveway."

"You think he's a crook, Herman?"

"I think he's too big to be a crook."

"What does that mean?"

"Guys who control that much money, so many companies, and thousands of jobs are considered untouchable because if they go to jail, it could screw up thousands of innocent lives. Remember those guys at AIG? They were the biggest crooks since Capone. They ripped off thousands of people, but did any of them ever go behind bars? No." He continues, "These Wall Street bankers, hedge fund players, VPs at Goldman Sachs know how to skirt the rules because they not only helped write the rules but know where all the loopholes are. Millions of people lost their homes in the Great Recession, but did any of the bankers who set all the old ladies up for the fall get punished? Of course not. Worst thing that happened to them was they went off and found bigger jobs and made even more money."

"Sheckle is one of these guys?"

"Google *financial felon*, and you'll see Sheckle's picture."

Doesn't sound like Mr. Wonderful to me.

Herman and I talk a few more minutes. He tells me he's lost two more pounds. He must have one of those scales with a swinging seat underneath a dial and a red arrow that points to big numbers around its edge hanging from a rafter.

"Keep up the good work, Herman."

After I hang up with Herman, I call Ms. Ramona Missy.

"Hello, this is Ms. Ramona Missy."

"Hi, this is Richard Sherlock."

"I've been waiting for your call," she says.

"Mr. Al Zazou gave me your..."

She cuts me off. "I'm glad you called because there is no better day than today to make your move into the wonderful world of real estate."

"I'm supposed to..."

She keeps talking, "And I'm the one who can move you into the home of your..."

I'm talking to an answering machine.

I wait for her sales pitch to finish and leave my name and number, and ask her to call me back.

Two minutes later, I get a text. *Be at my office at three.*

Ms. Missy's busy and wants to save time.

***

For the remainder of the morning and early afternoon, I continue to call the charities on Chester's list. Out of the twenty-six charities I speak with, twenty-four give me the same story as I heard from Use Used Food and Rescue the Little Ones. "He's just wonderful." The other two, Streetsmart Smarts and Heal the Heroes, have disconnected phone numbers.

I Google Streetsmart Smarts first and get no direct hits. I go through thirty-seven sites ranging from controlling traffic flows and tutoring to self-defense lessons and a revolutionary new cement compound made from discarded plastic water bottles, which "Thinks like a street should think, if a street could think." I call a couple of these, and the people I talk with probably consider me a crackpot or idiot. This isn't the first time this has happened and won't be the last. Next, I go through the State of Illinois' charities website and find a Streetsmart Newspaper listed but no Smarts. The address on Chester's list doesn't match any from the state, and there is no charity license number for Streetsmart Smarts.

Heal the Heroes is a different story. There are three sites with this name. The first, and biggest, has a very professional website detailing their mission to help veterans from Iraq and Afghanistan suffering from PTSD, post-traumatic stress disorder. There is a video, a listing of the doctors and psychologists on staff, a history of the organization, and a complete review of the Board of Directors, highlighting a number of the movers and shakers. The organization is based in Florida. It is especially proud of being awarded a Bill and Melinda Gates grant the past two years.

The second Heal the Heroes charity I find also seems legit. Not as big and flashy as its namesake, but it has a website, address, license number, contact information, and a PayPal link to donate. This Heal the Heroes' mission in do-gooderism is to help police and fireman who have been injured in the line of duty, a noble cause in my book.

Neither of the first two matches the address on Chester's list.

I may have hit pay dirt, or the lack of pay dirt, with the third Heal the Heroes. The website is at least three years old. Although it is concerned with aiding the victims of Hurricane Sandy in New Jersey, the address is on the South Side of Chicago. I try the phone number listed, which is different than the one Chester gave me, and it, too, is disconnected. The website has a collage of pictures of the Jersey Shore devastation but lists no names of principles or board of directors, has no mission statement on its banner, no contact link, or financial information. Anyone who would fork over money to this charity based on the appeal of the website, should quickly sign up for the Free Financial Advice nonprofit which also received some of Sheckle's sheckles.

***

Ms. Ramona Missy has had so much plastic surgery only her lips move when she speaks, and she can be a little difficult to understand. "You changed your name when you became a detective?" is her first question after I give her a brief personal background check.

"No, it's always been Richard," I tell her with a chuckle.

She doesn't get the joke, or she does get the joke but can no longer smile.

"You know what the biggest problem I have selling real estate is, Richard?"

"No."

"Parking."

I'm not sure what she means. "Parking spaces?"

"No, parking when I'm showing properties."

I don't understand.

"There's no place to park when I'm showing properties," she further explains.

"Oh." Now I get it.

"You're a cop, can you fix parking tickets?" she asks.

"I'm no longer a cop, and I couldn't fix parking tickets when I was a cop."

"Well, that's too bad. If you're going to make it in this business, you got to have parking."

"Thanks for the tip."

"You got a gimp sticker?" she asks.

"No."

"If you're going to make it in downtown real estate, you better get yourself a gimp sticker. I got one from my doctor."

I didn't know plastic surgeons could issue parking passes. "I'll see what I can do."

"Now, are you ready to go to work?" she asks without facial emotion.

"Ready to learn."

Ms. Missy hands me a stack of pink phone messages. "Call these idiots back, find out what they want. If any of 'em seem to have any money or a property they want to list, let me know right away. The rest, blow off."

"Yes, Ms. Missy."

She leads me to a corner desk in the farthest corner of the sales room and deposits me in front of a multi-line phone. "You ever drink pureed pomegranate extract juice?"

"Ah, no."

"You should," she says. "There's a place across the street that sells 'em; go get us a couple."

I'm waiting for her to drop at least a ten-spot to cover the cost, but she turns and walks across the room and disappears into a corner office.

While I wonder if I made a good first impression, I page through the sixty or so phone messages that all came within the last twenty-four hours. I don't get this many phone calls in a month, much less a day; it must be nice to be popular. I decide I better do the juice thing first, so I walk out of the LPRE office and onto Clark Street. The juice bar is across the street, next to Frances' Food Shop, a Lincoln Park restaurant institution known for great corned beef sandwiches. I walk in, stand in line with other juice aficionados, and see on the menu board that the large Pureed Pom is eleven dollars. I pull out my weekly budget of mad money and add it up: nineteen bucks. Two Pureed Poms are out of the question. I buy one and march back across the street.

When I return to drop off the juice, Ms. Missy is in her corner office, sitting in her oversized leather desk chair, and getting her fingernails done by one tiny Asian woman and her toenails done by another. The two traveling mani/pedi-curers converse in a tick-tocky, click-clacky language I can't understand. I place the drink on the desk in front Ms. Missy. "Here you go."

Ms. Missy has added a chin strap wrapped around the top of her head, which pushes the folds on her neck upward. She's now even more difficult to understand. "Where's my stwaw?" she asks.

Because of all the water splashing around, the filing, and the fact that Ms. Missy can barely move her mouth when she speaks, I think I heard her say, "Where's my squaw?"

The two Asian mani/pedi-curists certainly don't look Apache to me. So I ask, "Are you also expecting a medicine woman?"

"Wha?"

"I need a stwaw, a stwaw." She motions with her hands to outline the item of which she speaks.

"Oh, a straw."

I find the office lunchroom and start rummaging around in the drawers but find no straws. One of the secretaries, or assistants, as they are now called, enters and asks, "What are you looking for?"

"A straw."

"For Ms. Missy?"

"Yes."

"She likes the ones that bend."

"Thanks for the tip. I'm Richard."

"I'm Jeanne. You must not have your license yet."

"How'd you know?"

"Just a hunch. Good luck with Ms. Missy." She turns and leaves the room.

There isn't a straw to be had, but I do find a BIC pen. I pull off the top, yank out the point and the thin inside plastic tube that holds the ink, and pry off the back plug. I take it back to Ms. Missy. "There weren't any straws in the lunchroom, but this'll work."

She loosens her chin strap, and peers through the hollow plastic like it is a miniature telescope. She puts one end in the pom and the other end in her mouth. Ms. Missy adjusts it to where her lips have the tightest suction and sucks. A little pom juice comes out of the tiny hole in the side of the tube, but it works great.

"Refreshing?" I ask.

"It's gweat fo cwensin' yer inswides," she tells me. "Your wiver will tank you."

I wonder if it will be verbal, or in the form of a thank you note.

"You din't get pwomagwranate for you?" She asks, sipping away.

"No, I'm allergic to biblical foods," I explain.

"Get twose calls dun?"

"I'll get right on it, Ms. Missy."

Before I'm out the door, she removes her chin strap and says, "I owe you an apology, Richard. I forgot something."

I come back into the room and put my hand out to get the eleven dollars, but instead, she hands me a beige pair of high heels.

"When you went out to get the juice, you should have dropped these off at the cobbler's. It's very important in real estate to multitask."

I look down at the expensive shoes.

"Tell the guy I need tips."

I exit the office with shoes in hand. Both Asian women speak as I leave, but I have no idea what they're saying.

About 75 percent of the numbers on the pink sheets are from telemarketers. I try to call them back, but none have phone numbers that get connected to a real person. Telemarketers have our numbers, call us at all hours of the day and night, but we can't call them; something is wrong with this picture. Six messages are either personal calls or non-telemarketer/regular people-telemarketers trying to sell something. Three people called wanting to know the price of a north side mansion up for sale. With the last group, I use a listing sheet tacked up on the wall and inform them of the $12 mil price tag. One person asks if the "price is negotiable," one hangs up in shock, and one says "that's one too many zeros for me."

I get the shoes over to the cobbler, who has a sign in his storefront window reading: Time Wounds All Heels. By the time I get back to the office, Ms. Ramona Missy has left for the day.

It's too early to call it a day. I call Tiffany.

Wonders never cease; she calls me right back. "I can't talk right now, Mr. Sherlock, I'm at the spa."

"I need to check out a few addresses, want to come along?"

"I'm pretty busy right now," she tells me. "I'm right between my massage and my eyebrow tweezing."

"Well, I'd hate to squeeze your tweeze, Tiffany."

She hesitates for a few seconds and then says, "You know, I will go along with you."

"Want to take my car or yours?"

"Your car? You have got to be kidding."

This is exactly what I wanted to hear, since I left my car at home.

I take the No.22 bus downtown. Thirty minutes later, Tiffany comes out of the Re-New-Me Spa's lobby.

"I love what they did to your brows," I tell her.

"You noticed? How nice," she says.

We take the Dan Ryan south and get off at 57th. We travel west, the only way you can travel unless you want to drive into Lake Michigan.

"I'm really kind of glad you called, Mr. Sherlock," Tiffany tells me. "I needed an excuse."

"Excuse for what?"

"To leave the spa," she explains. "After I thought about it, I really wasn't in the mood for a colonic today."

Too much information.

"Go left on Cottage Grove," I tell her.

We go south a few miles. "Slow down," I plead as we pass the 6400 block. I look closely but can't find 6410 S. Cottage Grove. "Turn around, go back."

"You sure you got the address right, Mr. Sherlock?"

I reread the list. "It's what Chester has on his list."

Sixty-four twenty Cottage Grove is a liquor mart on the ground floor and what looks like a few offices on the second floor. Tiffany parks her new Lexus 450, and we go inside the store. We wait in line behind two guys buying one bottle of Mad Dog 20/20 with handfuls of small change. The counting seems to take forever.

"Excuse me," I say to the man sitting inside a square of bulletproof glass, "we're looking for Heal the Heroes."

It must be hard to hear through the glass because he responds, "Hero sandwiches?"

"No, Heal the Heroes," I say as distinctly as possible.

"Does it come in a half pint?" he yells back.

I give up. "How do we get to the offices upstairs?"

He points. We turn to exit the store. Tiffany asks, "I wonder what the man does when he has to go to the bathroom."

We go out the door to our right to the alley and to our right again. At the back of the building is a dilapidated stairway up to the second floor. Between us and the stairs are the two guys who bought the Mad Dog. They sit beside the trash dumpster enjoying their afternoon libation.

"Tiffany, maybe you should wait in the car."

"Or maybe I should have stayed for the colonic," she says, noticeably scared.

"I'll walk you back."

"No," she says holding onto my arm, "in for a dollar, in for a million."

As we pass by our fellow shoppers, they give us a not-so-pleasant sneer. I say, "We'd love to join you, but we have a prior invitation." We go up the creaky stairs.

There are three doors along the exterior hallway. The lettering on the first reads Wonderful Weaves by Wanda. I knock on the door, no answer. I put my ear to the door and can hear music inside. I knock again. No answer. We are about to walk to the middle door of the trio when a black woman the size of Rhode Island squeezes out the door. "You wanna a Wanda weave, woman?" she asks Tiffany.

"Ah, maybe."

"No betta weave than a Wanda weave," she says. "Dat pretty blond hair Wanda would weave wonderful for you."

"I was thinking just a couple of strands on the left side?" Tiffany asks.

"No problem. Come on in to Wanda's."

We enter.

On one side of the room there are two couches that were obviously dropped off at the dumpster downstairs but saved from destruction by Wanda. A sleeping woman, who rivals Wanda in size, occupies the couch on the left. On the opposite side of the room is a table with what I guess are weaver's tools. In the center of the room is one old office desk chair. On the back wall is a huge HDTV with a large black woman on the TV. I wonder if there is a size requisite required in Wonderful Weaves by Wanda. "Who's that?" I ask, pointing at the TV screen.

"Queen Latifah."

"Shouldn't she be wearing a crown?" I ask, but get no answer.

Wanda escorts Tiffany to the middle of the room. "Sit down here, honey, so Wanda can get at you."

Tiffany sits. "Could you do it so I could maybe put a few diamonds in as highlights?"

"Wanda can do that."

"Excuse me," I interrupt, "is this 6410 South Cottage Grove?"

"No."

Wanda takes a hunk of Tiffany's blond hair, divides it into three, and starts to weave the strands together.

"Ouch."

"Darlin, Wanda gotta make it tight to make it wonderful."

"Excuse me," I repeat, "do you know of a business called Heal the Heroes?"

"No."

"It was a charity, address was 6410."

"Check next door. He be here longer than me."

I leave Tiffany in the capable hands of Wonderful Wanda and go next door to Elmo's Entertainment, a division of E. Elmo Escobar Enterprises dot com. The door is slightly open, so I walk in.

"Excuse me."

The man behind the desk reaches for a Glock and points it at my chest. "You here to rob me?"

I jump back with my hands up. "No."

"Good." He puts the gun down. "What can I do for you?"

I wait until I'm breathing somewhat normally and say, "I'm looking for the Heal the Heroes charity."

"Oh man, that dude hasn't been here in months."

"So, you know him?"

"We did some bizness."

"My name's Sherlock, I'm investigating—"

He picks up the gun and points it at me again. "You a cop?"

My hands rocket back to the sky. "No."

He puts the gun back down. "Good."

"You know Heal the Heroes?" I ask, lowering my hands slowly.

"I knew the guy who used to run it."

"What was his name?"

"Louie."

"Louie, what?"

"Louie the Louse," he says. "At least that's what his friends called him."

"You know what his enemies called him?"

"A crook."

"You think he was a crook?" I ask.

"Yeah."

"Why?"

"It takes one to know one."

"Or a cop to know one," I add.

He picks up the Glock again.

"But that wouldn't be me," I quickly say.

During our conversation my hands have gone up and down so many times I might as well be at a Bears game doing the wave.

"Could you tell me something about Louie?"

"Salty guy who liked pepper," Elmo says.

"He ran a charity?"

"Something like that."

"Was it a scam?"

"Some people thought so." Elmo gives me a bit of a shoulder shrug.

"You know where I could get in touch with him?" I ask.

"Try Stateville or Joliet."

"Thanks for your time." I pause before exiting. "By the way, what kind of entertainment do you provide?"

"What kind do you want?"

I leave Elmo and proceed to door #3. I knock. No answer. The door is locked and sports no sign or name. It has been a while since this place had a tenant. Office space in this neighborhood must be hard to rent. I take out my one overcharged credit card, slip it inside the doorframe, and I'm in.

Inside, beneath enough dust to start an allergy epidemic, there is an old, dented, metal desk. Somebody must have taken the chair, and I suspect Wanda. I open the middle drawer slowly and find little or nothing of interest, unless you consider two pens, dental floss, and two size-D batteries a treasure. I open the right-hand side drawer and get much of the same nothing. I open the file drawer—empty. I push the file drawer halfway in, find the catch, and pull the drawer all the way out of the desk. I peer inside the empty abyss and way, way in the rear, I see what I expected. I reach in and pull out a few crumpled pieces of paper. One is a pink bill for propane, and another is a piece of stationary with the Heal the Heroes logo, address, and phone number on the top and the name Louie Leftalone on the bottom. I fold the paper and put it in my pocket. I replace the drawer, leave the office, and relock the door on my way out.

Wanda has done a wonderful job weaving three crisscross braids on Tiffany's left side, giving her kind of a 1960s hippy vibe. "Very attractive."

"Thank you, Mr. Sherlock," Tiffany says. "I'll stick a few carats in and light up the next room I'm in."

"That'll be twenty-five dollars," Wanda informs her.

Tiffany pulls out a fifty and tells Wanda "Keep the change."

To show her appreciation, Wanda gives her a coupon for *Three wonderful weaves for the price of two.*

Tiffany smiles, "Thanks, but I don't do coupons."

One empty bottle of Mad Dog 20/20 rests next to two satisfied liquor mart customers who have passed out against the side of the dumpster. "I believe they call that 'slumping,'" I tell Tiffany.

"I call it 'dumb,'" she tells me.

We walk to her car, which, *hallelujah*, has no tires, batteries, or parts missing. We get in. "Where to now, Mr. Sherlock?" Tiffany asks.

"Lincoln Park."

"Are we going to the zoo?"

"Maybe."

***

The offices of the GWWC are in a converted brownstone on Sedgwick, a few blocks north of North Avenue. Even Tiffany is impressed as we enter the front lobby area. "This is my kinda charity," she says.

"I'm Richard Sherlock," I tell the receptionist as I check the list Chester supplied. "Is a Mr. Alfred Murtaugh in?"

"And what is this concerning?" she asks.

"Sterling S. Sheckle."

She makes the call, and a well-dressed, middle-aged man of maybe fifty appears in seconds. "Hi, I'm Alf Murtaugh. Are you from the press?"

"No."

"TV station?"

"No."

"Radio?"

"I'm Richard Sherlock, and this is my assistant, Tiffany. We're on a special assignment for Sterling Sheckle. We'd like to ask you a few questions."

"Hold my calls," Alf tells his receptionist and leads us past smaller offices where the young people inside type furiously into their computers. We end up in his office, which was once the master bedroom of the brownstone. It has a marble fireplace, sitting area, a massive teak desk, high-back chairs, and original art on the walls. One of which is an oil portrait of Alf Murtaugh. Very impressive.

He sits behind the desk; we take the chairs. "What can I do for you?"

I consult my list one more time before speaking. "What exactly does the GWWC do?"

"The Global Warming Warning Committee is made up of a group of individuals and scientists who will alert the powers that be of the growing threats caused by the smoke of burned fossil fuels rising into our atmosphere."

"You're a nonprofit?"

"Yes."

I'm also a nonprofit but certainly don't live this well.

"And Mr. Sheckle has been a supporter of your efforts for how long?"

"Two years."

"And those people we passed in the hallway, are they busy alerting people that need to be alerted?" Tiffany asks.

"No."

"What do they do?" I ask.

"Their job is to write grant letters."

"They work weekends?"

"Volunteers."

"So," Tiffany asks, "do you have big horns or speakers to alert people that a cloud of stinky pollution is on the way?"

"Not quite," he says. "We sponsor meetings, symposiums, and gatherings of individuals who carry out our message to the corporate community."

"So, you don't, like, use sirens?" Tiffany tries to understand.

"More like we alert the alerters," Alf says.

"Oh, I get it."

I continue, "I have a figure here that was given to me by Sheckle's people, and I'm only asking for confirmation of the amount given to you."

Alf becomes a bit uncomfortable in his very comfortable surroundings.

"Three hundred thousand dollars?"

Alf's eyes perk up like a kid on Christmas morning. "I'm not at liberty to release financial information."

"Four hundred thousand dollars?"

"Sorry."

There is an uncomfortable silence to go along with the rest of the discomfort in the room. I suspect Alf suspects I know something he doesn't really want me to know, but I know nothing of the sort.

"Thanks for your time," I say, standing up.

"You're welcome."

I hustle Tiffany out of the brownstone. On the sidewalk outside, I comment, "Nice digs, huh?"

"Feng-shuied to a tee."

"I should live so well, Tiffany."

"Well, you two share at least one thing in common," Tiffany says.

"What?"

"You're both charity cases."

"Wait," I say, pulling out my phone. "I have to make a phone call."

I dial a number I know by heart, hear the ringing, and the connection's made. "Hello..."

"Lester."

"Phone call from Sherlock on weekend, like black cloud over picnic."

I'm calling Lester Oland, a detective on the Chicago P.D. who claims he was a descendent of Warner Oland, an actor who played Charlie Chan in the movies.

"I need a favor, Lester."

"Favor and Saturday make for bad bedfellows," Lester tells me.

I tell him all about Louie Leftalone. He pulls him up on the computer and confirms Elmo's suspected address. "People incarcerated easier to find than people who deserve incarceration."

"Thanks, Lester, and as soon as Mitchell's has their *Return to 1968 Prices* Day, I'll treat."

I hang up with Oland, which signals Tiffany to start up the Lexus. "Okay, so where to, Mr. Sherlock?"

"Tiffany, how would you feel about going to prison?"

CHAPTER 8

Sunday is visiting day.

As prisons go, Stateville, located close to Joliet, is quite famous. Built in 1925, it was the brainchild of a Briton, Jeremy Bentham, who designed a totally new circular concept for housing society's most, or least, wanted. Affectionately known as the "roundhouse," Stateville prison was erected as a panopticon, where a guard tower sits in the middle of several tiers of jail cells. Thus, one set of guards in one tower can watch over all the prison cells at the same time. It was heralded at the time as a state-of-the-art, revolutionary design, but evidently didn't weather the test of time because Stateville is the only panopticon prison in existence today. Besides its architectural significance, Stateville is also known as the home for many famous or infamous inmates, including Richard Speck, Leopold, Loeb, and it was the last residence of John Wayne Gacy. As they say, neighbors make the neighborhood.

The only addition to Stateville in the past twenty years is the Stateville Farm, a section devoted to minimum-security prisoners. That's where Tiffany and I sit at a picnic table with Louie Leftalone.

"How'd you ever get the name 'Leftalone'?" Tiffany asks.

"I must have been feeling sorry for myself the day I made that one up," he tells her.

"That's not your real name?"

"I've had so many names I can't remember my real name, darling."

"Don't call me *darling*."

Louie is obviously not taking advantage of the yard, gym, or tennis courts on the Farm. He's pudgy, all over pudgy. There isn't a part of his body that doesn't have a pudge.

"Do you remember getting any money from Sterling Sheckle?"

"Maybe."

"It would have come in the form of a check."

"I cashed them checks quicker than a holdup man runnin' out of a 7-11."

"It would have been a pretty substantial amount," I say to him, knowing the dollar amount on Chester's list.

"Let me tell you," Louie says, "during Katrina and Hurricane Sandy, I was making some serious coin." Louie sits back and explains. "There's nothing like a national disaster to get them bleeding hearts writing checks. I'm hopin' and prayin' to be out of this place before the *Big One* hits in California."

"Well, it's always nice to have something to look forward to," Tiffany says.

"Tell me how your scam works."

Louie's proud to expound on his specialty. "Ya got to jump on it quick. As soon as the fire hits, the tornado levels the town, or the water takes out the levee, ya get yer website up and running on the Internet. Ya got to have a lot of pictures of dead people, kids sufferin', destroyed homes, and dead pets; dead pets really crank up the ante in my business. You write some crap on there about how bad things are, money is needed right away, and whatever they give is going to go right to the disaster area; it gets 'em every time." He stops, gets a little more excited, and says, "And it used to be they had to send a check to a PO Box, but now with PayPal and smartphones, they just shoot the money right through cyberspace. I'm telling you, there's nothing like technology when yer scammin' folk."

"What's the biggest donation you ever received?" I ask.

"I think it was two grand," he says, which is a zero away from the number on Chester's list.

"Who was it from?"

"Who cares?"

"Did you ever call or contact people to get donations?" I ask.

"Naw, too much work."

"Fill out grant money forms?"

"No way."

"So, how did you keep the money flowing?" I ask.

"There are three keys to the business. The first is to name your charity a name close to another big one doing the same disaster. The second is to keep the pictures coming, ya got to keep the disaster disastrous. The third is to keep Googling your own website and get other people to do the same. The most Google hits, the higher the site shows up on the net. The higher the site, the more clicks you get and the more money you receive."

"Do you have a conscience?" I ask.

"Who'd ever want one of those?"

***

We're on the Interstate heading back to Chicago. Tiffany has to be doing at least eighty. "You know, Mr. Sherlock, this should be a wake-up call for you."

"Why?"

"Because your lack of text-nology in the world of technology is embarrassing. You're so far behind the times, you're like a flip phone in a 4G sea of androids."

"It would be a total waste of my cerebellum activity, Tiffany."

"What?"

"What's the benefit of filling my head with a load of technological mumbo jumbo when it's all going to be irrelevant as soon as the next big thing comes along?"

"Speak English, Mr. Sherlock."

"What's the point of learning to do something when it is going to be obsolete in a few months?"

"That was a little clearer, but I'm still not sure what you're talking about."

"Remember Myspace?"

"Of course."

"You use it anymore?"

"No. Only weird people who don't have friends use Myspace."

"Do you ever IM anymore."

"Nobody IM's anymore."

"Napster, Aereo, or pet any pets on Pets dot com?"

"No."

"My point exactly. Why fill your head up with tech stuff that in three or six months will be out of business, or you won't do anymore?"

"Mr. Sherlock, you're not making a lot of sense."

"A brain is like an attic, Tiffany. If you keep throwing junk in, it'll fill up, and pretty soon you won't have room for the important stuff you need to know." I tell her this, well aware she has lots of room to spare in her attic.

"No, Mr. Sherlock, you're totally wrong. First of all, if you live in a penthouse, you don't have an attic you have a rooftop deck. And secondly, the reason they invented self-storage units was for people whose attics are already filled up."

Why do I bother?

We travel a few miles in silence before I ask, "By the way, Tiffany, how old were you when you started dating?"

She pauses for a few seconds. "Let me see," she says, "guys started chasing me when I was about twelve."

I interrupt, "Twelve?"

"Your mother let you date at twelve?"

"Sure."

"Don't you think that's a little young?"

"You're making it sound like I'm from Kentucky, Mr. Sherlock," Tiffany says. "Actually, Mom was pretty strict about who I could date. Like she wouldn't let me date anyone in high school until I was in high school."

I can't believe I'm hearing what I'm hearing. "Who'd you date?"

"Let's see… there was the quarterback on the football team, the lead in the school play, and two rock stars." She pauses. "A couple of them overlapped, but not all at the same time."

"Rock stars?" I question.

"That was in my *bad boy* phase. Every teenager goes through one."

"They do?"

"Of course."

I picture in my mind a bedroom-on-wheels van pulling up to my apartment with rap music blaring and a scruffy, long-haired freak puffing on an e-cigarette and festooned with tattoos and more piercings than a pin cushion stumbling out. He lumbers to the door, can't figure out how to ring the buzzer, and instead calls out, "Yo, Kelly, I'm horny."

I start to sweat.

"Dating was really no big deal, Mr. Sherlock, until I started to get my equipment when I was about fourteen. Once that arrived, the phone really started ringing," she says proudly. "And after I got my first boob job at sixteen, the floodgates opened up."

"You got enhanced when you were sixteen?" I can't believe I'm asking this question.

"I went away for two weeks, and when I got back into town, I told everybody I had a growth spurt."

"At sixteen you were still a child."

"It's the same principle as stuffing socks in your training bra," Tiffany explains. "I merely substituted silicone."

"Your parents let you do that?"

"Mom had a pair. Why shouldn't I?"

This is scary.

"Mom passed her *desire-to-have-great-breasts* gene on to me. I think they call it boob-eredity."

"Oh my God." I'm now sweating profusely. Talk about differing parenting styles.

"And she taught me how important it is to get the implants changed out every couple of years to keep a *fresh, natural* look."

I get yet another image of my first daughter in my mind, but it is so frightening I can't verbalize it. I feel faint.

"Mr. Sherlock, you don't look too good. You okay?"

"No, I'm not okay." I pull down the visor and glance at myself in the small mirror. I resemble a sick, worn, aged Casper the Unfriendly Ghost.

"Should I pull over?" Tiffany asks.

"Yes."

"Where?"

"At a convent that takes in fourteen-year-olds."

CHAPTER 9

When in doubt, visit the wife.

Rosemary Sheckle lives in Evanston. The house is a Queen Anne, complete with a wraparound porch. It has a set of double front doors, a large foyer, and three fireplaces on the first floor. It is not huge, opulent, or the best house on a block of pre-1900 Victorians. It is merely a nice, warm, comfortable home.

"I appreciate you seeing me," I tell her as we sit in the sunroom of the house and sip ice tea.

"I assure you, I do not make a practice of doing this," she says in a soft-spoken tone.

Rosemary is a small, petite woman of maybe sixty, sixty-five at the far end. She immediately exudes a comfortable confidence in herself.

"I love your home."

"So do I," she says. "There is a certain comfort in living in a house with a history."

"It's not what I expected."

"Disappointed you're not in a midwest Taj Mahal?" she asks.

"No, but it is interesting that a person of your husband's stature wouldn't live in more substantial surroundings."

"Maybe that's why he's never lived here," she says with a smile.

This is news to me. When Chester told me Sheckle's family was "currently inactive," I didn't consider the length of the inactivity. "I was told you were still married," I say in explanation.

"We are."

"Actively?"

"Even when we were actively married, it wasn't very active," she laughs.

"I'm confused," I admit. "Your name is on all his personal accounts."

"As it should be."

"And you have full access?"

"Yes. I take what I need and have a savings account to see me through my golden years."

I see why she is relaxed and confident.

"You know why I'm here, Mrs. Sheckle?"

"I was told there are funds missing from Sterling's account."

"Six million dollars."

"I assure you, I have no need for six million dollars."

Wish I could say the same. I wonder if she has any idea what kid's clothes cost these days.

"If I wanted a fortune, I would have divorced Sterling years ago."

I have to ask, "Why didn't you?"

"My husband would have fought me to the death. He would have gone to any lengths to destroy me and prove I didn't deserve a dime. That's what Sterling does. He loves a good fight. And it has nothing to do with money; my husband couldn't spend one percent of what he's made." She gives me a small smile. "It's funny, but I've never been able to figure out if it is that he has to win, or he just hates to lose."

"You have to admit it is an awful big pot of gold to pass up, Mrs. Sheckle."

Rosemary takes a sip of tea. "Our son is a urologist in Cleveland, and our daughter teaches at Bates College in Maine. Both are married with families, enjoy their careers, and have lives with purpose and dedication. Unlike their father, uncountable wealth has little allure."

"Could someone have gone through you to get to him, moneywise, I mean?"

"Between Chester and the thousands of accountants Sterling has, I would doubt it."

"Do you have any connections to his business or any of the businesses he owns?"

"Not really."

I stand. "Thank you for your time."

"You're welcome," she says. "I hope you catch the crook, and if you do, I'll probably end up feeling sorry for him because my husband will make sure the person is mercilessly punished."

On my way out, I consider mentioning, "If you ever consider selling your home, I'd be happy to provide an up-to-date appraisal at no charge," but I don't. Best to wait until I'm a licensed, official real estate professional.

***

On my way back to the 'L' station, I turn my phone back on and notice I have a text message. It's from Tiffany. It takes me a while to get it on the little screen. *TTUL*. Whatever that means.

I don't consider texting back. I call, get her voicemail, and leave the message, "It's Sherlock, call me." She doesn't call in the ten minutes it takes to walk to the station, so I call again and end up leaving the same message."

She calls me seconds later, "Why didn't you text me, Mr. Sherlock?"

"Because I hate texting."

"You just have to get used to it."

"What's up, Tiffany?"

"We have an appointment today at four."

"We do?"

"With my dad's tailor."

"You think he's a suspect in the case?"

"No, you need new clothes. We're attending a benefit Wednesday night at the Drake."

"What's the event?"

"Some medical thing I can't pronounce. They're honoring Sheckle."

"Good job, Tiffany."

"We got premier seats," she says. "I just hope they don't have diseased people parading up on stage for everyone in the audience to feel sorry for. I hate that."

"Yes, that pity stuff can be trying," I tell her.

She gives me the tailor's address, tells me how hard it was to get the appointment, and that I shouldn't be late. This is the pot calling the kettle "black is the new black."

Before she hangs up, she tells me, "You know that nerdy guy, whose parents wanted a girl, we met at Sheckle's company?"

"Leslie Ambrose."

"Wasn't it Lindley?" She asks.

"I know of whom you speak. What about him?"

"He disappeared."

***

I planned to take the 'L' to Belmont, transfer to the Brown Line, take it home, get my car, and stop by Herman's, but I stay on the Red Line all the way into the Loop and make an impromptu visit to my favorite CFO, C. Franklin Witherington.

"I heard you were missing someone."

"What a sleuth, Sherlock," he says in a not-so-pleasant tone.

"What happened?"

"The nerd emptied out a petty cash account and split."

"How much did he get?"

"Around sixty grand."

"You keep sixty-thousand in petty cash?" Yet another accounting un-believability in my realm of personal savings capability.

"Yes."

"You keep it in one of those metal boxes in the bottom drawer of your desk?"

"No."

"Then how'd he get it?"

"You're the detective, you figure it out." C. Franklin isn't the most cooperative of clients.

"You report it to the police?" I ask.

"No."

"Are you going to?"

"No."

"Wouldn't that be the logical thing to do in this situation?"

"No."

"Why not?

"Because it isn't, Sherlock."

C. Franklin Witherington wasn't real friendly when we first met, and our relationship isn't improving. Maybe I should consider asking if he'd like to "Take in a Cub game some afternoon?"

"You just don't get it, Sherlock," he spits out at me.

Evidently, I don't. "Why are you being so difficult?" I ask. "I'm only here to help."

"You can help by keeping your mouth shut."

I pause to think it through for about three seconds. "You're not going to tell Mr. Sheckle, are you?"

"Not yet, and neither are you."

I learned a long time ago that when you're not sure what to do, don't do anything. I'll wait to rat out C. Franklin to Sheckle until I know more. "Fine, I'll hold off, but only because I really believe that under your gruff exterior you're a *softie* at heart."

I leave the CFO to stew in his own negative juices and go down a few floors. I walk the aisles of cubicles until I recognize Leslie's fellow techie, the one who ran into his office during my last visit to announce the Chinese cyberattack.

"Remember me?"

"You're the guy who was here the other day with the hot white chick."

"So to speak."

"She's gorgeous."

"Yes."

"Totally gorgeous."

I sit in the one chair across from his desk. I have to look around the massive computer screen to see him. "Where's Leslie?"

"Don't know."

"You're lying."

"No, I'm not."

I've haven't met a lot of computer people, but the ones I have met are terrible liars. They are probably excellent liars in cyberspace, but not so good face to face. "Come on, I know you're lying."

"No, I'm not."

"Yes, you are."

"Well," he says, "I'm evading the truth, but I'm not lying."

I give him a few seconds, "Come on..."

"I don't know where he is..."

"But..."

"I have a pretty good idea where he isn't."

"And where's that?" I ask.

"I doubt if he's attending his Gambler's Anonymous meeting."

Enough said. I rise and find my way off the floor.

If I was a smarter, more savvy businessman, I would have a face-to-face meeting with Mr. Sheckle and inform him of the progress I'm making finding the missing six million, but I'm also a lousy liar, so I take the elevator down to the Willis lobby. I get lost in a crowd of mostly foreign tourists who mill about waiting for their turn to go up to the observation deck. I take a few moments to contemplate the case.

Here is what I know so far: Six million dollars has been stolen. It came out of Sheckle's personal account, but nobody knows how it got pilfered. Sterling employs hundreds of accountants to watch his corporate money but only one to guard his personal fortune—a bit incongruous. Around town, Sterling is known as Mr. Wonderful, but I certainly haven't seen that side of him. Herman seconds that belief, and the current, non-active Mrs. Sheckle didn't place absent hubby in the *Wonderful* category either. Chester is in charge of doling out millions of dollars of Sterling's money, but some of his choices seem odd. I personally believe the Richard Sherlock Fund would be a much better choice than Louis Leftalone's Heal the Heroes. I do have one suspect, the head computer guy at SSS, who obviously would know how to make the right keystrokes, but, for some reason, that seems too easy.

The reality of the situation is I have little information to go on.

Although you never see this on TV, what real detectives do when they have little to work with is to look for holes in what they do have. Something that doesn't fit, isn't explained, or makes little sense. This is always boring, arduous, frustrating, and time-consuming work. On TV, something always seems to happen right before a commercial that takes the case/show into another place or into some unforeseen action, but in reality, this rarely takes place. Instead, a detective has to sit around thumping his head, thinking, re-thinking, and overthinking everything he has already thought to death about. Is it any wonder I hate my job?

My thought patterns are interrupted by a foreign man asking, "How best get to Wrigley Building made of chewing gum?"

I tell him, "He who take cab finish first at destination." Lester Oland has had a bigger effect on me than I realize.

I stand around looking stupid for a few minutes, but the electrical impulses go to work in my brain, and a hole in the case dawns on me like sunshine after a thunderstorm. I make a call.

"Hello, Chester. It's Sherlock."

"Mr. Sherlock, I certainly hope you're calling with good news," he says.

"Well, not yet, but I do need to speak with you. Mind if I stop by?"

"I'm not in the office," he says. "I'm working out of the house today."

"Wife?"

"Yes."

"Mind if I stop by?" I ask, knowing I have no other place to go or holes to fill today, except my appointment with Tiffany.

"I'm not much of a housekeeper, Mr. Sherlock."

"Compared to me, I bet you are."

He gives me his address. He lives in Edgebrook. This is a problem.

I call Tiffany. I get her voicemail. I call her again. Leave another voicemail. Three times...

And she finally picks up. "Mr. Sherlock, what do you want?" she says as her "Hello."

"I need you to accompany me to see Chester." Actually, I need her to drive me because Edgebrook is way up by O'Hare and not easily reached by the 'L'.

"I'm busy."

"Doing what?"

"Swatching."

"What?"

"Swatch shopping."

"You're shopping for cheap watches?"

"No. I'm seeing a stack of swatches."

"You're looking for Bigfoot?"

"Who?"

I give up.

"Tiffany, I need a ride to Edgebrook."

"Where's that?" If it isn't downtown or a big-money burb, Tiffany has little use for it.

"It's where Chester lives."

"Do I have to?" she asks.

"Tiffany, you're rich. You don't have to do anything."

"That's true."

"But I could use a ride. If I have to take the train, I might not be able to get back in time for our appointment." I hit her where I know it will hurt.

"That won't work. Meet me at my building, Mr. Sherlock."

"Thank you, Tiffany."

I have to take two busses, but I'm at the door of Tiffany's lakefront, high-rise condo building in thirty minutes. I give the uniformed doorman my name.

"Mr. Sherlock," he tells me, checking his computer screen, "you're not on Ms. Richmond's allowed visitors list."

This is hardly a surprise. "Is Kelly or Care Sherlock on her list?"

"Yes."

"They're my daughters."

"Are they with you?"

"No."

"Just because you're related to someone doesn't put you on her list," he informs me.

"She's expecting me. Would you call her please?"

"No can do."

"Why not?"

"It's the rules. People who live here don't want just anyone stopping by. That's why they give us a list. Duh."

"But I'm not just anyone," I try to convince the doorman.

"Who are you?"

I give this some thought before answering. "I'm her boss."

"You're Ms. Richmond's boss?" He looks me over like I'm spoiled cheese.

"Yes."

"Tiffany has a boss? I don't think so." He gives me one more once-over and scrunches up his face. "Hit the bricks, buddy," he says. "You're the reason we have rules in this building."

"Yeah, well, watch this."

I take out my phone and call Tiffany, who doesn't pick up, but the doorman doesn't know this. "Tiffany, it's your boss, Sherlock. I'm in the lobby, pick me up, quick."

I give the guy one last look. So there.

I go wait outside. Five minutes later, Tiffany's Lexus comes up out of the underground parking garage and drives up the condo's half-circular driveway. "That wasn't a very nice message you left, Mr. Sherlock."

"I apologize, but I was merely proving a point."

"You should have texted me."

There is a big, thick, two-foot long, bound book on the passenger's seat. I pick it up and lay it on my lap as I sit. "What's this?"

"Swatch book."

I open to the first page. It has a four-by-four inch, pasted-on piece of cloth and a corresponding description. At least two hundred like pages follow.

"What's it for?" I ask.

"Your new suit," Tiffany says. "If you think I'm taking you somewhere and you're not going to look your best, you're in the wrong line at the Walmart, Mr. Sherlock."

I give her Chester's address. She punches it into her GPS, and a lady starts telling us where to go. "In two hundred yards make a left..." Even if I had a GPS system, I doubt if I would use it. I've never been very good when women tell me what to do.

"By the way, Tiffany, how did you know Leslie Ambrose disappeared?" I ask as Tiffany zooms onto the expressway.

"A text."

Here we go again. "A text from whom?"

"Daddy."

It is hard to believe that Jamison Wentworth Richmond, the CEO of one of the biggest insurance conglomerates in the world, would be notified of one employee, from one company, from the thousands of companies he insures, leaving without giving two weeks' notice. "How did he know?"

"I don't know, but Daddy is very savvy when it comes to technology—unlike you, Mr. Sherlock."

"Did you ask him?"

"You mean did I text him back?"

"Whatever."

"I don't remember."

"Could you call him and ask him?" I would call and ask, but Mr. Richmond never takes my calls.

"I'll text him." Tiffany pulls out her phone.

I quickly grab the phone out of her hand. "Not while you're driving."

Tiffany's mad, but she knows I'm right. A few minutes later, we exit, as per verbal instructions, and drive a few more miles.

"You have now reached your destination," the lady tells us.

I return Tiffany's phone, she texts. Less than a minute passes, and her phone beeps.

"Sheckle's woman called," Tiffany reads off her phone's little screen. "Sheckle wants to add sixty grand to the total."

I should have seen this one coming.

Chester lives on a quaint, tree-lined street. Most of the houses are of the 1950s ranch variety, but Chester's is brick with bay windows in the front, a stone walkway, and shrubs needing a haircut. I rap on the storm door.

"Mr. Sherlock, I'm sorry you had to come all this way," he says as we enter.

"No problem. You remember Tiffany?"

"It would be hard to forget such a beautiful woman," Chester says, shaking Tiffany's hand and giving her a short bow."

"I know," Tiffany replies. "I get that a lot."

The house matches the neighborhood in quaintness, but as I look closer, I see the place is a bit tired. The carpet is worn, the couch has a tear, and there has been some shoddy plastering done on the wall to my left. "How's your wife?"

"She's sleeping now; we had a bad night."

He leads us into the front room, where he motions for us to sit on the couch. "May I offer some tea?"

"No, thanks. We'll only be a minute," I say.

"Is it green or regular?" Tiffany asks.

"I'm not sure to what you are referring," Chester tells her.

"I better pass then," Tiffany says.

I get to the point of our visit. "Chester, I need to understand the criteria used in choosing the charities and groups in handing out Sheckle's money."

"I'm not sure we had one," he tells me. "We would search for applicable candidates, do some due diligence, and if they proved to be honest and forthright, I'd add them to the list."

"And were the grantees approved by Mr. Sheckle before the money was dispersed."

"Not always."

"You wouldn't tell him?"

"We'd provide a list twice a year."

"Did he ever request a donation to a particular organization?" I ask.

"At times."

"But for the most part, he left it up to you?"

"Mr. Sheckle's interest in the gifting is not a major priority. He has more important matters to deal with."

"He must have a great deal of trust in you."

"It is a job. I perform a function he'd rather not deal with."

Tiffany must be bored. She gets up and wanders around the room, stopping to fondle a few knickknacks and run her finger on dust settled on the side tables.

"Chester, do you remember the Heal the Heroes charity?"

He ponders and says, "No."

"How about Use Used Food?"

"The guy who picks up the leftover charity dinners?" he answers rhetorically. "I liked that idea."

I see out of the corner of my eye Tiffany has made it to the opposite side of the room, near the hallway door. She is perusing the few, mostly black-and-white, photos on the wall. "You got any kids?" she blurts out.

"No, we were not blessed with a family."

I am, but right now I'm not sure I'd use *family* and *blessed* in the same sentence.

"You know," Tiffany says, "there's some real weird noises coming from the bedroom. You got exotic pets?"

Chester jumps up from the couch, runs across the room, past Tiffany, and down the hallway.

"Was it something I said?" Tiffany asks.

I follow Chester. Tiffany follows me. We end up in the far bedroom.

"Claire!"

Chester's better half is lying on a hospital bed making gurgling sounds. Her lips are bluish.

"It's her heart," Chester diagnoses, but he is too panicked to do much else.

She can't breath. "Call 9-1-1," I order.

Tiffany whips out her cell. Chester shakes and shudders as if a massive electrical current shoots through his entire body. Reminds me of me getting hit with the first bad back spasm of the day.

"What do I tell the lady?" Tiffany asks me, her phone pressed to her ear.

"Cardiac arrest, patient having trouble breathing, and give them the address."

As Tiffany relays the message, I go to work. I grab Claire's wrist. There's a pulse but not a good one. I sit her up and begin to tap on her back to try to free up the passageway. My taps turn into thumps. Chester is horrified. Claire spits up ugly fluids. Tiffany is horrified. As the flow slows from out of her lips, so do my thumps. Claire struggles for breath. I lay her back down. Her body stiffens. She lets loose again with a mighty heave. She ate eggs not too long ago. I tilt her head back, place one hand on her forehead and one on her chin, and wedge her jaws open. I take a deep breath and begin CPR.

Chester collapses facedown on the bed. Tiffany moves to help, but before touching him, she takes a long look at his face.

"Is he breathing?" I ask between Claire-blows.

"I think he fainted." Tiffany pats him on his back, for what reason I have no clue.

I hear the siren approaching. "Tiffany, go. Let them in."

It takes the paramedics less than five minutes to stabilize Claire and three minutes to get Chester back to reality. Once all is calm, I head for the bathroom. In the mirror, I look like I'm the winner of a no-hands, pie-eating contest. I splash water on my face, find some soap, and do a thorough wash job. After I towel off and wash out my shirt, I look around and see more vials of pills than at my neighborhood Walgreens.

Clumped together with little rhyme or reason, the vials are all labeled C. Longtooth. I read over the names of the medications and recognize none. I open the medicine chest. There's more prescription vials labeled C. Longtooth.

By the time I am out of the bathroom, Claire is being pushed out of the house on a gurney. Chester follows close behind. Tiffany holds the front door open as the group heads for the ambulance. "Don't worry, we'll lock the place up," I yell from the front porch as Chester is helped into the back of the vehicle to sit next to his wife.

The siren wails as the ambulance drives down the block.

"Wow, Mr. Sherlock, you were, like, amazing," Tiffany tells me. "I couldn't have done what you did."

"Sure you could have, Tiffany."

"No way," she says. "I could never allow my perfect skin to come in contact with the disgusting chunks that lady was putting out."

"If I ever have a heart attack, Tiffany, I'll make it a point not to have it around you."

"Excellent plan, Mr. Sherlock."

We go back into the house and back into the bedroom. I strip the sheets off the bed to prevent any seepage onto the mattress. Tiffany remains in the hallway. She's allergic to household chores. "These sure are weird pictures to have up in your house."

Finished with the housekeeping, I join her.

"These people are all so pale and drab. They should make a group visit to a tanning salon," she says.

"Those pictures are in black and white, Tiffany."

They are family photos, circa 1920s to the 1950s. Parents, grandparents, and the numerous offspring are all represented. "I'll bet that's Claire," I say as I point to one of the eight children in one of the group shots.

"She certainly looks much younger," Tiffany says, "especially without the chunks."

Chapter 10

"Eet's eempossible."

"I don't want to hear it." Tiffany holds her hands to her ears.

"I be wake up eentire night."

"You can sleep when you're ninety, Alphonse," Tiffany replies.

I'm up on a two-foot platform wearing borrowed dress shoes, black socks, a new white dress shirt, but no pants—only my boxer shorts to keep me decent. A man with big thick hands stands beneath me arguing to no avail. "Eempossible, Mees Teeefanny. Eempossible."

If Alphonse were wearing a pair of lederhosen, he'd be a dead ringer for Geppetto. He's maybe five foot tall, round in the waist, bald on the head, wire rims hanging almost off his nose, and a tape measure slung around his neck like a diva's silk boa.

"If you want to keep making my daddy's suits, I suggest you put that measuring tape into overdrive."

"Mees Teeefanny, you eeempossible."

I've never had a suit custom-made, and I doubt if I ever will again. This is not a pleasant experience. The guy takes more measurements than a survey team on a winding road. The seam calibration is particularly unpleasant, but Alphonse asking, "You wear yourself left or right?" is absolutely embarrassing.

After about an hour, all my inches have been tabulated, and Tiffany tells Alphonse, "All right, get out the bolt and start cutting."

"You'se eeempossible, Mees Teeefanny."

"You can charge him triple," she replies.

"Happy to be of serveeese," Alphonse says with a broad smile. Amazing how money can quickly change an attitude.

I get down from the perch and quickly re-don my attire of slacks, chunk-stained polo shirt, and loafers. "Tiffany, how much is this going to cost?"

"I don't know."

"I'm sure I can't afford it."

"Mr. Sherlock, when it comes to looking good, you can't be worried about what it is going to cost."

"Yes, I can."

"Daddy will just add it to whatever you already owe us, and it will all work out."

After I lost my CPD job and was getting fleeced in my divorce, I was not only forced to take the job as the on-call detective for Richmond Insurance but also to borrow money from my new employer so I could feed my kids and myself. I've been working for the company store ever since. Is it any wonder I hate my life?

"I'm trying to work off my debt, not add to it, Tiffany."

"Think about how good you're going to look."

"On my way to the poorhouse?"

"No, at the charity banquet tomorrow night," she says. "Don't forget you'll be walking in with me, so there is no room for a fashion brain freeze."

I give up.

After I tuck in my shirt, my phone pops out of my pocket, and I notice I have a voicemail message. Thank God it's not a text. It's from Al Zazou. As the message plays, I can almost see his teeth lighting up a darkened room. "Richard Sherlock, do we have an opportunity for you! Drop by the office tonight before seven, and Ramona Missy will tell you all about it. And remember, Richard, a salesman without enthusiasm is just a clerk."

"I have to go, Tiffany."

"Where?"

"To my second job. The one I have to have to help pay for the one I already have."

"Ta-ta."

***

By the time I get over to the LPRE offices on Clark, it is close to seven. The front door is open, but inside there isn't a human at a desk. All the agents are probably out making big commissions. I walk toward the Ms. Missy corner. Hearing faint sounds from inside, I knock on the office door before I enter.

A woman dressed in a lab coat, protective eyewear, latex gloves, and a hairnet opens the door a crack and says, "Yes?"

"I'm here to see Ms. Ramona Missy."

She opens the door wide, and, not being one to be easily shocked, I'm shocked. Ms. Missy is lying on a portable table wrapped up in white sheets like a mummy from toes to neck. On her face and neck is a black paste caked on thicker than drywall compound. Covering her eyes are two round slices of what looks like bread and butter pickles. Her hair is covered with a teal, skin-tight skullcap, which has some smelly chemical oozing out. In total, she's a bald, comatose, Egyptian minstrel show performer with an ecological streak getting ready for her spot in the pyramid.

"Is that Ms. Missy?" I ask.

"She can't talk," the lady tells me. "She's in stage three of her skin rejuvenation regimen."

I make a quick decision not to ask about stages one or two. "I need to speak to her."

"She can't talk."

"I was told by Al Zazou she wanted to see me."

The lady reaches down and removes one of the pickle slices. Ramona's left eye peers my way. She winks once, then twice, then once again. I wonder if she's using Morse code. The lady puts the pickle back on Ramona's eye.

I see a movement underneath the sheets, and seconds later hear my cell phone buzz. Oh no, a text message. "I'm having trouble with my phone," I tell the lab coat lady. "Could you help me get the message?"

She takes the phone in her hand and in six seconds shows me the message: *U sit on Open house Wed.*

I'm not sure what to do. I ask, "Could you help me text her back?"

"Why? She's right here. Nothing's the matter with her hearing," the lady says as if I'm a total idiot.

"Sure, Ms. Missy. I'd be honored."

My phone buzzes again. The message pops up below the last message: *12 2 2.*

I wonder if this is a secret real estate language. I don't want to seem dumb, but I also can't afford to hire a text translator. "I don't understand," I tell her.

My phone buzzes. *Noon 2 2,* the message reads. I still don't get it.

"Noon to two," the lady in the lab coat says.

Now I get it. "It would be my pleasure, Ms. Missy," I tell her, trying to sound as accommodating as possible.

Another buzz, another message: *Now Go.*

I'm wondering if she wants me to go and get an early start. I look at the lady for an explanation.

"She wants you to get out of here."

"Yeah," I say, trying to be convincing as possible, "I knew that."

***

I don't sleep well. I wake up in a cold sweat after dreaming of a punk rocker with enough metal on his face to cause a lock down at O'Hare when he goes through the TSA scanner. He's holding hands with Kelly as they enter a tattoo parlor. It takes me an hour to get the image out of my head and back to sleep. Later, I wake up screaming after dreaming of the punk rocker and Kelly leaving the tattoo parlor sporting the same multicolored tattoo of the punk rock band the Ramones, with the caption *"Joey will never die"* in a swirling serif font. The ink covers their entire backsides and makes my mind ache worse than my aching back. I don't even try to go back to sleep.

I get up and wander into the front room of my apartment. I do a few stretching exercises to keep my bad back from getting worse. I make some coffee, and while it is brewing, I reach into the top cupboard and retrieve a tin recipe box. In it are blank 3x5 cards, push pins, and recipes I will never attempt.

Years ago, at a sidewalk art sale, for the grand total of eight dollars, I purchased a large painting of a brown, dilapidated barn with four red mailboxes in front against a bright yellow sky. Why the barn needs four mailboxes or why the sky is yellow is almost as big a mystery as why Carlo, the artist, signed the horrendously ugly painting. The only change to this masterwork of art has been the addition of hundreds of little holes made by tacking 3x5 cards onto its canvas when I use it as a crime scene bulletin board. I refer to the painting as *The Original Carlo*.

I start to label individual cards with names, facts, suspicions, whatever comes into my head, and stick the cards onto the yellow sky. I don't get very far. Once I have Sterling, Witherington, Leslie Ambrose, Chester, and a few others tacked up, *The Original Carlo* is still seen in all its glory. The lack of information in the case is depressing, but not nearly as depressing as the image of Joey Ramone and his band on my daughter's backside. I go take a shower. By the time I'm done, the sun is up. Hello, Tuesday.

***

"I've lost another pound, Sherlock."

"Good for you, Herman." Herman losing a pound is akin to Gutzon Borglum chipping a pimple off Teddy Roosevelt's Rushmore nose.

"Want some açaí berry puree or a flaxseed muffin?" he asks. "Both are excellent internal cleansers."

"No, thank you. I already had my internals cleansed this morning."

"Okay, but you're passing up some very effective roughage, Sherlock."

"Too much information, Herman."

I enter his apartment.

I sit. He sits across from me. I see his computer screen on the table doing financial jumping jacks. "What can you tell me, Herman?"

"I made another nineteen grand off Sheckle. He's making a run at a company that raises Vietnamese frankenfish."

"Herman, I don't need to hear that."

"Then why did you ask?"

"You're supposed to be looking at his charitable gift giving," I admonish the financial whiz, "not delving into his secret business negotiations."

"If I happen to run across something interesting while I'm in there working for you, Sherlock, what could be the harm in that?"

"Plenty," I inform him. "I need to know what's gone down with all the money he's given away."

"Just get his tax returns. That'll tell you everything you need to know," he tells me. "You have to provide a written receipt for every dime you give away now."

I, of course, wouldn't know this because I belong on the receiving end, not the giving end, when it comes to donations.

Herman schools me, "A few years ago, the IRS decided to clamp down on all the phony deductions people were claiming and required proof of all the benevolence going on. Guess what happened?"

"Gift giving dropped like a stone?"

"No, but the reporting of gift giving fell faster than a stockbroker off a ledge on Black Friday."

Chester's been accommodating thus far, but I doubt if he'd let me see Sterling's tax returns. "You wouldn't happen to have any window into the world of tax returns, would you, Herman?"

"Sorry, Sherlock," he says. "Get caught hacking into the IRS, and you'll be wearing stripes for the rest of your life, and stripes make me look fat."

There is not a covering on earth that wouldn't make Herman look fat, except maybe a teepee.

I contemplate my situation for a few seconds. "Herman, six million was lifted from Sheckle and another sixty grand from petty cash, but Witherington refuses to call the police. Why?"

"If Wall Street gets wind the SSS Corporation is bleeding money from an internal breach of their bank accounts, the brakes will go on, the SEC will come in, and every deal SSS is making will come to a screeching halt."

"Sixty grand to them is pocket change."

"Sixty grand to them is lint. Six million is pocket change."

I lean back on the couch. "I got to follow the money, but I can't if there's no road to drive on."

"Yeah, I say you got a problem."

"What I really can't figure out," I admit, "if six million is walk around money for these guys, why is Sterling so dead set about getting his money from Richmond?"

"Beats me," Herman says. "What you need is a guy on the inside who can give you the straight dope."

Yeah, that guy is going to pop up out of nowhere.

"Try Max," Herman suggests.

"Max who?"

"I found him when I was snooping around," Herman says. "Max Sheckle. He's Sterling's idiot brother."

CHAPTER 11

I'm driving on Western Avenue on my way to the expressway when I look up to see a billboard. It shocks me to the point I have to stop the car. The poster must be sixty feet wide and thirty feet high. It is a photo of a petite teenage girl with a protruding pregnant belly. She sports multiple ear, nose, lip, and eyebrow piercings, has filthy, stringy, cornrow hair, and wears shredded, dirty Levi jeans. Her T-shirt advertises Megadeath's *Rust in Peace* album. The only finger on her left hand without an oversized skull and crossbones ring is her wedding band finger. Behind her is the daddy, a tatted-out, hip-hop version of James Dean, puffing on a self-rolled cigarette. The message on the poster reads in huge letters: Abort your Abortion and Adopt Adoption.

Oh jeesh.

There's only one thing to do. I put the pedal to the Tercel's metal, and rush back to my apartment. I double-park, rush up the walkway, and take the stairs two at a time. Inside my apartment, I spin the dial on the combination lock, reach inside the safe, and pull out my service revolver. I remove the cartridges from the magazine and the chamber, double-check that the weapon is empty, slip it into my shoulder holster, and don my one old sport coat for cover.

In an hour, I'm creeping along in the pick-up line at the girls' school. Care waits patiently, and when she sees me, she hustles to the car, opens the front door, tosses in her backpack, and sits in the front passenger seat.

"Can we stop at McDonald's?"

"No."

Care slumps in the seat.

"What did you learn today at school?" I ask.

"Nothing. Can we stop at Burger King?"

"No."

We're moving again. I see Kelly on the sidewalk ahead of us talking to You-Know-Who. When the Toyota is parallel to them, I stop the car, stomp on the parking brake, and hop out.

"Dad, what are you doing?" Care shouts.

"I'll be right back."

The car horns blow from behind.

Kelly doesn't see me until I'm standing almost face-to-face with Cameron. "Hi," I say to the young lad with acne on his face and buds in his ears. "Just wanted to introduce myself."

Kelly has turned a shade of bright crimson. She's so shocked she can't speak.

I thrust my hand out to shake and at the same time make sure my coat opens wide enough so Cameron can't miss seeing my gun. "Hi, I'm Kelly's daddy."

His eyes are the size of Frisbees as he stares at my hardware and limply shakes my hand. "Is that a real gun?" Cameron asks in 33 1/3 rpm instead of the usual 45.

"Oh, yeah," I say. "Trouble is my business, especially people who get other people in trouble." I give him a big Al Zazou smile.

Tessie the Terminator is on her way over, ready to whack my car with her sign. "Well, got to be going. Sure was nice meeting you, Cameron."

"Nice to meet you."

"Sir," I add for his grammatical benefit.

I pull Kelly along and get back to the car before Tessie can dent the hood.

"That was the most embarrassing thing that's ever happened to me," Kelly wails out from the back seat. "How could you do something like that, Dad?"

I was just being friendly, Kelly. Don't you want me to know the man of your dreams?"

"Not now, I don't. That was, like, so totally uncool. It was, like, total humiliation. I bet it's already gone viral."

With few cars ahead of me, I drive out of the school pick-up zone quickly.

Kelly sits in the back seat, still shaken but aware enough to start punching out messages on her cell phone.

"Hey, Kelly," Care says, "maybe this would be a good time to tell Dad about your date this weekend."

In the rearview mirror I see Kelly's face register 100 percent in the rage factor.

"What date?" I ask.

"Tell him, Kelly," Care says, zinging her harder than if she had a cattle prod.

"What, Kelly?"

"Cameron and I are going out this Saturday," Kelly announces in the most forceful tone she can muster.

"I told you 'No dating,' Kelly."

"He asked me last night," Kelly says.

"I don't care when he asked you. I said 'No dating'."

"Mom said I could go."

"And I said you couldn't."

"When I'm with Mom, it's Mom's rules. When I'm with you, it's your rules. Monday is a Mom's rules night."

"Well, this weekend you're with me, so it will be my rules, and I say: no dating."

"No," she says, and pulls a folded sheet of paper out of her back pocket and throws it into the front seat. "Mom said she has to switch weekends this weekend because she has to study for her new job."

"I don't believe you."

"She's right, Dad," Care says. "Mom has to switch."

My ex, instead of having the decency of calling with her schedule changes or school news, sends me last minute notes. I'm so mad I don't bother reading this one. I grab it, crumple it up, and shove it in my pocket.

"So, Saturday is Mom's rules and not yours," Kelly says with total disdain.

I hate this. She's got me. What can I do? Being a part-time, divorced dad is impossible.

"This isn't right, Kelly, and you know it."

"I didn't make the rules, the judge did."

The rest of the ride home is as quiet as a deaf-mute's funeral.

***

"Don't feel bad, Dad," Care tells me after dinner. "Kelly's not talking to me either."

"This is not good, Care. Nothing destroys a relationship faster than silence."

"I kinda like it." Care sits next to me on the couch, which will soon be my bed.

"Does your mother really have to switch weekends?" I ask, although, I really shouldn't.

"Yeah, the next weekend she's taking a test."

I'm hoping it's the civil service exam. "A test for what?"

"Her career."

"Your mother doesn't have a career; she has alimony."

"I think she called it astrocology."

It doesn't sound like it has anything to do with the post office.

"Mom's going to become a doctor of astrocology."

I can imagine my ex doing a form of proctology. But astrocology? "What's that?"

"Mom said it's where you mix your astrological sign with psyche psychology, and come up with solutions to problems."

"You've got to be kidding?"

"Mom says it's the latest, newest, big thing in the world of therapy."

"They bring the patient in, lay him on the couch, and ask, 'What's your sign?'" I continue speaking in disbelief. "Is the second question, 'Do you come here often?'"

"I don't know," Care says. "I'm having a hard enough time with geography to worry about anything else."

"What kind of questions do they ask on the test? 'Which one is more sensitive, a Gemini or a Moon Child?'"

Only my ex could find a career this absurd to pursue.

"Mom's real worried about passing the test," Care tells me.

"If she flunks, does she get thrown out of the solar system?"

"I don't know, Dad."

My ex is almost as bad a test taker as I am, one of the few traits we share. I had to take the detective exam three times before I passed. "Well, wish her luck for me."

"I will," Care says.

As I take a minute to corral my negative thoughts and calm down, Care gets up and walks to *The Original Carlo.* "On a big case, Dad?"

I start to answer, but stop.

Kelly comes out of the bedroom and sits as far away from us as she can, which isn't far since the rooms in the apartment are each the size of a postage stamp.

"I'm trying to find six million dollars," I say.

"You are?" Care asks.

"Do we get to keep it if you find it?" Kelly pops into the conversation.

"We?"

"Yeah, do we? I could really use some new shoes," Kelly gets up to come closer to the bad painting as if spurred by the chance at easy money.

"No."

"Why not?" Kelly asks disappointed.

"Because it's not my money that got stolen." I add, "I don't have any money."

"How'd it get lifted, Dad?" Care asks.

"They think somebody hacked into the computer and stole it."

"I can't wait to tell Cameron, he's an awesomely famous gamer on the computer."

Great, just what I need, a son-in-law who spends all day playing *Donkey Kong*.

"You want us to help rearrange the cards on the *Carlo*, Dad?" Care asks.

"That's the problem, I don't have enough to rearrange."

Care points to the cards. "Any of these guys do it?"

"Maybe."

"If I were you, I'd check to see if any of them are dressing a lot better all of a sudden," Kelly says.

"Thanks. I'll do a thorough check of their closets next time around."

"Don't forget under their mattresses. A lot of criminals hide their money there," Kelly adds.

"Go take your showers. It's time for bed."

***

I'm up at five thirty. I stretch, shower, get dressed, and make PB&J sandwiches. In their brown bags, I add an apple, granola bar, no-sugar candy, napkin, and note saying "I love you." At a few minutes before seven, I go into the bedroom to awaken my sleeping beauties. "Rise and shine."

Neither stirs.

Louder, "Time to get up."

"Dad, leave us alone," Kelly mumbles.

"Wake up. Education awaits you."

"We don't have to go to school today."

"Yeah, right," I tell Kelly, who has buried her head beneath her/my pillow.

"We don't," Care says. "It's a teacher service day."

I repeat, "Yeah, right."

"It is," Care moans out.

"It's on the note," Kelly says.

"What note?"

"The note from Mom."

Oh no. I rush into the bathroom and pull yesterday's shirt out of the hamper. Crumpled in the pocket is the note. I read.

Oh jeesh.

I return to the bedroom. The girls are sound asleep. "I got a big day today." The girls hunker down into the covers. "Can't your mom watch you today?"

Care lifts her head and says to me sleepily, "No, Mom said she's in the middle of her Venus retrograde and is extremely sensitive to any changes in her schedule."

I give up.

Care rises from the netherworld at eight and Kelly at eight thirty. "I don't have time to watch you today, girls. I have a meeting and I have a great opportunity later that could be a big plus in my new career."

"You have a new career too, Dad?" Care asks.

"I'm working on it."

"Are you going to become a shrinking-astrologicalist like Mom?" Care asks.

"No, I'm going into real estate."

"That sounds boring," Kelly comments.

"Good, then you won't mind waiting here while I'm sitting on an open house today."

"No way," Kelly says. "We hate hanging around here. This place is, like, totally boring."

"What do you want me to do? I have to work today," I tell my two girls.

"Call Tiffany," Care shouts out.

"Yeah, we'd much rather hang out with her than you."

"Thanks, Kelly. You're all heart."

I call Tiffany. As is her MO, she texts me back an hour later: *What?*

I give up. "Care, text Tiffany and tell her you two want a play date at her house this morning."

Three minutes later, Care announces, "We can stay with her until noon, then she has to start getting ready for tonight."

"Whoopee," I comment sarcastically.

***

At ten, I drop the girls, with lunch bags in hand, off at Tiffany's condo. My doorman buddy is working. "They can get in, but you can't," he tells me.

I tell the guy in no uncertain terms, "Well, I wouldn't want to get into any place that would consider letting someone like me in anyway."

CHAPTER 12

Jimmy Carter had Billy. Bill Clinton had Roger. Richard Nixon had Donald, who was so dumb that Tricky Dick wiretapped him. Max is Sterling Sheckle's dumber brother.

Sterling has him tucked away in an office between the Xerox room and the men's room.

"I don't know what the big deal is," he tells me. "I'm going to get money anyway."

"So, you used to handle part of the family trust fund your brother set up?"

"I did. It was a family trust, and I'm family."

"And now you don't have access?"

"No."

"Why not?"

"There was a slight disagreement on my investing techniques."

Max is at least ten years younger than Sterling. He wears an open silk shirt, beltless slacks, and what looks to me to be alligator shoes. If you saw him on the street, his appearance would answer the question: What does a past-his-prime gigolo look like?

"And before you ask about the money from the Arron stock deal," he tells me, "I was framed."

"And that kickback a few years ago?"

"I was framed for that one, too."

"From what I've heard about you, Max, you've been framed more times than a Monet."

Max pushes the Sun-Times, which is the only paper on his desk, to the side. "I got bad karma. What can I say?"

"Do you have any access to any funds?"

"No. But I should," he tells me. "Sterling's locked them up tighter than John Gotti."

"Why?"

"It's a trust fund. I trust the fund, it should trust me."

"Did you ever have checkwriting privileges?"

"Yes."

"When did that end?"

"After I invested in the Fisherman's Third Hand Corporation."

Max's office is so small there's no room for a chair. I have to stand.

"I'm telling you, if they had given the invention more time, we would have made a fortune. You can hold the pole, bait the line, and drink a beer all at once. It was genius."

"And now you're employed here?"

"Yes."

From the emptiness of his desk and office, it doesn't look like work. "What do you do?" I ask.

"I'm the Vice President of Special Projects."

"Which projects are you working on?"

"The Costa Rican Tidelands Recovery Project."

"What's that?"

"I don't know. They haven't explained it to me yet."

"Whom do you report to?"

"That cheapskate Witherington. The guy is tighter than a clam encased in concrete."

"No expense account in Costa Rica?"

"None."

"Thanks for your time, Max."

"No, problem. Time is one thing I got plenty of."

This visit to SSS has been a total waste so far. I take the elevator to the security floor and ask the receptionist, "Did they ever find Leslie Ambrose?"

"Not that I know of."

"Who replaced him?"

"Lew."

"Lew who?"

"Ling Lew."

"Ling Lew?"

"That's who," she says.

"Is he in?"

"I'll ring Ling."

Hiring a Chinese guy to counter the Chinese seems a bit unfair, especially to Ling Lew. I meet Ling in Leslie's old office, which Ling has not had time to remodel, or has no interest in remodeling. There is only so much you can do with a room filled with computer stuff. If I were Ling, I'd paint.

Little to my surprise, Ling Lew is the same Asian guy who ran in sounding the alert on the Chinese hack attempt the day Tiffany and I visited Leslie Ambrose.

"How is the threat-thwarting going?" I ask.

"Long lineup of threats for Ling to lessen."

"Sorry to hear that."

"Where's Tiffany?"

"She's on assignment." Watching my kids is a chore, so I'm not lying.

"She's hot."

I don't agree or disagree.

"What did she think of me?"

I don't understand his question.

"Is she engaged, have a boyfriend, going out with anybody right now?" he asks.

"Not that I can recall."

"Do you think she'd want to go out with me?"

Being maybe 5'2" in elevator shoes, I would doubt if Ling would fit into Tiffany's dating profile, but it's not my place to play Cupid. "Ling, I really can't say. You'd have to ask her."

"Oh boy," he says, "I don't know if I could do that."

"By the way, Ling, has Leslie surfaced?"

"No, probably still floating in cyberspace."

"How about the sixty grand from petty cash?"

"Probably floating around up there, too." Ling likes to chew on the frame tips of his designer glasses.

"Ling, here's what I can't figure out," I admit to the guy. "If somebody did, in fact, breach the system, got inside, and started stealing, why would they stop at six million when the corporation is worth billions?"

"Yes," he says, "why settle for bitcoins when real dollars are available?"

I have no clue what he is talking about. "So to speak."

"I personally don't believe anyone broke our firewall, Mr. Sherlock. If they did, the place would have already gone up in flames."

"Thanks, Ling."

"No problem," he says. He pauses and adds, "Think you could ask Tiffany what she thought about me. I'm sure our eyes met the day she was here, and I felt an instant connection, Mr. Sherlock."

"I'll see what I can do. Good luck in the new job thwarting those threats."

"I'll zap those Chinese right in their dim sum dumplings."

I leave Ling, exit cyberspace, and get back into the elevator. While in Rome, I might as well visit the fiddler. I go up instead of down, get off, go down the hall, and poke my head into door #1. "Mr. Sheckle, do you have a minute?"

"You find my money?" He looks up from the flashing on his telephone console.

"Not yet."

"Then what do you want?"

What I want is to get on his free money giveaway list, but this doesn't seem to be an apropos time to ask. "I need to know why you have hundreds of accountants for your business but only one for your personal fortune?"

"One's a lot easier to watch than twenty," he tells me.

"Anybody ever steal money from you before?"

"People try to steal money from me every day."

"Why?"

"Because I got a lot of money!" he shouts. "Why do people rob banks?" He doesn't give me a chance to answer. "Because that's where the money is, Sherlock."

Evidently, he doesn't think much of my detecting skills.

"Mr. Sheckle, do you know how much money you have?"

"Of course not."

"Then how would you know if you're missing any?"

"Because when I went to look for it, it wasn't there."

Good answer.

"Mr. Sheckle, do you recall anyone being successful stealing money from you?"

"Yeah, the guy you can't seem to find. Why don't you get that skinflint Richmond to settle the claim, and we can be done with each other?"

"I'll be more than happy to mention it the next time we chat, but I can't promise anything." It's best not to inform him that Mr. Richmond and I have never had a face-to-face conversation.

"You get my money, Sherlock, and be quick about it."

Before he punches a blinking line, I ask, "One more question, sir?"

"What?"

"How'd you ever get the name Mr. Wonderful?"

"Believe me, it wasn't my idea."

***

The condo is on the 19th floor of a building on the 200 block of Chestnut Street, right behind Water Tower Place between Michigan Avenue and Lake Michigan. It's a Streeterville address, one of the toniest in the city. The unit has two bedrooms, two baths, a nice-sized living/dining area, and small kitchen, but it's closet space challenged. The building was constructed sometime around the early sixties, so its vintage has another fifty years to go before it's *vintage*. The present owners of the unit are the original owners, and they weren't big on updating.

I arrive thirty minutes early, put out an Open House sign in the building's front lobby, tip the doorman a twenty to assure easy entrance, and go upstairs to the condo unit. I use a dishtowel to dust the furniture. I find Windex in the cupboard and clean all the mirrors. I spiff up the bathrooms by polishing the plumbing fixtures. I decide it would be best to pull the curtains in the front room halfway because half the view is of the building next door. The other half of the view is the darkened street below, which runs north between multistory buildings—an urban chasm if there ever was one. I put out the one-sheeters Al Zazou had printed up, place the leather sign-in book on the dining room table with two pens, and wait to sell, sell, sell.

At twelve thirty, the first guests arrive.

"Oh my God, this place is old enough to be a museum."

"Thank you for the compliment, Tiffany."

Care and Kelly carry the brown bag lunches I had made that morning. "There's a McDonald's in the Water Tower," Care informs me. "Can we go there?"

"No."

"Could you give us money and we can go shopping in the Water Tower?" Kelly asks.

"No."

"Why not?"

"Because I don't have any money."

"The only person who would buy this place would be, like, Stevie Wonder," Tiffany tells me as she wanders around. "Whoever picked this paint?"

I take a closer look at Kelly. "What's that stuff on your face?"

"Makeup."

"You're fourteen, you don't need makeup."

"Tiffany gave me a makeover."

"Why did you do that?" I ask Tiffany. "She doesn't have anything made to be made over."

"Now that she's a woman, Mr. Sherlock..."

I cut Tiffany off, "Did she tell you that, or did you read it online?"

"I could tell. We women have unspoken bonds between us," Tiffany informs me.

Two old ladies come in the front door. "Is this the open house?"

I move quickly to greet them with a big Al Zazou smile on my face. "Welcome, welcome. Please come in, and sign in please." I must sound like a game show host.

"We're just looking."

I hand each a listing sheet. "If you have any questions, please don't hesitate to ask."

The ladies wander off toward the bedrooms.

"I have to go, Mr. Sherlock, to start getting ready for tonight."

"Thanks, Tiffany," the girls say in unison.

"Alphonse has everything. All you have to do is get over there."

"Yes, Tiffany," I say. "Are we taking my car or yours?"

"The only place I'd ever take your car is to a junkyard."

"I have a hard time imagining you in a junkyard, Tiffany."

"The only reason I'd go is to see your car in one of those machines that crush them up and squeeze them into a little square," she says.

"I'll let you know so you can buy a ticket."

"Make it in the front row." Tiffany makes her way out of the condo. "Ta-ta, little dudettes."

"Bye, Tiffany. Thanks."

As Tiffany and the girls exchange air kisses, I go to check on the potential buyers. I am a bit amazed to find them going through the dresser drawers in the master bedroom. "Excuse me..."

"Oh, hi. We were just looking," the leader tells me.

"Obviously."

The other lady keeps on rifling the underwear drawer.

"Excuse me, you're not supposed to be doing that."

"Why not?"

"You're supposed to be looking at the unit, not the unit's contents."

"We don't care about the unit."

"Then why are you here?"

"We live in the building, and we like to know our neighbors," the leader continues.

"We want to see if she wears Depends," her cohort admits.

"Out."

I escort the two out the front door.

"Are they going to buy the place, Dad?" Care asks after the Snoop Sisters leave.

"I doubt it. You two eat yet?"

"Tiffany made us wheat grass protein shakes, but we flushed them down the toilet when she was busy texting."

"I can't say I blame you."

Nobody shows up in the next half hour. The girls are pretty much finished with their lunch when a middle-aged couple enters.

"Hi, how are you?"

"We're just looking," the man says.

"Please sign in."

The man goes to the book while the woman heads for the bedrooms. For some reason Kelly follows her. As I chat with the hubby, I can faintly hear their conversation.

"Is this shag carpeting gross or what?" Kelly says.

"It's different," the lady says.

"It belongs on a rerun of *That '70s* TV show."

"Or in a disco," the lady says, laughing along with my daughter.

"You see the shower in the bathroom?" Kelly asks.

"It looks like something you'd see in a prison movie."

"How about the light fixture in the other bedroom? Ga...rooooose."

"Excuse me," I jump into the room and conversation. "Kelly, you have a phone call in the other room."

"No, I don't. My phone is in my pocket."

"Then go into the other room and wait for one." I give Kelly my *What in God's name are you doing* look. Kelly gets the message and leaves the room.

"I apologize for my child's poor attempt at humor." I attempt to undo Kelly's damage. "The unit does need a bit of updating."

"I'll say."

"You won't find a comparable unit in this neighborhood for the price," I assure her.

"I can see why."

I try to think of what King Closer would say in this situation and come up with, "Location, location, location." Not real good, but I'm just a beginner.

The woman walks back into the front room and finds her husband peering into the window of the building next door. "Ah, honey, that's tacky."

"I thought I saw a crime taking place," he says.

"Yeah, right, dear." She pulls him toward the front door.

"Thanks for stopping by," I say. "If you're in the market and you need an agent, I would be more than happy to be of service."

"Our name is on your sign-up sheet, but you probably have plenty to do trying to sell this place," the woman says. "But I do have one final question."

"Yes."

"Do the children come with the unit?"

"Yes, or you can buy them separately."

The woman laughs at my sarcasm, "I bet you're a good dad."

"Would you mind telling them that?" I plead.

The couple exit. Care goes over to the sign-in sheet, reads, then asks, "I wonder if the guy is related to the real Abe Lincoln?"

I read what she just read. "If he is, I have a feeling he didn't inherit Abe's honesty gene."

For his phone number he wrote: *1-800-You-got-to-be-kidding*.

I look over at my oldest, "Kelly, you're not supposed to point out the negatives of the unit to the potential buyers."

"Oh, Dad, that shag carpeting sucks."

"Don't use that word."

"Sucks?"

"Yes. I hate that word."

"Why not? Everybody says 'sucks'."

"Not in this family we don't."

"Why not?"

"Because I said so."

"That's not a reason."

"When you're an adult, Kelly, you can use any word you want, but as long as you're under my roof, 'sucks' is off-limits."

"I'll wait to use it at Mom's house." This kid really knows how to get me.

"Dad," Care says, "the shag carpeting really is disgusting."

"Care, some people might like shag carpeting."

"Multicolored shag carpeting with stains and bare spots?" Kelly questions.

"Yes!"

"Good luck finding them, Dad."

She has a point, but I refuse to acknowledge it.

Nobody else shows up for the open house. We sit around for the next ninety minutes. Ms. Missy is going to be so disappointed her face might crack.

"Are you still going out on your date this weekend, Kelly?" I ask.

"Yes."

"You know I don't approve."

"Mom said it was okay, and it's Mom's time, so I'm going, Dad."

I hold my anger in check. I take a deep breath. "Let me give you a few dating pointers, Kelly."

"What?"

I stand right in front of her and demonstrate as I speak. "Now, always remember to keep both your arms bent at the elbow so if he tries to sneak a feel, you slam your elbow down on your ribs, and stop his hand from going anywhere it shouldn't be going." I show her the move using both right and left elbows. I must look like I'm doing the Funky Chicken dance. "You try it."

"Oh my God," she says.

"And if he's squeezing you too tight, take your thumb and push it into his eyeball." I demonstrate this maneuver too. "That'll stop him."

Kelly is staring at me like I'm the Ebola virus.

"Kelly, you have to learn these tactics if you're going to start dating."

"I can't believe I'm hearing this," Kelly says in absolute awe.

"What should she do if their braces get locked together when they're making out?" Care asks.

"Call me. I'll be there in minutes with a set of pliers."

"Dad, are you for real?"

"I'm only giving you these tips for your own protection, Kelly."

"How do you know all this stuff, Dad?" Care asks me.

Her question catches me a little off guard. "I read a lot."

***

I drop the girls off at their mother's house at four. The minute the Toyota squeals to a stop, Kelly jumps from the back seat quicker than if she's fleeing an oncoming acne epidemic.

"Kelly, wait." I jump out of the driver's side and catch her before she can get into the house. I crouch down to her level.

"Dad, please, no more advice."

I place my hand on her shoulder. "Listen, Kelly, I want you to know this. If at any time, or any place, you find yourself in a situation you don't belong, all you have to do is call me. No matter what it is, what's happening, or what situation you're in, just call. I promise there will be no questions asked or punishments doled out. All I care about is your safety. If you need me, call me. That's what dads are for."

Her facial expression changes slightly. I know she heard me. I lean over and kiss her forehead. "I love you."

Kelly walks into the house.

Care follows up the path. "Hey, Dad," she says, "what's the difference between french kissing and regular kissing?"

CHAPTER 13

Alphonse's suit fits like a body glove. I never knew clothing could make you feel this good. He's provided everything. Shoes, shirts, socks, tie, suit, belt, and hankie are laid out for me like I'm Prince Charles. He even helps me get dressed, holding my pants so I can step in.

"Eees perfect," he says and stands back to admire his own work.

"I have to agree with you, Alphonse."

"Mees Tiffany will be pleeesed."

I stuff my other clothes into a plastic Jewel shopping bag, thank Alphonse, exit, and get to my car as the meter maid is approaching. The first time I turn the ignition key, it merely clicks. The second time, the engine kicks over. I wave to Rita as I pull out of the spot.

The CCCCC is the Chicago Community's Call to Cure Cancer. It's an organization made up of Chicagoland corporations who give and raise money to cure the horrible disease. It was formed years ago by a number of CEOs of the big medical companies and healthcare organizations, including Baxter and Abbott Labs. In the past few years, the big guys stepped aside, and the CCCCC is now fronted by a number of the newer medical biotech companies, who have hit the fundraising trail with more zeal than Lewis and Clark. They put the arm on anyone and everyone with a spare dime in their pocket. Tonight, the $500 a plate dinner is in honor of a $500,000 matching donation campaign headed by none other than Mr. Wonderful himself, Sterling S. Sheckle.

The event starts at 7 p.m. I'm at the Drake Hotel at 6:45. Tiffany meets me at 7:45. She takes one look at me and immediately straightens the knot in my tie, repositions my hankie, and tugs on my lapels. "Anybody who can make you look this good is a genius, Mr. Sherlock."

For once, I totally agree with her.

Tiffany is ravishing. Her long blue dress accentuates every perfect curve of her body. Her jewelry must be worth millions, but it seems only a subtle addition to her overall beauty. Her long blond tresses cascade down her back without a hair out of place. Her hint of a suntan makes her radiant. No one is perfect, but Tiffany is about as close as you can get, at least in the looks department.

We proceed to the check-in table where we find our seat assignments, and are given a tacky stick-on badge that reads: *Hi, my name is.* Tiffany not only refuses to write in her name, but also refuses the badge itself. "Everybody who knows anybody knows me," she informs the hostess. I fill in my Richard Sherlock and slap it on my chest. Tiffany immediately rips it off. "Putting that thing on an Alphonse is a crime against fashion, Mr. Sherlock."

I wonder why they have these silly name badges? Nobody wants to wear one. They don't go with anything, and people rarely print their names big enough for others to read. If you're a woman in a formal, there is no good place to put it. If she sticks it on her chest, it gives every guy a reason to stare at her breasts. I have to remember to tell Kelly never to wear a name badge. For five hundred bucks a plate, they should at least have a better way of identifying the participants.

The ballroom at the Drake is *the* place for the best of the best. If you are a mogul who's daughter is getting married or a charity looking for the big bucks, the Drake is the place to be. The bar at the far end of the room is filled. There are waitresses passing out fancy appetizers, waiters with trays of white and red wine, and other servers taking special drink orders. The massive chandeliers are brightly shining down on tables for ten set with the finest linen, china, and silverware, just like in my apartment. It is easy to see the real movers and shakers. They are forty-plus men in groups of three, talking and sipping expensive scotch. Their wives are also in groups, but sipping martini concoctions and staring at each other's jewelry. The last grouping is a younger crowd of thirty-something, obviously on the prowl.

"These events are a great place to scope out men, Mr. Sherlock."

"Think any women will scope me out?" I ask.

"If they don't, I can't say I have much hope for you, since you've never looked better," Tiffany tells me.

Tiffany scans the crowd like a Secret Service agent looking for weirdos. "I hate to admit this, Mr. Sherlock, but my dating pool has run dry. For some reason, I've been attracting the wrong crowd lately. My planets must be out of alignment or something."

I should refer her to my ex-wife.

"That guy looks pretty hot," Tiffany says, pointing out one young man.

"The guy with the greasy hair pointing upward in the middle of his head?"

"Yeah, check those pecs."

"Tiffany, his head looks like its ready to take off."

"The Rolex he's wearing says a lot too."

I watch as the guy gives her a smarmy smile. Tiffany doesn't smile back, but gives him a slight head flip to acknowledge his liking. "Let's see how serious he is," Tiffany says to me. "Stay here, don't move, Mr. Sherlock."

Tiffany moves very casually from my side and sets herself adrift as if bait on the end of a fisherman's line. She doesn't look the guy's way, but puts herself in a position so he can easily make his way over. It doesn't take more than a minute for him to take the bait, and she reels him in.

My attention is diverted when I hear, "Hi, I'm Roger Korman." The guy puts out his hand. "Who are you?"

"Richard Sherlock."

"I'm with Platalette Diagnostics. You?"

Probably not good to admit I'm not with anyone. "I'm on a special project for Sterling Sheckle," I tell the guy.

"We have a new blood-checking device that's going to revolutionize the finger pricking of every diabetic in the world."

"Really," I say.

"We're going into stage one trials, and we're looking for funding." He pauses. "Is this what you do for Sheckle?"

"No, not really," I say.

"How well do you know him?"

"I know him, but I wouldn't call us 'tight.'"

"Can you get in to see him?"

"Sure." All I have to do is knock on his door.

"Tell you what," he says softly to me, "you get me in to see Sheckle, and if he invests, I'll cut you in on the deal."

"Really?"

"But your finder's fee will have to be our little secret."

"I'm good at keeping secrets."

"So am I."

He hands me a business card. It has his name, the company name, and a WWW website; all that is missing is an address. I should ask if he has any pressing real estate needs, but I don't. "So, you're here to raise money for your company?" I ask.

"That's why everybody's here."

Roger walks away and hits on another guy adrift in the sea of do-gooders. I see Mr. Greasy Point chatting up Tiffany. To my left, a group of three men exchanging information suddenly breaks up. Each of these guys wears a special, big, pre-printed badge on their lapel, which must signify something more than their dislike for tacky stick-on name badges, but I'm too far away to figure it out. One guy heads for the bar, so I follow him.

"Hi," I say, catching up with him, "I'm Richard Sherlock."

"Johnnie Walker Black," he says. I wonder if his parents had drinking problems when they named him, then I realize he's speaking to the bartender and not me.

"Hello, again."

His badge reads: Nick Klink, Chicago Pharmaceuticals, CCCCC Member of the Board. If anyone should have a classy badge, it's Nick Klink.

"Quite a donation Mr. Sheckle is making to your organization," I say as my conversation starter.

"We'll see."

"Are we any closer to finding a cure?" I ask.

"Cure for what?"

"Cancer."

"I thought you were talking about Sheckle." He watches the bartender and not me.

"Any progress at all in the fight against cancer?" I ask again.

Nick motions to the bartender to *hurry it up*. "We funded a company that has separated a gene from the poison of the Gila monster, which looks promising as a beta blocker for breast cancer."

"The poison from the Gila monster is going to cure cancer?" I ask.

"No."

"What is it going to do?"

"It will arrest some of the symptoms of the disease and maybe keep it from spreading." He catches the bartender's eye. "Make that a double." So far, Nick hasn't impressed me as a real benevolent type. He seems a bit restless waiting for his scotch.

"If it works, are there enough Gila monsters in the world to keep up with the new demand?" For me, this seems like a logical question.

But not to Nick, "I wouldn't know, that's not my problem." Nick grabs his drink and walks away.

It's always fun to get to know new people.

The chandeliers blink. It's time to sit. I look around for Tiffany. I don't see her because she's behind me. "New money, Mr. Sherlock."

"What?" I ask, spinning in her direction.

"New money isn't as good as old money, but it is better than no money," she tells me.

The latter would be the category I'm in. "He looked a little bit on the slimy side to me, Tiffany."

"Mousse."

"Mickey?"

"No, it was mousse in his hair."

"Yeah, I knew that." I pause. "Maybe I should try some of that stuff in my hair?"

"That would be like you wearing an Abboud tie with your Members Only jacket."

I follow my protégée to table #9, which is dead center in the room, one table from the front row. We sit in the two chairs facing the stage where a long dais has been set up. These dais eaters sit like the apostles did at the Last Supper. Sheckle's in Jesus' chair.

There are seven others at our table, including three men with the initials M.D. after their names and three women. The three men tell me they own biotech companies. The final fellow works in research for the SSS Corp, and has Ph.D. after his name. All four men stare at Tiffany and barely notice me. The women are the wives of the three M.D.'s. One seat remains empty. This is not really a singles event. As we get comfortable, each of the ladies leer at Tiffany, noting immediate dislike, envy, fear, or any combination of A, B, and C.

After the introductions, I decide to break the small talk iceberg. "So, how is the race for the cure going?"

"What race?" the bigwig next to me asks.

"The race to cure cancer," I answer.

No one answers. Maybe they didn't understand my question. "Are there any miracle drugs out there that people will be able to take and get rid of their cancer?"

"Not that I know of," the fat cat on the other side of the table says.

"I heard they're having some success with the DNA of the Gila monster," I add to keep this fascinating conversation going.

"Who'd ya hear that from?"

"A guy at the bar named Nick."

"Did he ask you to invest?"

"No, but another guy did."

"Did you?" the fat cat on my left asks.

"I'm thinking it over," I say.

"Let me know how it works out," the big wig says.

Appetizers are served, squishy little white things wrapped in bacon. I pass; bacon has no nutritional value whatsoever. Bread rolls are passed around the table, but by the time it rolls to me, the basket's empty. All three of the docs took seconds before the rest of us got firsts. Same story with the butter. Wine is served, but two of the docs tell the waiter they want something better. One doc talks with his mouth full of hard roll and spits out crumbs like a seed spreader on a spring lawn. If my girls were this impolite, I'd make them take etiquette lessons, if I could afford etiquette lessons.

A lot of people, especially patients, complain about the ungraciousness, boorish behavior, and poor conversational skills of our medical professionals. There is a theory for the cause of the disease of "impolitis mannerosis." It is said that to become a doctor in America, the competition is so great, potential doctors have to spend an inordinate amount of time studying to achieve superlative grades to get into a good medical school. And because there is only so much time during the day, something has got to go, and that something is knowledge of displaying proper manners and learning positive communication skills for effective human interaction. So, maybe it's not the fault of many doctors who can't eat, speak, and explain things like us normal polite folk. If these uncouth docs can cure cancer, I'd be the first to forgive them their frailties.

During the salad course, the three docs step all over each other trying to impress the SSS research guy, treating him like he's King Midas with an open checkbook. The three women clink their jewelry while they nibble. Tiffany continues to scope out the male talent in the room. I merely take it all in. Each doc talks about developing a drug to help people fight cancer. One guy explains how his pill helps lessen the pain of chemo treatments. One guy is effusive about the progress his company is making in the search for a treatment that will lessen symptoms of hair fallout, and the last guy says they are "that close" to a stem cell treatment that will hide the appearance of ugly melanoma moles.

Something seems wrong with all of this.

They talk all through dinner, which is a surf and turf combo of salmon and filet. It's delicious. I wish I could have seconds or take what Tiffany hasn't picked at, but I'd hate to put myself into the same impolitis mannerosis category as some of the others at the table who scarf down the food like coyotes at a kill. I certainly wouldn't want to debase myself like that, but I will remember to call the guy at Use Used Food tomorrow to see where he'll be taking the extras.

During the Baked Alaska, which I am surprised the Drake would allow, not only because of the inherent fire hazard, but also the pollution the smoking ice cream causes, the show begins. The president of the CCCCC gets up, moves to the podium at the end of the table, thanks everybody, and introduces the other people at the head table. Nick Klink gets a big hand. The president goes on to talk about all the good the CCCCC is doing in the fight against cancer. I'm surprised he doesn't mention anything about the Gila monster, but poison is probably not a real good after-dinner conversation topic. He does mention a few drug trials for symptoms of pain, lesions, and regurgitations, and that doesn't seem to bother anyone. What do I know?

"And now, ladies and gentlemen, I would like to introduce you to the man of the evening, who has pledged a matching contribution of one and a half million dollars to our current research campaign, Mr. Wonderful himself, Mr. Sterling S. Sheckle."

Sterling stands up. Applause, applause, applause. I'm not sure how many other people notice, as I do, but a man magically appears behind the speaker's podium and places a square something on the floor. And thank God he does, because no one could see Sterling if he didn't step up on it. But even with the box beneath his feet, his head peers over the top of the podium like a little old lady behind the steering wheel of her late husband's Coupe de Ville. I also notice Sterling did not have Alphonse make his suit. His suit hangs on him like a wet horse blanket.

"What do you think of his suit?" I whisper to Tiffany.

"Hideous."

I have not been to a lot of charity dinners, but the ones I have been to follow pretty much the same pattern. Drinks, schmoozing, appetizers, more schmoozing, dinner, dessert, a couple guys get up and ask for money, and the man being honored is introduced. The honoree speaks for about ten minutes about how great the charity is, sits, gets some award that will end up in his closet, and it all ends with a couple more guys asking for more money and last minute schmoozing.

But not this event.

Sterling Sheckle starts talking, and after the usual ten minutes, he's still talking. Ten minutes becomes twenty, and twenty becomes forty. The Lord's Prayer is recited in thirty seconds. The Gettysburg Address was less than two minutes. Sterling obviously hasn't read either, nor does he know the powers of brevity. It is well over an hour before Sterling Sheckle shuts up. Not only is the speech lengthy, it's awful. Sterling gives what seems to be a forty-year, day-by-day, descriptive rendition of what made him the man he is today. If I were to critique his speech, I'd call it: self-centered, self-possessed, self-satisfying, and totally boring. Not once does he mention a mentor, wife, family member, executive, employee, or friend who may have had some influence or been a help in his life. He uses the word "I" so many times, we could be at an optometrist convention. Sterling tells no jokes, recalls no anecdotes, nor utters any word remotely related to humility.

Tiffany is one of the first people to get up and head for the bar. About five single guys are next, following her like a school of fish. Nick Klink is so bored he nods off sitting at the head table, and no one has the slightest inclination to wake him; thank God Nick doesn't snore. The three docs at our table make it through about fifteen minutes before they split, leaving their wives to whisper to each other. The SSS Ph.D. at the table hangs in because he knows what would happen if he left.

The pain is finally over when the president bestows upon Sheckle the CCCCC's Man of the Year Award. He hangs a gold-plated medallion over Sterling's neck, which unfortunately doesn't rest on his chest, but all the way down to his navel; it resembles a thin yoke on a starving oxen. There is little applause at the end because so few hands are left in the room. Most of the attendees are busy knocking them back at the hotel bar, trying to raise money for eradicating the symptoms of cancerous cuticle fungus.

The house lights go on, and oddly enough, I see someone I know. It's Morton DeRuth, towering above all the others, making his way to the stage with a huge smile on his face to shake Sheckle's hand. The two of them together look like Mutt and Jeff.

I wonder what Stretch is doing here.

CHAPTER 14

Another nightmare.

Kelly is pregnant; it looks like twins. She's dressed in rags, on her knees beating wet clothes against a washboard with one hand while she texts on her cell phone with the other. She's living in a house that looks like a shoe. Her four kids, three wearing diapers made of discarded gunnysacks, play in a mud puddle. All three *dads,* Joey Ramone and his two brothers, lounge around on dilapidated lawn furniture in front of rusted out pickup trucks. They strum their guitars, pass around a joint, and giggle in their communal drug-induced stupor. To help round out the scene, there's a few mangy dogs wandering around, an eviction notice tacked on the front door, and hundreds of empty Fruit Roll-up boxes litter the yard.

I awaken in a cold sweat.

I'll never get back to sleep. It's a little past 5 a.m. I get up and notice that my cell phone on the table beside the bed is not blinking. It ran out of juice again. I take it into the kitchen, plug it into the charger, and get the coffee started. I walk back through my apartment, stop to see the dearth of clues on *The Original Carlo*, and return to the bedroom. The pain in my head, caused by not being able to escape the image of *Kelly who lives in a shoe*, overcomes the pain in my back as I stretch on the floor, like a yogi with muscular dystrophy, which helps a bit. I shower, getting the water as hot as freshly brewed tea and having it hit my back like a sci-fi laser beam destroying New York City. Physically, I feel better. Mentally, I'm as burnt as the toast I eat for breakfast.

I once again pick up the list Chester provided. I don't know why I do this, because I already have it memorized. I retrieve my cell phone and see it has enough juice in it to listen to the one voicemail message I received. "Yaa, dis is Sven. You called 'bout Sheckle money. Yaa, but naa. Check bounce."

I'll return the call at a decent hour. I spend the remainder of my pre-morning staring at *The Original Carlo*. I am not having a good time.

I wait for the sun to rise before I leave the apartment, and I'm glad I do because the Toyota won't start. I try the ignition about thirty times, but the only sound is a *click*. Why I repeat this process over and over either speaks volumes of my unflagging optimism or to my total idiocy of auto mechanics. I get out and open the hood. This is also stupid because I have no clue of what to look for. I close the hood. Thankfully, I parked with no one in front of me. I return to the driver's side, reach in, and turn the ignition key back on. I release the parking brake, put the car in neutral, and push. When I get it going down the street at about three miles per hour, I painfully jump back into the driver's seat, depress the clutch, jam it into second gear, and set my left foot loose. The car jerks, engine catches, and I'm off sputtering down the street like an epileptic breakdancer on pep pills.

I take the long way to where I'm headed to hopefully charge both the car and my batteries. I stop at MechanicsRUs.

"Looks like you got yerself a real classic," the guy tells me as I park in front of the service bay. "Haven't seen one of these since Christ was a corporal."

I decline informing him that there is no passage in the New Testament about Jesus joining the armed forces. "It wouldn't start this morning."

"Personally, I hate that," he tells me, opening the hood.

"What do you think the problem is?" I ask.

"It wouldn't start this morning," he says.

"Okay, what do you think the solution is?"

He peers around the engine, as if he's looking for a scavenger hunt item. "It could be the Lamsky connection."

"The what?"

"Lamsky rod. It's the connection from the igniter, through the pressure cap, into the solenoid, and through to the battery. Common problem in these Toyotas."

"It is?"

"See it all the time."

"And what is the solution to the problem?"

"About three hundred bucks."

"You know," I say, "it happened one other time, but it did kick over on the next try."

"Yeah, Lamsky's can be finicky."

The truth is, I don't have one problem with the car, I have two. One, this Lamsky thing, and two, the problem of not having enough money to get my Lamsky fixed.

"I'm going to have to think about it," I tell the guy.

"What's to think about?" he asks.

He's got me there. "I'm not sure. I'll let you know after I think about what I have to think about."

Luckily, I kept the car running. I climb back in and motor on over to Herman's. I park on the end of the block so if I have to push, I'll have a clear path ahead of me.

"What got you up so early?" he asks, opening his door.

"Don't ask."

"I already did."

I enter Herman's apartment.

"I made another thirty grand off Sheckle."

"Herman..."

"He's about to make a hostile takeover of a new upstart biotech firm."

"Does it have anything to do with Gila monsters?"

"How'd you know?"

We take our usual seats. Me on the couch, Herman in the swivel chair in front of his computer. "Have breakfast yet?"

"Yes."

"What did you have?"

"Burnt toast."

"If you want to regulate your metabolism, Sherlock, you have to have a good breakfast."

"Thank you, Jenny Craig."

Herman offers me a stalk of celery, dried prunes, and a small bottle of 5-Hour Energy. "These'll get the old system into overdrive," he tells me.

"That's not breakfast, Herman. That's a ticking intestinal time bomb."

He bites into a handful of prunes, stuffs them into his mouth, and chews away like a third base coach chomping on a wad of chewing tobacco. Yet another image I won't be able to get out of my brain.

I sit back on the couch, sigh, and admit, "I'm lost, Herman."

"You look lost," he says while prune-laced spittle runs down his chin and into the folds of his neck fat. Ditto on the brain image thing.

"I got no leads, no answers, and another sixty grand has disappeared," I tell him.

"Too bad."

"I went to this charity event last night, honoring Sheckle, and it doesn't make any sense."

"That they're honoring Sheckle?"

I start at the beginning and take him through the entire event. By the time I'm finished, he's eaten a tree's worth of prunes. I end with: "Can you hold off on the 5-Hour Energy until I'm ready to leave?"

"First of all, Sherlock, they don't want to cure cancer. There's no business if they cure cancer. The business is treating cancer." He's not speaking; he's lecturing. "Do you have any idea of how many people would lose their jobs if they cured cancer?"

"Are you telling me 'It's too big to succeed'?"

"Exactly. All that money for drug research goes into finding drugs to treat the symptoms, not finding a cure."

"That's not right."

"Right has nothing to do with it. It's a business. Being a part of the CC-whatever organization gives Sheckle an inside line on every company on the edge of a breakthrough."

"That really doesn't seem fair."

"Fair also has nothing to do with it," Herman says.

All this medical research stuff is making me sick.

"Now, you really don't look well, Sherlock," Herman tells me. "Have a prune."

I decline. "Have you checked out Chester yet?"

"He's as clean as a new chip in an Intel factory."

Whatever that means. I sigh again, "Nothing?"

Herman opens five small 5-Hour Energy containers and pours their contents into one glass. "Well, I do have one small, nagging feeling," he tells me.

After he downs that energy drink, he's going to have a lot bigger feeling than a small nag. "What?"

"Two sets of books. They're keeping two sets of books."

"Who?"

"Witherington, Chester, or both. And if it's both, that'd be four sets of books."

Once again, it's the power of compounding.

"Why do you think they'd keep two sets?"

"The discrepancy in amounts Chester listed, and old Chuck seems like the kind of guy who would keep two sets of books."

"I can't believe a corporation the size of SSS could, or would, do that."

"What financial rock have you been sleeping under, Sherlock?"

"None, because I haven't been doing too much sleeping to be honest with you."

"It's because you're not eating a good breakfast. Have some prunes."

"Pass."

"Witherington didn't become Sheckle's CFO by never telling a lie," Herman says between chomps of a celery stalk, the leaves of which flutter down onto the keys of his computer.

"Chuck does have a history of malfeasance in his past, but if you can't find out what he's up to, there's no way I'll be able to find out what's really going on," I tell him.

"Call that buddy of yours at the IRS. Maybe he'll help you out, Sherlock."

"Oh yeah, that's going to happen."

"You get the IRS numbers, I'll get what I can get, and we'll be able to compare prunes to prunes."

Herman stirs the 5-Hour Energy with the end of a celery stalk as if it is a Bloody Mary. "Do you think you can hold off drinking that stuff until I'm out of here?"

Herman doesn't listen to me. He eats another two prunes. "I sure am glad they invented the pitted prune," Herman says. "Think of the time I save."

While Herman chews, I sit back and think. The numbers discrepancy I've found with the charities is maybe just the tip of the iceberg. "You really think Chester could also be keeping two sets of books?"

"Everybody cheats. It's only a matter of how much and how often."

"Even Chester?"

"He's an accountant, Sherlock. It's in his blood."

"I can't believe Chester's a crook. The guy goes to church five times a week. What's in it for him?"

Herman swishes the energy drink around and around in the glass. "Beats me."

"I just can't buy Chester fudging."

"But, if he is fudging," Herman says, "he'd write them down somewhere."

"Why?"

"He's an accountant." Herman swigs the 5-Hour Energy like a thirsty cowboy.

The clock is ticking, the fuse lit. I begin to fear for my life.

"So how do I find Chester's second set of books?" I ask, speaking much more rapidly than before.

"You figure out when he's not going to be in his office, pick the locks, break in, rifle all his drawers until you find what you're after."

"That's against the law, Herman."

"Duh."

I hear a gurgle from his stomach. It sounds like distant thunder. A storm is coming, and it's gonna be a whopper.

"Thanks, Herman, but I better be going."

"So soon?"

Another gurgle—this one rumbles like an impatient Harley Davidson at a red light.

I'm out of there before Vesuvius erupts.

***

Outside Herman's, the Toyota doesn't start. Dead. But now is not the time to deal with the problem. I walk six blocks, and take the 'L' downtown. My destination is at the south end of the Loop. A notice on the front of the building informs it's scheduled for demolition.

The offices of DeRuth and Associates, Public Relations are thankfully on the second floor, because the elevator is out of order. The door is unlocked. I don't bother knocking.

Morton DeRuth is at least six-eight in height and weighs less than twelve pounds. He's so thin he has to jump around in the shower to get wet. Feed the guy some ketchup and you can use him as a thermometer. He's seen his shadow fewer times than Punxsutawney Phil has on cloudy days.

Morton probably got the nickname "Stretch" when he was about three, but he picked up an additional moniker when he was one of the press people working for the Chicago P.D. We called him "Stretch the Truth" DeRuth.

"Sherlock, I haven't seen you since you got kicked off the force. Does your hand still hurt?" he says as I enter his place of business.

"Nice to see you, too, Stretch."

"If I would have been you, Sherlock, I would have sued the city for the partial use of a hand after you coldcocked that idiot captain of yours. You could have claimed you injured it in the line of duty."

I hate being reminded of the lapse in judgment I made the day I got so frustrated with a superior I socked him in the jaw. I'd still be on the force today if I would have held back, with money coming in every two weeks, a pension, chances for advancement, etc., etc., etc.

Dumb.

"Why didn't you mention it then, Stretch?" I ask. "I could have used the money."

"Because I was too busy trying to bury the story."

"It was shown everywhere, from the national news to YouTube."

"Yeah, your story kind of got away from me, Sherlock."

"I'll say."

Stretch's neck is so thin his Adam's apple bobs up and down like a rubber ducky in a river rapid when he speaks.

"What were you doing at the Sheckle event last night?" I ask and sit down in one of the two chairs across from his desk in the only office in the *Offices*.

"That was beautiful, wasn't it?"

"No."

"I thought his speech was moving."

"The only thing moving during his speech were all the people trying to avoid hearing it."

"That whole event was my idea," Stretch says triumphantly. "It made the Trib, Sun-Times, and had hundreds of tweets."

"For a half a million bucks it should."

"He'll get out under two fifty. For that kind of publicity, it's a pittance."

"I thought it was five hundred," I admit.

"Fine print, Sherlock, fine print."

"He won't have to match a half million in donations?"

"No way."

"So maybe he should be called 'Mr. Half-Wonderful'?"

"You know, I gave him that name," Stretch says as proud as a peacock. "It stuck like gum on a gumshoe's shoe."

"Doesn't sound to me that Mr. Wonderful is all that wonderful."

"It's all in how you look at it, Sherlock."

"Please, tell me."

"It's not the present inside, but the gift-wrapping, that's important, Sherlock. It's not the amount you give away, but the amount you promise to give away, that gets results," Morton "Stretch the Truth" DeRuth schools me in the fine art of public relations. "Sheckle has been doing this for thirty years. He's a modern-day Robin Hood in the eyes of all the little people out there."

"He's not supposed to break his promises."

"He's a hell of a lot better than most of the gazillionaires in this town who go into convulsions every time they have to part with a dime."

"I'm not buying it, Stretch."

"I don't care, Sherlock, because there's only one opinion that counts," Stretch says. "Public opinion."

"You're telling me that Sheckle's giving away millions is nothing more than an advertising campaign?"

"It's beautiful, isn't it?"

"No, it's sneaky."

"Your opinion, Sherlock, which doesn't count for anything."

He's right. "Then why does he do it?" I ask.

"There's this billionaire in LA who owns more rental property than a business savant playing Monopoly. The guy takes out full-page ads in the LA Times, almost weekly, telling the city what wonderful things he is doing for them. In reality, he's an evil slumlord. He's an admitted racist with more lawsuits filed against him than Bernie Madoff. He'll lock you out of your apartment if you're late more than three minutes with your rent. He treats renters' complaints like they're the plague, and on top of all that, his wife, who helps run the business, is worse than he is. And this guy shells out less than 25 percent of the money he says he's giving away."

"Why?" I ask.

"When he needs a variance on a piece of property, an inspector to look the other way, or a slight change in zoning, they got a rubber stamp OK with his name on it. You can't do the kind of business Sheckle does without the right kind of karma working for you."

"It's not karma; it's a brand of extortion," I say.

"Call it what you want, Sherlock. All Sheckle's doing is doing business."

"You're saying Sterling Sheckle is in the same league as this guy in LA?"

"Sheckle's in finance. So, same league but different division."

"And you helped put him there?" I rhetorically ask Stretch.

"Put him there, keep him there, and keep his rent real low."

I've heard enough.

If I wasn't depressed enough with the image of Kelly and the Ramone Brothers outside the shoe house, the meetings with Stretch and Herman certainly haven't done much to lift my mood. It's not yet nine thirty, and I still have the whole day in front of me for more rotten things to happen.

"See ya, Stretch. It's been a slice."

"Ya know, if you would have had someone like me working for you when you punched your captain, you'd still be on the force today."

"Yeah, right." I'm outta there.

To make myself feel a little better, I walk through the Loop toward Michigan Avenue to the Chicago Cultural Center, one of my favorite places in the city. The building always puts me in a better mood. I hope it does the trick today.

The Cultural Center was built in 1897 at a cost of two million dollars. Two million dollars today would barely get you a small, two-bedroom lakefront condo on a low floor with a halfway decent view, but back then two million was a substantial chunk of change. It was designed in the neoclassical style with everything from Vermont pink marble and blue limestone to mosaics of Favrile glass. The place is a treasure. Once the home of the Chicago Public Library, it's currently used for art exhibitions, dinners for dignitaries, meetings for people who need to be impressed, and offices for many of the city's cultural movers and shakers. The best part of the building is that it has a multitude of rooms, most of which don't get used on a regular basis. I find one and close the door behind me.

I sit behind a table, once used by Ulysses S. Grant in the Civil War, and take out my phone. I call the number on the screen.

"Hello, is this Sven?"

"Yaa," he says.

"This is Richard Sherlock. Thanks for returning my call."

"Yaa."

"You got money from Sheckle?"

"Naa."

I'm not sure I hear him correctly. "Was that a yaa or a naa?"

"Yaa and naa."

"Okay." Now, I'm really not sure what's going on. "Can we get together and talk about it?"

"Yaa."

"Today?"

"Yaa."

"I'll see you at lunchtime."

"Gud."

I bet Sven is an excellent texter.

I don't have a lot of time to contemplate what Sven said because my phone rings seconds later.

"Hello."

"Mr. Sherlock."

"Chester, how's the little lady."

"Richard, you saved Claire's life."

"Let's just say 'I was happy to help out.'"

"I owe you so much."

"Not really, Chester. How is she doing?"

"Much better, she wants to meet you and thank you personally."

"That's not necessary."

"I'm bringing her home today."

"So you won't be in your office?"

"No."

"How about tomorrow? Will you be in then?"

"I won't be in until we can find some daytime help."

"And when do you think that will be?"

"I'm not sure," Chester says.

Herman's suggestion of breaking into Chester's office bothers me. I spent nineteen years upholding the law and to be breaking it now, just to make my job easier, isn't right. Plus, I have a hard time believing Chester is a crook. Guys who wear tweed sport coats are never the bad guys in the story, but it sure isn't stopping me from sneakily finding out Chester's itinerary for the next few days.

"Claire would really love to see you and thank you, Mr. Sherlock. Can you stop by the house?"

"Again, it's really not necessary."

"Please," he says, "it would help in her recovery."

This has turned into one of those *There's no way to 'say no'* moments.

"If I can fit it in today, I will."

"Claire will be thrilled. Thank you."

"You're welcome."

There is a short pause.

"How is the investigation going?" Chester asks.

"I've got a new lead I'm about to pursue."

"Good luck."

It is probably best not to tell him the new lead is him.

"Let me know if there's anything I can do to help."

I feel like a real schmuck after I hang up.

Again, I don't have to feel lousy for long because the phone rings thirty seconds later. Suddenly, I'm popular. Why, I have no clue.

"Hello."

"Richard..."

"Mr. Zazou.

"Call me Al."

"Al."

"Just wanted to call and tell you how impressed we all were with the way you handled the open house."

"Really?"

"We think you have real talent for this business."

"But only one couple showed up to see the place." I decide it is best not to mention the Snoop Sisters.

"Quality, not quantity, Richard."

"If you say so, Al."

"Ms. Missy and I want you to come in and begin to familiarize yourself with some of our office procedures. This kind of knowledge can give you a real leg up on the business once you pass the test, get your license, and bore full speed ahead into the world of Chicago real estate."

"I'd like to Al, but I still have to make a living. I'm currently on a case."

"At your convenience, Richard, at your convenience."

"Okay."

"Can you be here today?"

"I just said—"

"Anytime, Richard. Anytime works for me."

The shine from Al's teeth emanates through my cell phone. "Well, maybe late, late afternoon."

"That would be super," he says. "The more you learn now, the quicker the commissions will roll in when you hit the streets."

"I'll call you."

"Remember Richard, nothing starts in business until somebody makes a sale."

A group of tourists enter the room. One asks the tour guide, "Is that General Grant?"

"If it is," the tour guide answers, "he's out of uniform."

"I was just leaving," I say, getting up.

On my way to find another empty room, I make a decision. "Don't tempt fate or the Lamsky on the car unless it is absolutely necessary.

The room I find empty is a small theater. I sit in the back row and start to dial Tiffany's number, but I quickly consider it a waste of time. I try to text her, but that is even more problematic since I can never get my thumb or finger to touch the right letter in the exact right spot. What happens is I write messages with so many misspelled words it comes out in Greek gobbledygook. When I go back and try to correct the errors, I make more mistakes, erase more than I want to erase, and end up with a message only a Native American codebreaker could decipher. So far, I've spent triple the amount of time it would have taken me to call and leave a voicemail. I hit send but don't know if it went anywhere, so, I call and leave a voicemail anyway, which Tiffany will probably ignore. I should invest in carrier pigeons.

CHAPTER 15

I always tell my daughters that the most important thing you can do in life is try. If the odds are insurmountable and success is a pipe dream, and even if you fail miserably, as long as you try your best, you will never feel like a failure. It is not what you may accomplish in life, but the desire, willingness, and effort that go into a challenge that makes life purposeful and worthwhile. This is a time I should heed my own advice.

I really don't want to go to the IRS. My one contact there hates me. If I ask for help, he'll not only turn me down, but also browbeat me, call me names, and insult my intelligence; and this is what he does on his good days. Also, when I do visit him, I put my life into his hands, which carry more deadly viruses than the Do Not Touch vault at the Center for Disease Control.

But I have to try.

"Excuse me," I say to the receptionist on the 4th floor of the Klucynski Building, "is Lloyd Holler in?"

"Who should I say is calling?"

"Richard Sherlock."

Before she dials her phone, she looks up at me and asks, "Are you sure you want to see *him*?"

Lloyd Holler, that's two L's in Lloyd and two L's in Holler, has spent his whole life as an auditor for the IRS. His career has made him meaner than Dick Butkus in his prime, the shark in *Jaws*, and my 4th grade P.E. teacher combined.

"You, what do you want?"

"Hi, Lloyd."

"The last time I saw you, you almost got me killed," he screams at me. He is referring to an unfortunate evening where one gang member decided to thin the gangbanger herd by eliminating his competition with one shot between his rival's eyes.

"That certainly wasn't something I planned," I try to explain. "I thought you were retiring to a quiet life in the country, Lloyd?"

"Naw. Decided against it."

"Why?"

"I'm still having too much fun."

In his left hand, Lloyd holds a wet, wadded up handkerchief filled with bodily fluids from his nasal cavities. He dabs at the torrent, which flows faster than the Big Muddy. "Hurry up, what do you want? I got cheats to catch."

"A favor."

"I hate favors."

"Sterling S. Sheckle," I label the favor.

"I hate that guy worse than I hate favors."

This would be a damning comment from most people, but Lloyd hates babies, flowers, music, little dogs, and just about every human being on the planet.

"The SSS Corporation might be keeping two sets of books."

Lloyd's watery, bloodshot eyes bore into me like a high-speed drill boring through cheap pine. "You got proof?"

"I'm working on that."

"How?"

"I've found some discrepancies in the amounts he's given to charities."

Lloyd swipes his nose, which does more spreading than absorbing of his mucus. "And what do you want me to do about it?"

"If I give you my list, would you compare it to his returns?" I ask.

Lloyd's watery, bleary eyes somewhat focus. A downward snarl forms on his mouth. He coughs and says, "Bring it on. If he's cheating, I'll break him in two." Lloyd sneezes, sending a plume of snot into the air equal to a spring Chicago thunderstorm. Charming.

I hand over the list and run from the room before the cloud hits me and I become a One Mile Island.

***

It's not even ten thirty in the morning and I've already had the

absolute pleasures of watching Herman chomp prunes, listening to Stretch stretch the truth, and having Lloyd Holler spray me with infectious diseases. And people wonder why I hate my job.

A weird sound comes out of my phone. It's a text from Tiffany telling me that she can't understand my text and to text her back. What would be the point of doing that?

I call her. She picks up; she must have forgotten to look on the screen and see it's me.

"Tiffany..."

"I'm really glad you're texting, Mr. Sherlock, but I can't read Pig Latin."

"Neither can I."

"So you can write something that you can't read, Mr. Sherlock? Wow, that's weird."

I don't answer. Some responses are better left unsaid.

"Tiffany, how would you like to join me for lunch today?" I ask and add, "It's on me."

"I'm not going to any place that has a drive-up window, Mr. Sherlock."

"And after our delicious lunch, we can take a nice, pleasant drive out and see Chester." In a way, I feel like "Stretch the Truth" DeRuth, tricking Tiffany into driving me out to the burbs again.

"Is that the people with the old pictures on the wall?"

"Yes. This time we get to meet the little lady when she's fully functioning."

"Well, I certainly hope she doesn't have another one of her chunk snafus. The last one was disgusting."

"I'm standing outside on the corner of Dearborn and Adams. When can you pick me up?"

"Fifteen minutes."

Tiffany arrives forty-five minutes later. The second I hop in her Lexus, she informs me, "I don't have a lot of time. I got a hot date tonight, and I have to have time to get ready."

"What time's your date?"

"Eight."

"It's not even noon yet."

"It's never too early to start looking more beautiful, Mr. Sherlock."

"Tiffany, you're beautiful without doing anything."

"I know, but staying perfect is just as important as becoming perfect."

"That, I wouldn't know."

"Where are we going?" she asks as she pulls into traffic and cuts off a cab.

"West on Madison. We have to get to Randolph."

By the time we exit the Loop, I ask, "Are you going out with Mr. Pointy Hair?"

"Yes, and his hair isn't pointy; it's stylish."

"It's greasy."

"No, it's mousy."

"What happens, Tiffany, if you find out it's not his hair that's pointy but his head?"

"Yes, that would definitely be a red flag."

"I hope you have a great time." We proceed down Randolph Street past Halsted. This used to be a neighborhood where fishmongers, meat-packers, and vegetable peddlers plied their trade in the early mornings. There are still a few around, but now the area is dotted with expensive, classy restaurants, high-rise condo buildings, and sleek office spaces. Progress.

"Are we going to the Packing House?" Tiffany asks, noting the most expensive restaurant on the block.

"No, keep going."

In a few more blocks we come to the end of the gentrification. Urban decay replaces urban renewal in the blink of a pothole. "Pull up over there, and park in the street."

"Are you sure we didn't already pass the restaurant?"

As soon as the car comes to a stop, I jump out, causing Tiffany to hurry to catch up with me. "Wait. Where are we going?"

"To Sven's."

"What's a Sven?"

"I'm not sure."

"I don't eat meatballs, Mr. Sherlock."

There are about twenty-five homeless men and women lined up in front of the Tabernacle of Ebenezer, Tender of Jesus' Flock storefront church, ministry, and shelter. Tiffany grabs my arm for protection as we pass by hungry parishioners and head for the front door. "Isn't this great, Tiffany, we don't have to wait in line?" I say facetiously.

"Are we still in America?" Tiffany asks as we enter the filthy, but hallowed, grounds.

"Excuse me," I say to the first person I see wearing a pair of shoes that fit. "Where can I find Sven?"

"End of the line."

It doesn't take much dragging to bring Tiffany along. She clutches onto me like a barnacle to a pier. We pass two cafeteria-like tables of food. There's soup, or what I hope is soup, black beans, kidney beans, tube steaks, commonly referred to as hot dogs, rolls, and other assorted but necessary goodies. Behind each food item, a former homeless person is ready to serve up a portion to a current homeless person.

"Mr. Sherlock, I think I'm going to gag." Tiffany speaks with one hand over her nose and mouth.

"Before or after we eat?"

"You mean we're going to actually eat this slop?"

"Sure, they promised me we'd get one of the better tables."

"Oh my God."

We reach the end of the line, where there is one guy about fifty, tall, blond, and with blue eyes. "Are you Sven?" I ask.

"Yaa."

"Sherlock." I put out my hand to shake his. "This is Tiffany," I introduce my protégée, who looks two shades past pale.

"Yaa, yaa."

"Mr. Sherlock, I can feel my skin is beginning to molt from the stench of those bean things. If it keeps up, I'll need a bee venom facial on my entire body."

"Take a deep breath, Tiffany, you'll feel better."

"No."

The line of men and women with plates full of beans and ballpark *filets* is moving toward us. "Yaa, gloves," Sven says, handing over the latex. He positions me next to him and Tiffany next to me. I'm going to be handing out new syringes. He puts Tiffany in charge of condom distribution.

Tiffany pulls on two pairs of latex gloves. "God," she says, "what I wouldn't do for a full body condom right now."

The lunch crowd starts moving past us.

"You got a check from Sheckle that bounced?" I ask Sven, who is busy handing out miniature bibles. I didn't know Matthew, Mark, Luke, and John came in a CliffsNotes format.

"Yaa."

"How much was it for?"

"Forty tou-sand."

"Ouch."

"Yaa. Ouch."

"What happened?"

"He hold it."

I'm not sure what he means. "He put a hold on it?"

"Yaa."

"Why?"

"Naa." Sven shrugs his shoulders.

"Did you ever get money from Sheckle before?"

"Yaa."

"How much?"

"Forty tou-sand."

"And this time when he sent you the money, you went to deposit it, the check was no good."

"Yaa."

I hear one of the homeless guys ask Tiffany to show him how to put the condom on.

To my surprise, Tiffany rips open the condom packet, removes the rolled up latex, takes one of the man's tube steaks off his plate, and demonstrates proper condom application and etiquette. "Make sure you roll it all the way down, as far as it can go." She is quite emphatic in her instruction.

And while that show goes on, I continue with Sven. "Were you ever contacted by anyone from Sheckle's?"

"Naa."

"How about from the SSS Corporation?"

"Naa."

"A guy named Chester?"

"Naa."

Tiffany is now waving the wrapped, phallic *T-bone* for all to see. "And that's how you keep little homeless buns out of the oven."

Sven doesn't have much more to add to the little he had to say to begin with. If nothing else, he's given me a new angle to pursue. We wait until the line depletes before we pack it in and say "Ta-ta" to the Ebenezer Tabernacle and Jesus' now well-satiated flock.

Yaa, gud.

***

We stop at Tiffany's favorite health food emporium, and I treat her to a pomegranate-persimmon power drink. I settle for Vitamin Water because they don't have regular water in the place.

We arrive at Chester's house early in the afternoon.

"Thank you so much for coming," Chester greets us at the door.

"How is she doing?"

"Right now she's sleeping."

"Can I get you anything?" Chester asks.

"Regular water," I request.

"Tiffany?"

"No," Tiffany says, sipping on her power concoction. "I'm good."

While Chester fetches my water, Tiffany goes back to the wall of photos. For some reason she's fascinated by the pictures. "A lot of these people look alike," she says.

"I think they call it 'family,' Tiffany."

"Here." Chester hands me the H2O.

"Before we look in on Claire, can I ask you a few questions, Chester?"

"Certainly."

"Do you ever remember giving money to a guy named Sven at the Ebenezer Tabernacle?"

"Yes, he feeds, clothes, and cares for the homeless."

"Do you ever remember sending him a check, then canceling it?"

Chester answers immediately, "No."

"Chester, I know this is a difficult question, but I have to ask it."

"Go ahead."

"As Sterling's tax preparer, did you ever, shall we say, do a little fudging on his behalf?"

"Never," he answers without hesitation.

"How did you report the charitable contributions to the IRS?"

"A detailed listing was provided year after year."

"Is that a standard practice?"

"It is now, but I've been doing it for years."

I sip the water. "Here's another question that's a bit difficult to ask."

"Go ahead."

"Do you believe Witherington fudges a bit in reporting Sterling's corporation's return?"

Chester hesitates. "Unless you have something nice to say about someone, it is best not to say anything at all."

"I agree with you, Chester, but that doesn't work real well in my business."

Chester moves his body around as if the conversation is causing him physical pain.

"Does he cheat, Chester?"

"He puts in mistakes," Chester says with a grimace on his face.

"What?"

"He puts mistakes into the return that the IRS will catch when they audit the return."

I don't get it, so I say, "I don't get it."

"A corporation the size of SSS is always audited, and it is the job of the auditor to find the errors, assess the penalties, and bill the business. An auditor is always under intense pressure to move the file along as quickly as possible. So, Witherington loads the return with easy-to-catch fudges, hoping the auditor will catch those and miss the real whoppers he's got hidden where the big money lies, no pun intended."

"Don't you think the IRS would be smart enough to know that trick?" I'm thinking Lloyd Holler, with two L's in Lloyd and two L's in Holler, would be on this like snot on his nose.

"It's a game."

"A game?"

"Many CFOs believe if they don't take chances, they're not doing their job."

"But if you figure in all the time, effort, and expense, do you really save any money in the long run?"

Chester looks at me like Herman looks at me when I'm too naïve to be believed.

"Sorry I asked."

A faint voice is heard from down the hall, "Chester."

I follow Chester out of the front room and into the hallway, where Tiffany stops him by pointing to one of the pictures. "Is this your family?"

"My wife's."

Tiffany points to a small name listing printed on one of the group shots. "The Geltalinski family?"

"Yes."

"I bet she was glad to become a Longtooth."

"I certainly hope so."

Claire is sitting up in the hospital bed as we enter. She doesn't look all that bad considering what's she's been through. She has better skin tone than Tiffany had during Sven's lunch for the homeless, and I'll bet she doesn't use bee venom.

"How are you feeling?" I ask.

"Better, so much better," she says. "I can't tell you how sorry I am that I had to put both of you through all of that."

"It was nothing," Tiffany says.

There's a pair of reading glasses, a plastic water bottle, and three or four prescription vials on the bedstand.

"Would you please remind her take her medicine, get plenty of rest, and stay in bed until the doctor says she can to get up and move around?" Chester asks us. "Claire wants to be her own physician."

Tiffany starts to repeat Chester's instructions, but defers to merely saying to Claire, "What he said."

We hang out a few more minutes, chitchatting about stuff none of us care much about, until Claire starts to yawn.

"We'll leave you now so you can get some rest," I say.

"We both cannot thank you enough," Claire says.

"Again," Tiffany says, "don't mention it."

We make a hasty retreat out of Chester's home. He's given me a lot to think about and another stop to make today.

Once we're in the Lexus, Tiffany says, "Was that gross or what?"

"What?"

"The smell," Tiffany explains. "She had that 'old lady' smell. My grandma Moomah has it, and it totally grosses me out."

"What was worse, the smell from the homeless lunch or Claire's old lady odor?" I ask.

"Each had its own characteristics of puke, but I'd have to go with the beans; they were truly disgusting."

"You don't mind if I make a note of that for future reference?"

"I'm only here to help, Mr. Sherlock."

"Want to make one more stop today?" I ask as she zooms into traffic.

"I don't know. Right now I have only four hours to get ready for my date."

"Then could you drop me off at the Willis Tower? I'd like to stop in on C. Franklin Witherington."

"What are you going to say to him?"

"I'm going to see if I can shake his windows and rattle his walls."

"You know," Tiffany says, "that might be fun to watch."

CHAPTER 16

There is a theory, belief, or rumor that after a few years of being a policeman, one will develop a certain sixth sense about people, especially bad people. A veteran cop can be cruising down the block on regular patrol, spot a person walking along, give him a look, and immediately tell this individual is up to no good or that it hasn't been long since he was up to no good. A good cop will slow down, follow the person until he or she looks back, and then the two will exchange stares. At this point, or soon after, the perp will get scared, take off running, and the cop will have cause to take chase, catch the person, and begin questioning. Nine out of ten times the cop's instincts are correct. Call it intuition, a knack, skill, magic, or whatever. I can't put my finger on the when, where, and why it happens, but I'm living proof the sense exists.

Tiffany parks in a handicapped spot, as usual. And when we get to the main floor of the Willis Tower, we have to wait at the elevator bank that goes to our set of floors. When the Otis arrives, we squeeze in with a number of other people, almost all business types.

Nobody speaks as we hurtle skyward, except Tiffany. "How are you gonna get old Chuck to spill his guts on how he cheats the IRS?"

"Shhhh."

"How? Tell me."

"Shush!" I raise my voice to her. "How many times have I told you not to talk in elevators?"

"I don't know. Why would I ever count something as stupid as that?"

"People can hear you."

"So?"

"It's none of their business, Tiffany."

"And how do you know that?"

Now she's got me talking a mile a minute in the elevator. I let out a big, "Quiet! Shush!"

Tiffany takes offense, "You certainly don't have to snap at me, Mr. Sherlock."

"I agree," the guy standing next to me says.

"Me, too," a lady says. "You didn't have to shush her."

"Do you some good to be a little nicer, buddy," another guy says.

"Yeah," a few more passengers add.

One lady calls me a "creep."

During the verbal lambasting by my fellow riders, I notice one guy on the other side of the car who doesn't voice his opinion. He's dressed poorly, even by my standards, and he's disheveled. He needs a haircut, shave, and a sports jacket that both fits and goes with his pants. He stares into the wall to his left and not at the front of the elevator car, as is the custom. As the car doors open and passengers exit, many turn around to give me a final dirty look; everybody is a critic. When we get close to 104, Tiffany, I, and Mr. Disheveled are the only ones left in the car.

The doors open on Sterling's floor. Tiffany starts to exit, but I hold her back. "After you," I say to the man.

Tiffany reluctantly lets him exit before her, and she gives me a dirty look.

The three of us walk to the reception desk. "I'm here to see Mr. Sheckle," the man says uncomfortably to the receptionist.

"Do you have an appointment?"

"No," he says. Then he changes his answer to "Yes."

"And who should I say is calling?"

"Bengie Galusha."

"And you, sir?" the lady asks me.

"C. Franklin Witherington." I take one more look toward Mr. Disheveled. "We're here to see Mr. Sheckle, too," I tell her.

"Your name?"

"Richard Sherlock."

"I thought we were here to see that Worthington guy?" Tiffany asks.

"We're killing two birds with one stone," I say to my assistant.

"Oh," she says, "we're going to shake Sheckle down too. Cool."

I give the receptionist a slight smile. It's about all I can do after that comment.

Bengie is already shifting nervously in his chair as Tiffany and I sit across from him.

"My Dad would love to see you rip into Sheckle," Tiffany says.

My eyes are on Bengie, but I speak to Tiffany, "Too bad you didn't bring a camera..."

"I did," she says. "My phone."

Bengie gets out of his chair, goes back to the receptionist, and says something I can't hear. She points, and he disappears down the hallway to my left.

"Mr. Witherington will see you now, Mr. Sherlock," the lady kindly informs me.

We stand. "Dissing Witherbottom should be a good warm-up before you rip into Sheckle," Tiffany says, following me into the floor's office area.

We walk, with me in the lead, down an aisle of office cubicles. To my left, I see Witherington step out of his office, notice me, and give his assistant some instruction. To my right, I see something that sends the hair on the back of my neck up and into a point worthy of Tiffany's soon-to-be date.

I take a right instead of a left, away from Witherington, and into the aisle that leads to Sheckle's corner office.

"Would you make up your mind, Mr. Sherlock, on who you're going to shake, rattle, and roll first," Tiffany admonishes me as she follows my quickly changing path.

I'm about ten feet away when I see the pistol come out of the back of the man's pants. He raises it to aim as he screams out, "Sheckle, you took my house away from me."

I take my left hand and give Tiffany a shove that sends her flying into an open cubical. I take two more steps and leap into the air, spreading my arms wide, and come down on Bengie Galusha like a parachute over a landed skydiver. Assistants scream as I lay on top of the guy, try to grab the gun, and get his free arm into a hammerlock. We must look like a short stack of pancakes being served by a waiter with epilepsy. Bengie swears up a storm. Screams fill the air. Workers take cover behind desks or hit the floor in fear. The gun is waving in his hand with his index finger on the trigger. I shift forward on his body and jam the tip of my little finger into the space between the trigger and the backstop of the firing mechanism. As he squeezes, the trigger has no place to depress and the gun can't fire, but it really hurts my finger. I try to shake the gun out of his hand, but he won't let go. My little finger is swelling up bigger than a diseased goiter because he won't stop trying to shoot. I don't have a lot of choices, so I open my mouth and come down on his forearm like a crocodile on a floating flounder.

Chomp.

Bengie lets out a wail louder than a B-movie actress in a low-budget horror film. The gun flies free. I release my incisors, scramble forward, and kick the gun under the desk outside Sheckle's office.

The next voice I hear is Sheckle's: "What the hell is going on? I'm on the phone trying to make some money in here!"

By the time Sheckle is back in his office, Bengie has pretty much given up the cause. I wrap him up in a submission hold worthy of Hulk Hogan and pin him down until he gives up the fight entirely.

"Somebody get some rope."

"We don't have any rope," a man says. "Where do you think you're at, a dude ranch?"

"Duct tape?" I ask.

"Sure, everybody's got duct tape," another guy answers.

"And somebody call 9-1-1."

I get help from some of the younger employees, and we strap a now compliant, weeping Bengie onto a stenographer's chair. Bengie now resembles a forced-to-submit, gift-wrapped typing pool member with silver trimmings. He blubbers on how he once had a nice home but lost it when the rate went up eight points and Sheckle's company refused to renegotiate.

"Another satisfied customer?" I ask rhetorically.

Two sets of patrolmen arrive in a few minutes and each compliments me on my duct-taping skills. They shackle up the suspect. Then they take a pair of scissors and cut the duct tape off. I feel sorry for Bengie. This guy is no criminal. He was probably told he could afford more house than he could and signed an adjustable mortgage with a balloon the size of the Graf Zeppelin. When he couldn't pay the new amount, foreclosure came quicker than a thief in the night. Hopefully, he is one of the last victims of the 2008 mortgage meltdown. The cops roll him down two aisles of cubicles like a shopping cart down the frozen food aisle, off the floor, and into an elevator.

Tiffany, when she feels the coast is clear, comes out from the cubicle and, although still shaken, screams, "Why did you have to push me so hard, Mr. Sherlock? If I get a black-and-blue mark on my arm, I won't be able to wear anything sleeveless on my date tonight."

I return her scream with, "What did you want me to do, Tiffany, send you a text that the guy had a gun?"

"No, because the way you text I wouldn't have been able to read it."

"Well, then please accept my humblest apologies for being so rambunctious in my efforts to save your life."

"Apology accepted," Tiffany remains in psycho mode, "but I will be thinking of ways on how you're going to make this up to me."

"I can hardly wait."

"And if I do bruise, I don't think there's time for me to go back and totally redesign my wardrobe for the evening, Mr. Sherlock."

"Then let me do it for you."

"Oh God, save me!"

I find a chair and plop down. My heart is beating faster than a metronome on speed. I'm waiting for the officer in charge to show up and start asking questions when Morton "Stretch the Truth" DeRuth comes on the floor acting like a bunkhouse monitor at a juvenile detention camp.

"Nobody leaves the floor until I say so," he announces to the workers. "You will all be signing a release, stating you will not discuss this matter with the press or anyone outside the company."

I would have thought "Is everyone okay?" would be his first question.

"There is no good that can come from any publicity concerning what just happened." He pauses and adds, "Anyone not signing the release will be dealt with individually."

I bet he's fun at the company party.

I turn quickly when I hear a familiar voice approaching.

"No, no, not you, Sherlock."

Neula "No-No" Newman evidently pulled the short straw and got assigned as the officer in charge of this case.

"Hey," Tiffany says to her, "I know you."

"Oh, yeah," "No-No" says, "the girl who weighs less than my right thigh."

"What happened to all that weight I had you lose?" Tiffany asks as she stands back, viewing Neula's considerable bulk.

"I found it."

During a previous case, Tiffany acted as a quasi counselor for Neula "No-No" Noonan and Detective "Wait" Jack Wayt, who were having relationship problems at the time. After the case was put to bed, I didn't find out, nor did I ask, if the two were still sharing one very large bed.

"Jack and I had dinner the other night," "No-No" tells Tiffany.

"Let me guess," Tiffany says, "it was a buffet."

Neula gets right to work. She bags the gun, gets statements from a number of eyewitnesses, takes measurements, and vacuums up dust from where Bengie and I did our dance. Neula saves my statement for last, and after I finish, she says, "You know, Sherlock, you got a real knack for being in the wrong place at the wrong time."

"Tell me about it."

The employees on the floor remain shaken up, and who could blame them. A nut job came into their workspace waving a pistol and trying to shoot their boss. Some of the workers are shaking, some are pale, and a few mumble to one another. I wait for an executive higher-up to stand on a desk and make an announcement, but no "Everybody go home" or even an "Everybody take ten," is broadcast. Stretch is running around passing out release forms to be signed and dated. There is a line-up at both the men's and ladies' rooms. The lunchroom is full, and the rule of *No cell phone use during office hours* is being openly broken repeatedly without any fear of reprisal.

Finally, Sheckle comes out of his office and announces, "Get back to work people. There's money to be made out there."

Sheckle notices me seated in a chair trying to get my breathing back to normal. "You find my money yet?" he asks.

"I had to take a break to stop some guy from killing you."

"No excuses, Sherlock," he says before retreating back into his office cave.

Mr. Wonderful.

The purpose of the visit today is to see C. Franklin Witherington, and time is a wasting. I find Tiffany. "Let's go see Chuck," I tell her.

"I can't, Mr. Sherlock. I'm starting to see a bit of discoloration on my tight and toned upper arm, and if I don't get it into a spa for some therapy, I could be in big trouble."

I look at her arm. "I don't see anything, Tiffany."

"You wouldn't because you're not a woman," she tells me.

"What? Do women have some special X-ray bruise vision?"

"I do."

"Have a nice time on your date, Tiffany."

"Ta-ta."

Darn, there goes my ride.

Witherington's assistant must be in the ladies' room line or in the lunchroom because she's not at her desk. I knock on the CFO's office door and wait.

"Who is it?"

"Richard Sherlock."

The door electronically opens. I walk in. C. Franklin Witherington is behind his desk, which has piles and piles of papers, reports, and office stuff, some a foot in height, scattered about. He looks out from behind the stacks at me. "What the hell was going on out there?"

"Some guy tried to shoot Mr. Sheckle."

"Who?"

"Some guy who lost his house."

"Did he shoot him?"

"No."

"Come close?"

"No."

Witherington seems a bit disappointed, but I don't want to assume anything, so I ask, "Disappointed?"

"Why the hell Sheckle ever bought the controlling interest of Mortgage for the Masses, is beyond my comprehension."

Witherington didn't answer the question, but I decide not to press the issue.

"I told him not to do it, but he didn't listen," he adds.

Welcome to my world. No one ever listens to me.

"You wouldn't believe some of the accounting gymnastics I had to do to some of those mortgage deals," he tells me and waits for a compliment, which I don't give.

It would be the easiest and the best use of time to ask the CFO, "Excuse me, Mr. Witherington, but do you cheat when filing the corporation's tax returns?" But I decide to take a different tactic. "Excuse me, Mr. Witherington, do you think Chester cheats filing Mr. Sheckle's personal IRS returns?"

"Of course he does."

"He seems like a pretty honest fellow to me."

"Chester's pencil slips more times than a comedian on a sidewalk of banana peels."

"Could Chester's be merely honest mistakes?"

"No."

Witherington gives me the *Look* I'm getting way too used to getting.

"Could you give me an example of a Chester mistake?"

"I could, but what would be the point?" He's being evasive.

"Well, would only a person who makes those kind of mistakes be able to recognize those kinds of mistakes?" I'm putting a shade of lipstick on a pig here, trying to disguise my outright calling him a mistake-maker.

"What is that supposed to mean, Sherlock?"

Evidently, makeup didn't work. "I'm not saying 'it takes one to know one,'" I relent.

"Like hell, you ain't."

I should have used another shade of lipstick.

"I've been trying to get Sheckle to get rid of the guy forever," Witherington says. "Why he keeps the old geezer around is anyone's guess."

"Would you like to make a guess?"

Witherington gives me the same stare as before. "No."

So far, I'd have to give my shakedown of Mr. C. Franklin Witherington a three on a scale of ten. Time to go for the jugular and up my score. "Chester says you're the crook, Mr. Witherington."

"Good for him," he says without emotion.

Make that a two on a scale of ten. "He says you intentionally put mistakes into your returns to camouflage the bigger evil deeds you're trying to slip past the IRS."

"He did, did he?"

"He certainly did."

"Maybe I should change my opinion of Chester," he says.

"How?"

"I didn't think he was that bright."

This is not going well. "So you do put in mistakes that they'll catch, so they hopefully miss the major financial transgressions you include in the return?"

He gives me the *Look*. I can't say I'm enjoying everyone peering down on me like I'm some incredibly naïve idiot.

"It's a game, Sherlock; that's all it is, one big game."

Revised score: One on a scale of ten.

"Thanks for your time, Mr. Witherington."

I need a new career.

CHAPTER 17

I call before I come over.

"Al, Richard Sherlock calling."

"Call me Al," he says.

"I did call you Al this time, Al," I explain.

"You're the man, Richard, you the man."

"I could get over there, but not until around five thirty or so, if that will work for you?" I ask.

"No problem, I'll be waiting."

"Okay, I'll see you in about an hour."

"And remember, Richard, the sale starts when the customer says 'No'."

"I'll remember that Mr. Zazou."

"Call me Al."

I need some time to decompress. I'm pretty close to the Harold Washington Library, so I walk over and sign up to use one of their computers. While I wait for my turn, I read a copy of last month's *Time* magazine and get more depressed. The older I get, and I am rapidly approaching forty, the more I realize there is no new news. It is all the same invasions of countries, horrific slaughters of innocent people, coups, atrocities, and crooks doing crooked things. It's just different people, countries, groups, factions, and crooks doing the same awful crimes over and over. Thankfully, it's not much of a wait, and I get on a terminal before I have to read about a natural disaster in some country I've never heard of before.

I log into the real estate website and see my test scores remain *In Progress.* Next, I re-Google Sterling Sheckle and find new articles on his do-gooder activities. Surprisingly, there is little on his business dealings. Next, I Google Leslie Ambrose and get hundreds of choices of reading material. I Google Leslie Ambrose, computer expert, Chicago, and get one hit referring to a computer game named *League of Legends*. I read the article, but it makes about as much sense as one of my texts when my finger doesn't hit the right letters. Next on my Google list is Cameron Jones, and I find no felonies, prior arrests, or misdemeanors. This makes me feel a little better, but I remember it is against the law to list a minor's legal infractions. He could still be a serial killer and I wouldn't know it. Max Sheckle comes up in a number of dating sites.

There are pictures of Max holding fish he caught, skiing down a mountain, relaxing in the hot tub, and sipping the bubbly. The description he's given himself: "A real fun frolicker, who could easily pass for thirty-something, who really knows how to make a woman feel special," doesn't match the man I met the other day. This has been pretty much a waste of public library computer time until I Google Sheckle's wife, Rosemary. The calm, cool, and collected Evanstonian is actually quite the business dynamo. She is on the board of a number of corporations, has been involved in the ownership of many diverse businesses, and most interestingly, has been named in a number of past and pending lawsuits. This is definitely unexpected. The mild-mannered Mrs., who I sipped tea with, is actually a bare-knuckled, corporate titan you don't wanna mess with. Who woulda ever thought?

A kid, who looks like he couldn't figure out how to type his own name into the computer, comes over, taps me on the shoulder, and tells me, "My turn." I get up from the computer, he sits down, and in less time than it takes me to tie a shoe, he's in the middle of a video game shooting zombies that pop up on the screen.

***

The sun setting in the west reflects off Al's teeth and almost blinds me for life.

"Richard, you're looking super," Al says as I enter the LPRE offices.

"So are you, Al."

The place is as empty as my checking account. I see only one woman in the far corner of the room at a desk talking on the phone. I've seen her before.

"Ms. Missy really wanted to be here, Richard, to give you a hearty handshake and other words of wisdom," Al tells me as we make our way to the back work area of the office.

"Where is she?" I ask.

"She was either getting a bikini wax or a face peel, I can't remember which."

I'm thankful he can't remember, but I do have to wonder exactly where her "words of wisdom" may have come from.

I follow Al into the mail room, in the middle of which is a large table with stacks of envelopes, an open box with pre-printed letters, and a larger box filled with two-by-two inch refrigerator magnets in the shape of a house with an inscription reading, *"You Can't Miss with Ms.*

Missy." The office phone number and LPRE logo make up the base of the little dwelling.

"Richard, I really want you to study exactly how we have laid out this very important, demographically targeted marketing plan."

It seems pretty obvious to me.

Al continues, showing me firsthand how to hit the marketing plan's target. "You take one letter, fold it in three, put it into an envelope, and add one magnet." He pauses and puts his one finished product on the far end of the table. "Stack them up like this," he continues the DIY, "so when they go through the mailing machine, they will automatically seal."

"Fascinating." What else can I say?

"I really want you to get a sense of exactly how we have designed this campaign," Al says as I take my first crack at stuffing.

"I like the design," I tell him. "The little house is really cute." I'm lying; the little house is dumb. What rich person would have this on their refrigerator or live in a house this small?

"Richard, you're going to make a hell of an agent," Al says on his way out of the room. "Just close the door when you leave, it'll lock."

"Okay, Al."

He stops before his exit. "And remember, Richard, the next house you're going to sell is right around the corner."

I start stuffing.

I'm about one hundred in when my mind has gone pretty much blank. This is actually a positive because with a blank mind there is nothing in your way, and you can do a lot of thinking.

What do I know: Six million Sheckle dollars remain missing, along with another sixty grand out of petty cash. Sterling Sheckle, Mr. Wonderful to millions, is hardly wonderful. He's a shrewd, calculating corporate raider who, more than anything else, loves money. I love money too, but in my case, it is a long distance love affair. Chester says Witherington is an IRS cheat and Witherington, who pretty much admits his questionable financial reporting, returns the favor. The head of Internet security at SSS took an unsuspected leave of absence and hasn't been heard from since. The new security chief would rather sack Tiffany than hack his fellow Chinamen. Sterling is married, but in name only, and his wife has access to a number of his accounts. Mrs. Sheckle, who I thought was a suburban garden clubber, is actually a corporate bigwig with a résumé and track record Donald Trump would envy. Sterling's younger brother, Max, is an idiot who spends most of his time searching for women dumber than him to date. Sterling has put him on a string so short he might not have enough rope to hang himself, if he so desired. There are a number of charitable organizations benefiting from Sterling's advertising-related benevolence, but some are questionable when it comes to just how charitable they may be. Some of Chester's figures don't match, but I got Lloyd Holler to figure that out for me. Finally, Herman continues to get rich off this case, while I'm having a hard time getting my Toyota started.

The only question that matters, and the last question I ask myself at this time is: "Am I any closer to finding the money and solving the case?" The answer is a resounding, "No."

My thought process, but not my stuffing, is interrupted.

"I certainly thought you'd be gone by now," she says as she enters the mailroom.

"Why?"

"Most don't last as long as you have."

This woman, the one I recognized walking in this evening, is the same woman I met in the lunchroom when I was searching for "stwaws."

"How long do the others last?" I put particular emphasis on the *others*.

"Depends."

"Depends on what?"

"When they run out of cash."

I feel pretty stupid, even after she says, "Don't feel too stupid. It was obvious you were trying to make a good impression."

"You only have one opportunity to make a good first impression."

"Gee," she says, looking up, "where have I heard that before?"

I laugh.

"Once you pass the test and get your license, you will be contacted by a number of brokers. They need you just as much as you need them," she says. "Commissions are split four ways in this business."

That was on the test; I hope I got it right.

"I have to be going," she says. "Just pull the door closed when you leave. And don't forget, the sale starts when the customer says 'No.'"

"Thanks for the tip," I tell her. "And don't you forget 'only dead fish go with the flow.'"

If I had a brain in my head, I would leave the remains on the table, free myself from the invisible shackles of slave labor, and walk out the door, but since I always preach to my kids to "Finish what you start," I'm in the LPRE office another two hours stuffing and stacking until all the envelopes are filled.

And during that time, I make two major decisions.

***

The 'L' doesn't get me home until close to nine, and I immediately call my girls.

Care tells me about Wilma Whiner's mother being the guest Room Mother for the Day and the arguments Ms. Whiner gets into with the teacher, claiming American education puts too strong an emphasis on the male influences on our society. "She said the reason the country is so screwed up is because men make all the decisions."

She might be right.

When Kelly gets on the phone, I tell her of my first decision.

"I'm not much on joining clubs or organizations, Kelly, but I have decided to join DADD."

"I thought you told me once, 'I wouldn't want to be in any organization that would have me as a member,' Dad."

"I'm making an exception," I pause, "for you."

"What's D-A-D-D?"

"Dads Against Daughters Dating."

"Oh, Dad, could you give it a rest?"

"I'm worried about you, Kelly. This is all happening too soon. Men are predators. They're only after one thing. You're not prepared for the dangers that lurk in the minds of young men."

"Dad, I'm almost fifteen—"

"No, you're not," I interrupt to correct her. "You're fourteen."

"I know what I'm doing. Cameron and I have already established an emotional bond between us."

"No, you haven't."

"We like to do the same things, go to the same places, eat the same food."

"What? Fruit Roll-ups?"

"Dad, you're not letting me grow up."

"No, I want you to grow up, but you're already in fourth gear in the expressway's fast lane when you should be starting off slowly, looking both ways before getting into traffic on a side street."

"Dad..."

"Where are you going on this date?"

"The mall to see a movie."

"Which one?"

"Mall or movie?"

"Movie."

"I'm not sure."

"Will you promise me it'll be G-rated?"

"No."

"Well, if it's PG, you'll need a parent or guardian to go with you, and I'll be more than happy to go along."

"Dad, would you stop?"

I take a breath. "I'm sorry, Kelly, but this is what dads do when their little girls stop being little girls. I can't help it."

"Dad, I know what I'm doing. Cameron and I are an item. We know each other, trust each other, and we're both very mature. Nothing bad is going to happen."

I give up. I don't say a word.

"I got to go and finish my homework," she tells me, breaking the silence.

"I love you, Kelly."

"Talk to you later, Dad."

After the conversation with Kelly, I'm no longer worried. Now, I'm petrified.

I sit around the apartment. I stare at *The Original Carlo* and get so depressed I drape an old sheet over it. I turn on the TV to get my mind off my troubles. For some reason, I stop channel surfing on the Lifetime channel and catch act one of the Man Hater's Movie of the Week where some guy is going through women like Sherman through the South. I turn it off when the scorned women join forces to catch the guy and wreak their own brand of scorched earth upon him.

This day started out bad and has gotten progressively worse.

There is no way I'm going to get any sleep, so I might as well make good on my other big decision of the day. I go into my closet, pull out a pair of jeans, my running shoes, a black sweatshirt, and an old Cubs hat. In the kitchen, I take my transit card and the last eight dollars out of my wallet and stuff them into my back pocket. In the other back pocket, I stuff my cell phone. Above the refrigerator, I spin the dial of my gun safe, and when it opens, I grab a gift given to me by Shervy Reckless, one of the better second-story men in the history of Chicago burglary. I leave the house before I have time to change my mind on what I'm about to do.

The 'L' is almost empty on my way downtown. I'd have the car all to myself except for the two homeless guys sleeping soundly in the last row. When it is real cold, or the guys can't find a good dumpster to sleep behind, they get on the 'L' and ride and ride until the sun comes up. When my phone rings, it wakes one of the guys up, and he gives me a dirty look. Will the *looks* ever stop?

I see the caller's name on the small screen.

"Tiffany."

"Mr. Sherlock."

"Tiffany, it's almost midnight, are you okay?"

"No."

"Where are you?"

"At the Palmer House."

"What are you doing at the Palmer House?" Tiffany is more a Ritz Carlton or Four Seasons person than the Palmer House.

"I'm depressed, Mr. Sherlock. I need somebody to talk to."

"How depressed are you?"

"I haven't retouched my makeup in over an hour."

This is serious. "What's the matter, Tiffany?"

"It was my date."

"Mr. Pointy Hair?"

"Yes."

"Did you find out it was grease instead of mousse?"

"No."

I hear her sniffle.

"Tiffany, wait there. I'm on my way downtown right now."

From the back of the car I hear, "Could you keep it down, buddy. I'm trying to sleep back here."

"Who was that, Mr. Sherlock?" Tiffany asks.

"Commuters make strange bedfellows."

"Mr. Sherlock, you're talking like you text."

Twenty minutes later, I find Tiffany in the Palmer House bar, slumped over a cosmopolitan. "Tiffany."

She turns and takes one look at me. "Where did you get that outfit? You look like a TV sitcom dad trying to impersonate a college kid."

"It's my uniform for the night."

"Are you going to a late-night kegger?"

"No."

Enough about me.

"Tiffany, what happened?"

"He was a creep."

"Mr. Pointy Hair?"

"Yes."

"I tried to tell you that, Tiffany."

"I never listen to you, Mr. Sherlock. You know that."

Duh.

"Was it his hair that was creepy?"

"No, it was his attitude," she says and launches into her diatribe, as I knew she would. "First, he picks me up in a two-year-old, domestic car with his stinky gym bag in the backseat. And you know where he takes me?"

"No."

"To a mall."

"To take you shopping?"

"That's what I thought at first, but no."

"Why then?"

"To eat at a chain restaurant." Tiffany is shaking, reliving the horror she suffered.

"Which one?"

"Olive Garden."

"Did you get unlimited salad and breadsticks?" I ask.

"We had to sit at this little table, next to the men's room, and had to listen to all the waiters sing "Happy Birthday" to some forty-year-old lady who was obviously lying about what birthday she was celebrating."

"Did they sing it in Italian?"

"You know there are only three words on the Olive Garden wine list, red, white, and rose."

"Keeps it simple." I'm being a bit flip with my responses since she's not listening to me anyway.

"The food was this fried, breaded piece of meat cut from between the cow's horns, covered with this cheesy concoction of heart-stopping cholesterol."

"Scrumptious."

"And then the real coupe-de-grappe, Mr. Sherlock..."

I interrupt her, "I think that's coup-de-gras."

Tiffany takes a deep breath before saying, "He used a coupon to pay the check."

Her head collapses into her hands, which were luckily lying on top of the bar. Her cosmopolitan goes flying. She's back up in a flash and waves quickly for another round.

"I can't believe it happened to me, Mr. Sherlock."

"I tried to warn you."

"But the worst was yet to come," she says and downs half the new martini. "He says to me on the way home..." She stops, as if she won't be able to verbally repeat the man's remarks.

"What?"

"He tells me a lot of hot guys are taking a lot of drugs to bulk up, and a lot of the abs I'm seeing are filled up with steroids instead of muscle. Well, those guys, he says, pay the price when they can't get it up anymore. And," Tiffany is talking a mile a minute, "'if I were you,' he says, 'I'd be giving guys a test before I made any kind of commitment.'"

"What kind of test?" I ask, thinking true-false, multiple choice, or essay.

"He says, 'what do you say we go back to my place, and you give me a run-through to see if I perform up to your sexual standards?'"

Tiffany has to take a breath before continuing, which gives me time to picture in my mind Cameron saying the exact same line to Kelly during the sex scene of the R-rated movie they're watching, unchaperoned, Saturday night at the mall.

Tiffany finishes off the martini in one gulp. "If the crummy Ford he was driving wasn't going forty miles per hour, I would have jumped out right then."

"What did you do?"

"I bolted the minute we hit the next red light."

"Right in front of the Palmer House?" I ask.

"I'm not sure how I got here, Mr. Sherlock. I could have been wandering for hours in the state of shock I was in." She signals the bartender for another.

But I signal, *No way*.

"I'm scared I'm losing my touch spotting available men. How could I have been so wrong? How could I have made such a mistake?"

I place my hand gently on her shoulder. "You made a mistake, Tiffany. We all make mistakes."

"Speak for yourself, Mr. Sherlock. I've never made a mistake this bad. The guy was one step away from a Walmart shopper."

"Tiffany, maybe you're looking at the wrong things when it comes to finding suitable men."

"He was at the right event, wearing the right clothes, looking right out of *Muscle & Fitness* magazine."

"With greasy, pointy hair," I remind her.

"It was moussed."

"Tiffany, you have to be more concerned with a person's values instead of his outward appearance."

"Yeah, about his values, his Rolex was a knockoff."

"How'd you find that out?"

"Phonies weigh a lot less than the real ones."

"The point I'm trying to make, Tiffany, is you only seem to care about what you see and what you assume their bank account may be."

"Yeah."

"But what's important is the type of person they are beneath their toothy smiles and moussed up hair. How do they treat their mothers, what do they want to accomplish in life, are they respectful, honest, trustworthy, and self-confident; these are the aspects of a person you want to look for."

"How am I going to find all that out?"

"Talk to them, ask questions, watch the way they carry themselves. Ask yourself: are they polite, are they nice to the waitress, do they pet little dogs? It's all these little things that make up a person's character. And that's the man you want to find, one with character."

"Oh, Mister Sherlock, this guy tonight was a real character."

"Not like a character in a comedy but character, as in personal values."

Tiffany stares at me. I can see she's hearing what I have to say, what a switch that is, but I'm not sure if her brain is taking it all in and synapsing it into some type of understandable sense.

"Do you understand what I'm getting at, Tiffany?"

"I'm trying, but it is quite exhausting."

Obviously.

"Why don't you go home and sleep on it?"

"No, Mr. Sherlock, I need a couple more cocktails to help me get my mind off the horror I've been through tonight."

"No, you don't. No amount of cosmopolitans are going to make you feel any better."

"What else can I do to erase the memory of Mr. Pointy Hair from my brain?"

I hesitate because I don't want to say what I am about to say, but I say it anyway, "You can come along with me. I could use your help."

"Where are you going?"

"I have to go break into somebody's office and steal a few files."

"Really?"

"I hate to admit it, but yes."

"Well, that sounds like fun, and it should certainly take my mind off Mr. Pointy Hair."

"I'm so glad I can be of service."

***

We are the oddball couple of the evening as we walk past the lobby of the Monadnock Building: me in my burglar getup and Tiffany in the stylish short skirt, four-inch heels, and gold jewelry embedded in her blond Wanda weaves. Inside the building, I can see the night guard/watchman has set up a desk and chair in front of the elevator bank. He sits, playing with his cell phone. There will be no going in or out the front door.

We walk around to the back of the building. One of the doors is wide open. I look for a janitor, cleaning lady, building engineer, or workman and thankfully see none. I put my finger to my lips to "shush" Tiffany, and we move forward slowly. Once inside, there are a number of filled plastic trash bags sitting next to the service elevator. Tiffany hits the Up button on the panel. "What are you doing?" I whisper.

"We want to go up, don't we?"

"Not that way."

I pull her away from the elevator bank as I hear the car coming down the shaft to pick us up. We hurry into a hallway that leads us farther into the east side of the building and to a door labeled *Stairwell.* It's locked.

Tiffany asks, as I'm pulling out my Shervy Reckless lock pick set, "We're walking up stairs?"

"Yes."

It takes me only seconds to open the door. I'm good. "Come on," I say to Tiffany.

"How many flights do we have to go up?" Tiffany asks.

"Six."

"Well, that's not going to be happening in these Jimmy Choos." Tiffany takes off her heels, hands them to me to carry, and starts up the stairway. "This isn't the preferred exercise I usually choose for getting my cardio, Mr. Sherlock."

"Sorry, Tiffany. Which exercise would you prefer?"

"The StairMaster."

"What's the difference?"

"There's no little electronic thing to tell you how many flights you've already climbed."

Another conversation that's pointless to continue.

My bad back is hurting by the time we reach Chester's floor. Tiffany, to my surprise, is huffing and puffing. "Little out of shape there, Tiffany?"

"That's the cosmopolitans talking, Mr. Sherlock."

Chester's office is on the other end of the floor. We creep down the marble hallway. At the ladies' room, I stop. "Tiffany, why don't you stay here? If you see anyone coming, duck back inside, call me on my cell phone, and warn me."

"No," she says. "I don't want to do that. Being the lookout is boring. I want to be a burglar just like you, Mr. Sherlock."

Again, there is no point in arguing. "If you insist."

It takes me about a minute to pop the lock on Chester's outside door, but I don't open it right away, as Tiffany wants me to do. I open it a crack, reach in, and wrap my hand around the door's bell so it won't tinkle when the door pushes past.

We're in. I relock the front door before I take another step inside. At the desk in the front office, I push the desk lamp down low so the light won't shine out, open the file drawer, and tell Tiffany, "We're looking for copies of the tax forms Chester filed for Sheckle."

"How will I know one? I've never seen a tax form before."

I should have known. "It'll have IRS at the top and lots of numbers and stuff all the way through it. It'll be pretty thick."

Tiffany sits down at the desk and starts going through the drawer. I go into Chester's office, closing the door behind me. I have to pick the lock on his desk. This is a good sign. I start in on the bottom drawer. After rifling through three or four files, I conclude that Chester could teach a class on organizational skills. The files are perfect. Each one clean, neat, and with correspondence on the left-hand side and accounting figures on the right. The most recent pages are on the top by date; older ones descend downward in the pile. The same holds true for the number pages on the right side. Chester got a lot of use out of his time and date stamping tool. Each file is so organized it's almost scary. This is the total antithesis of recipe cards tacked up on *The Original Carlo*.

The desk yields nothing of value. I jimmy the first lock on the first file cabinet against the back wall and slide open the metal drawer. This time I pull the drawer out as far as it can go and search in the back beyond the files. Empty. Darn, this is the usual place people stash the files they don't want anyone else to see. After the first drawer, AAA–CEI, I skip to the drawer where IRS would fall. I pick that lock and find not one file with any tax records. There are also no IRS returns in the TA–VAR file. Even if Chester filed Sheckle's taxes electronically, he has to have backup information, spreadsheets, handwritten forms, and other financial documents somewhere. I hear some movement out in the other office and pay it little attention, figuring Tiffany is walking around the room. I open one file drawer at random, the LEA–M file, hoping to change my luck and find a section filled with files concerning medical records. I pull out the first one, start reading, and my cell phone buzzes to alert me to an incoming text. I pull out the phone, flub around until I hit the right spots to pull up the message, and it reads: *Somebody is at the door*.

By the time I get to the inner door, open it, and step out into the front office, I see Tiffany opening the front door, hear the little bell tinkling, and hear her say to the person in the hallway, "I know you."

Next, Tiffany turns to me and says, "Look who's here, Mr. Sherlock, it's Agent Romo."

Oh jeesh.

Romo Simpson is your quintessential FBI agent. He's a fit, trim six-footer who would be on the front of the Studs of the FBI calendar, if one existed. I'm sure he lives in the suburbs, has 2.3 kids, his wife drives a domestic, oversized SUV, and he's only one or two successful cases away from a big promotion. Tonight, Romo is decked out in an all-black, skintight, slinky suit and joined by two junior agents in similar garb. This isn't the first time Romo and I have bumped into one another on a case.

"What are you doing here?" I ask.

"Freeze," he says, "you're under arrest."

Tiffany asks Romo, "Those black baseball hats with the FBI on the front are really cool. Could you get me one?"

"I told you to freeze."

"Does it look like we're going anywhere?" I ask.

"You're both under arrest," he repeats.

"For what?"

"Breaking and entering."

"How do you know we're breaking and entering? We might be here working."

"I don't think so," Romo says.

"If anyone is breaking and entering, it's you," I tell him.

The facial reactions of the two junior agents confirm my suspicion.

"Put your hands up," Agent Romo orders.

"No," I say. "You put your hands up."

"Are you making a citizen's arrest, Mr. Sherlock?" Tiffany asks.

"Exactly."

"I'm a federal agent of the FBI, and when I say 'Put your hands up,' you have to put your hands up." Romo draws his weapon.

"No, we don't."

"Yes, you do." He wags the gun at me.

"Put that away before someone gets hurt," I tell him. I hate guns, especially ones pointed at me.

"No."

"If you don't put it down, I'm going to write my congressman and tell him I caught you guys in a Watergate type break-in."

Romo lowers the weapon. "You're kidding, right?"

"Bad publicity can ruin a career," I add.

Romo puts the gun back in its holster. "Tell me what you're doing here," he says.

"Same thing you're doing here."

"Which is?" he asks.

"You're looking for evidence of a financial trail of questionable accounting practices of one Sterling S. Sheckle."

Romo's men give each other the same look as before. It's a different *Look* than the *Look* everyone is giving me, but a *Look* is finally off me and onto someone else.

"How'd you know that?" Romo asks me.

"Mr. Sherlock is the best detective on this block," Tiffany explains.

There is a noise from out in the hall. It sounds like the wheels of a janitor's cart coming down the hallway.

"Shush, everybody," I say.

Now we all freeze.

When the squeaky wheels stop, or get some grease, I say, "We should all get out of here."

I go to the door, hold it open slightly, not letting the bell tinkle, and see the janitor is ten or twelve offices away. He is just disappearing inside an office as I reclose the door. "You people get ready. When he goes into the men's room, go out into the hall, turn right, and go down the far stairwell."

Being the lookout, I wait. The group lines up behind me. When I see the janitor enter the restroom, I hold the bell, open the door, and let the four loose into the hallway. I close the door, go back into Chester's inner office, take a last look at the medical file I left open, and make my own escape out of the office.

I meet my fellow burglars outside behind the building.

"What took you so long?" Romo asks me.

"I stopped at the snack bar to get a smoothie."

"I'm not sure if that was a good answer or bad answer," Romo tells me.

"We should go someplace where we can talk," I tell him.

"The Palmer House has a nice bar," Tiffany suggests.

***

With three people dressed in covert operations outfits, me resembling a college kid, and Tiffany dressed to the nines, I am compelled to tell our waitress, "We just came from a costume party."

"Did you win?" she asks.

"No."

She peers at the FBI contingent at the table and says, "If you're not Asian, it's kinda dumb to dress up as ninjas."

I order coffee, Tiffany a latte, Romo a SoBe drink, whatever that is, and the two juniors order milk—growing boys, no doubt.

"So, what's going on with Sheckle?"

"Oh no," Romo says, "you first."

"Sheckle has been involved in some questionable business practices as of late, and you can't figure out what, but you know something is crooked so you're turning over every leaf in the forest trying to find something."

Romo gives me one of the better looks I've received as of late. "How'd you know all that?"

"Mr. Sherlock is, like, really smart," Tiffany explains.

"The problem is Sheckle's doing the same stuff all the other big banks and conglomerates out there are doing, but you need more proof to put him over the top, so you need to go through his personal records." I pause. "Right?"

Romo shifts around in his chair and says, "You're close."

"What'd I miss?"

"I can't say at the present time," Romo says. "Classified."

The two juniors, both now sporting white mustaches, exchange their *Look*.

"You should have broken into Witherington's office," I tell him. "He's the key to this puzzle." I really don't know this, but why not plant the seed in Romo's brain and keep him out of my non-moussed hair for a while.

"It's been considered."

The seed is not only planted but beginning to sprout.

"You know it's against the law for police to be breaking into places without a warrant," I remind Romo.

"Who says we don't have a warrant?" Romo asks me in his best *I'm the FBI* tone.

"Did you have one for tonight?" I hate when people answer my questions with another question, but I can't resist.

"It's in process."

Yeah, right.

Tiffany, to my surprise, asks, "Did you know about the missing six million, Agent Romo?"

"I do now," he answers.

"Who do you think took it?"

"I'm not sure," he says. "Who do you think took it?"

"This creep I went out with a couple of hours ago."

"Really?" Romo signals his minions to take out pen and paper.

"I'll give you his name if you promise to investigate him, convict him, and keep him out of the dating pool for twenty-five years to life." Tiffany is never one to shy away from a bit of revenge.

"So, where do we go to from here?" Romo asks me as Tiffany supplies info to the milkmen.

I start to tell him my plans, but I hesitate and then say, "You first this time."

Romo sips his weird looking drink, trying his best to fake enjoying it. "We're not alone in our search," he says.

"Is there alien life in this case too?" I ask.

Romo comes clean. "There's enough G-men after Sheckle to fill a Grant Park big ball league. The SEC, Justice Department, and IRS are all racing to be the first to fry this guy on a criminal bonfire. Whoever gets there first is going to hop up three ladder rungs in one step."

"And you want that to be you?"

"Yes. I cannot tell a lie."

"But you have no trouble with bending of the *breaking and entering* rules?"

"Some rules were meant to be bent," he says.

"Easy for you to say, being the guy who's in charge of enforcing the rules."

"As long as I'm bending and not breaking, everything will be fine."

"From your lips to J. Edgar Hoover's floppy ears."

"The Bureau will continue in the active investigation. And—" He pauses for emphasis. "Your actions will be carefully monitored. If I were you, Sherlock, I'd be watching my p's and q's."

"What are p's and q's?" Tiffany asks.

"Nobody knows," I explain. "It's one of those mysteries of the universe."

"And what you know, I better know," Romo tells me.

"I promise to keep you in the Loop." I doubt if he realizes I'm speaking geographical area—not the exchange of information.

"Ten-four."

I get up and help Tiffany from the table. I signal the waitress to bring the check to Romo. He can pay, and I can see my tax dollars hard at work.

Before we exit, Tiffany asks, "Now, when do you think I can get one of those hats?"

CHAPTER 18

Friday has got to be a better day than Thursday, but it doesn't start out with much hope.

Although I didn't have any dreams of my oldest daughter living in a shoe with sixteen kids, I barely slept a wink all night. I'm up and about well before dawn cracks. My back hurts so I do my stretching exercises, take a steaming hot shower, and feel a bit better. At least until I decide to go downstairs and out into the street to check to see if the Toyota starts and the car is nowhere to be seen. Then I remember it's sitting outside Herman's. Not good. I go back into the building, up the stairs, and into my apartment. I have my second cup of coffee for the day and sit in my front room.

The Original Carlo stares down at me like an angry babysitter. The few cards pinned up are spread about in no particular order, and I ask myself why this is so. Their haphazardness gets me thinking.

At times, the best friend a detective has is time. And I realize it is time for me to take the time to sit back and relive the life and times of this case. I start at the beginning when Tiffany and I first visited the SSS Corporation and picture myself going through every person, place, motion, question, comment, and happening—minute by minute, hour by hour, and day by day. I take my time and try to see what I've missed, doesn't fit, or needs further explanation. With my almost photographic memory, the sun is pretty far up in the sky before I get to Romo and me bumping into one another busting into Chester's office.

I certainly didn't figure out who did it, or how, or why, or when, but I was able to see a few aspects I hadn't seen before. This is good. It means my subconscious mind is hard at work even if my regular mind is in the same state as my Toyota.

I do come to a few conclusions. The first concerns the spread about cards on the *Carlo*. Nothing is connected. Chester has no reason or basis for being connected to Sheckle. He's hardly a high-level accountant capable of filing taxes for a billionaire. Sheckle and his wife are unconnected relationship-wise. Max, the idiot brother, may have an office but is unconnected to the business, especially when it comes to the family checkbook. There is no charitable connection to the charities except that they all share the same IRS designation. Usually, when billionaires like Bill Gates give their money away, there's a theme that runs throughout linking all the giving to an overall purpose. Sheckle's missing six million has no connection to any one business-charity or to a singular aspect of any one charity-business. It is merely money that disappeared. Witherington might be connected to Sterling by employment, but he sure isn't connected by respect or likability. And the biggest disconnect of all is from the powers that be in our society. If the SEC, FBI, Treasury, Justice, Bureau of Land Management, and Council on Indian Affairs are all after Sterling S. Sheckle in some way, shape, or form, why aren't they working together for the greater good and common goal? Nobody can do disconnect better than our government's entities.

The connection, and there has to be at least one, has to be money. For the life of me, I just can't see it. Maybe Herman can. I'd love to hop in the car and go over and ask him, but that's not going to happen.

I call instead. "Herman, it's Sherlock."

"I can't talk," he says and hangs up the phone.

I call back. "Herman..."

This time he just hangs up the phone.

I leave the apartment, walk to the 'L', ride for five minutes, and walk another six blocks. Instead of going right up to Herman's apartment, I stop at my Toyota. I unlock the door, put the key in the ignition, turn it one notch, and, just for kicks, push it down once more. The Toyota fires up like an Indy car at the starting line. Go figure.

I consider leaving the car running while I go in to visit Herman, at least until I check the gas gauge. I turn off the car.

I knock on Herman's apartment door and get no response. I pound on the door and the response un-repeats itself. "Herman, I know you're in there."

"Go away."

"Open up, I need to talk to you."

"Go far away."

My lock pick set is still in my pocket, so I let myself in.

Herman is sitting at his computer, pounding the keys like an angry, zoned-in novelist on a creative binge.

"What are you doing?" I ask.

"Selling short."

"Selling what short?"

"Sterling stocks are falling like frogs in a biblical plague."

"Why?"

"Who cares?" Herman continues to pound away, only taking a break to suck down 5-Hour Energy shots. "It took me an hour to get out of my existing positions this morning, and I've been selling short ever since."

Since I have no money to invest, I know little about investing. "What does that mean?"

"You can make just as much money on the way down as you can make on the way up."

"How do you do that?"

"You sell before you buy, so when it goes down, you buy to cover what you've already sold."

"Oh, of course," I say, "how could I be so stupid not to know that?"

"Go in the kitchen and get me my prunes," he orders. "I need sustenance."

When I come back with the dried fruit, his movements have diminished. "I could do another hundred grand if this keeps up."

"What keeps up?"

"Companies Sheckle has controlling interests in are falling like dominos. Something's happening. There's a tip out there that started as a loose pebble, and has turned into a rockslide," Herman says and bites into two prunes.

I'm thinking Romo lost the race. The guy or girl who beat him to it bragged about it, and the boast got all the way to Wall Street where it became fodder for profits to be won and lost.

"I really appreciate your tip, Sherlock. You really made my month."

"So happy to be of service."

Herman continues to play and trade on the computer as I converse. "Let me ask you something, Herman: Does all Sheckle's buying and selling, wheeling and dealing, vacuuming companies up then tearing them down, do any good for anyone besides Sheckle?"

"Probably not."

"So no new factories get built, jobs get created, or inventions get invented because of what Sheckle does."

"I would doubt it."

"So why does he do it"

Herman looks away from his computer screen to give me the *Look*. It's back, and back at me.

"So all these titans of industry, hedge fund owners, arbitragers, and corporate raiders merely pass millions of dollars between each other not for the common good, but for the good of themselves?"

"You're learning, Sherlock."

"It's a game?"

"Life's a game, Sherlock. You just have to know where to play."

"And sometimes they cheat at the game?"

"And," he continues his prior thought, "you have to know how to play."

I hear a rumbling, and it's not coming from his computer. "I better go, Herman."

Herman doesn't look up. His fingers are pounding the computer keys like hailstones in a freak spring storm.

***

Outside, my Toyota turns over smoother than a pancake at IHOP.

On my street, I park on the edge of the block, just in case the Toyota goes into ignition reverse.

I see a guy in a bad suit standing at the door to the 3-flat where I live. He holds an oversized envelope in his left hand while his right hand pushes one doorbell after another.

Fee-fi-fo-fum, I smell the blood of a salesman.

As I approach the door, he takes a quick look at the front of the envelope and says, "Are you Richard Sherlock?"

"Yes."

He holds out the package but doesn't hand it over. "My name is Clem LaBong. That's capital L, small a, capital B, small o, small n, small g. LaBong, Clem LaBong."

He hesitates. I wait for my package.

"Did you bring that for me?" I ask.

"Yes, it's for you."

Clem LaBong holds the envelope back and says, "But before we get into that, I want to tell you about an affordable life insurance policy that will not only protect you in your golden years, but will totally cover the cost of casket, embalming, postmortem makeup, graveside service, or cremation, if that's what you prefer." He puts the letter out for me to take, which I do, but he doesn't let go. As we both hold the package, he assures me, "Just listen to the entire plan. It won't take a minute because I promise I'm going to be brief, be good, and be gone."

I pull the letter from him, see no mention of death benefits upon it, and say, "Mr. LaBong, capital L, small a, capital B, small o, small n, small g, reverse your process."

I leave Clem at the door.

The envelope has no return address. It comes in a cardboard packet similar to a FedEx letter, but has no receipt, delivery slip, or computerized bar graph. It's flat. There can't be anything more than a letter inside this envelope. I'm still careful. Remember the ricin scare? I go into my kitchen, lay the parcel on the table, and find and put on a pair of latex gloves. I should probably also put on a pair of safety glasses, but I don't own any.

I carefully slit the edge of the cardboard with my trusty widget razor blade, pick up the envelope, squeeze its sides, and, as I suspected, a legal-size envelope falls out. There is no addressee, but I figure it must be for me. The envelope is not sealed. I take out one page, tri-folded perfectly, and read:

Mr. Sherlock, In exchange for you dropping your current investigation of Sterling Sheckle, $100,000 will be wired into a bank account, foreign or domestic, of your choice. Sincerely,

And they say no one writes letters anymore.

Of course, the letter isn't signed, but I do think the *Sincerely* is a nice touch.

Now, one hundred grand is merely chump change to a guy like Sterling Sheckle, but to a guy like me who doesn't have a grand, much less a hundred of them, it's a whole load of money. New car, better place to live, vacation with the kids, and presents under the Christmas tree that aren't pajamas, socks, or wrapped fruit are only a few items I would be able to suddenly afford. This is tempting. And, the amount of effort I would have to put in to garner this payout is minimal at best, especially considering I'm currently so far away from figuring this case out, doing nothing more is equal to what I've been able to achieve thus far in my investigation. This fact considered, the offer is even more tempting. I'd probably have to open one of those offshore bank accounts so there would be no red IRS flags for a Lloyd Holler to see, but I'm sure a Witherington, Sheckle, or Herman can help me out in that area.

I reread the letter a few more times. I feel like Adam in the Garden of Eden with an insatiable craving for apples.

The doorbell rings. I move to the intercom box on the wall. I push the button. "Who's there?"

"It's me, Tiffany."

"Is there anybody there with you?" I ask, thinking this could be a clever Clem LaBong ruse.

"Push the button so I can get in."

Buzz.

A minute later, I meet Tiffany at my front door. She's alone. "Why can't you live in a place with a doorman?" she asks, entering.

With a hundred grand I probably could.

"And to what do I owe this spur-of-the-moment, drop-in visit?"

"I couldn't sleep. The thought of that creepy date I was on kept me awake."

"Well, if it is any consolation to you, Tiffany, I couldn't sleep either."

"Oh, Mr. Sherlock, that's so nice for you to lie awake all night thinking about me." She hesitates, gets an odd look in her eye, and says, "But now that I think of it, you lying there all night thinking of me could be kinda creepy, too."

"I wasn't thinking about you, Tiffany."

"You weren't? Why not?"

Why do I get into these conversations?

"Tiffany, do you think your dad would consider a settlement for the six million Sheckle claims he owes him?"

"My dad?"

"Yeah."

"My dad didn't get filthy rich by paying out, Mr. Sherlock. He got rich by having people think he will pay out."

Darn. There goes one way of dropping the investigation without actually personally dropping my investigation.

"Would your dad consider putting another private eye on the case since I'm doing such a lousy job?"

"Of course not. Why would he fork out for someone else when he already owns you?"

Two down.

"How about if I call in sick?"

"You don't get sick days, Mr. Sherlock."

Three strikes. Bye-bye one hundred grand.

"We have to solve this case," Tiffany says. "It's the only thing that will take my mind off my current dating slump."

"Come on, Tiffany, you drive."

***

My phone rings on the way downtown. It's Lloyd Holler's assistant, telling me that Mr. Holler would appreciate me dropping by to discuss the Sheckle situation. From her manner and tone of voice, I get the feeling that this could be good. Lloyd may have come up with something that will open a new door I'll be able to go through and get me to a new and better place. Hope, hope, hope.

We arrive at our first destination of the day. "Find a place to park near that building."

"The sign says it's going to be torn down. I don't want to park real close if it is about to be hit by one of those wrecking balls."

"It doesn't look like it's coming down today, Tiffany."

She parks in a metered space. Before she gets out, she hangs the handicapped sticker on her rear view mirror. At the expired meter, I fish in my pocket for change, and, as is the rule, find none. "Don't worry about that, Mr. Sherlock. If you have a gimp sticker, you don't have to pay."

"You know, Tiffany, I really don't think it's fair that you use one of those to park your car."

"Mr. Sherlock, no one ever said life was going to be fair."

Tiffany is one of the few people in the world for whom that statement becomes a positive.

Upstairs, we enter the office and are met immediately. "And who is this beautiful little piece of heaven, Sherlock?" Stretch leans over, takes Tiffany's hand, and kisses it as if he's Prince Charming.

Tiffany treats his chivalry as if he's Prince Albert in a can. "Gross," she says, whipping her hand away. "You're so skinny you could pass as a pole."

"I'm a lean, mean, PR machine, you little sweet thing," Stretch tells her with a toothy smile.

We proceed into his office. "Stretch, I don't want to take a lot of your time, but I have to ask: If you're the one in charge of making Mr. Wonderful, wonderful, why aren't you the one picking the charities he doles out his money to?"

"I do pick them."

"All of them?"

"Far as I know," he says. "I find the ones that give us the greatest amount of exposure for the least amount of money."

"Chester, Sterling's personal accountant, tells me he picks 'em."

"Well, he might pick some, but I pick the big ones."

"Did you pick the Global Warming Warning Committee?"

"One of my favorites."

"Why?" I wonder, since this was the worst of the worst in my opinion.

"Their corporate board meetings are held at a Rock Resort in the Caribbean each year. And those folks know how to party."

"All for the good of humanity."

"Exactly."

If my new real estate career doesn't pan out, maybe I should go into the charity business.

My phone rings. I pull it out of my pocket, see who is calling, say, "I have to take this," and move to speak in another part of the office.

"You know," he says to Tiffany, "there's always room for one more at the Rock Resort."

"When you travel," Tiffany says, "do you go inside a straw."

"Hello," I start the conversation at the other side of the room.

It's Ling Lew.

"Mr. Sherlock," he says, "I thought you should know the sixty grand from petty cash got redeposited this morning."

I'm shocked. This is the last thing I expected.

"Nice job," Ling offers his compliments.

I wish I could take the credit, but I honestly can't. So I don't say anything and let Ling think what he wants, and hopefully he tells Sheckle what a great job I'm doing.

"Are you going to be around this morning?" I ask.

"Can't leave the castle when the Huns are invading."

"I'll see you in a bit."

"Bring Tiffany."

I hang up the phone. "Tiffany, we got to go."

"So soon?" a smitten Stretch asks.

"Not soon enough," Tiffany tells Stretch, totally un-smittening him.

As soon as we are out of the office, Tiffany says, "Another creep to add to my résumé. I attract them like Goths to a plane."

It's only a short walk to the Federal Building, but Tiffany insists on driving. This time she parks in a handicapped space. "If I were you, Mr. Sherlock, I'd invest in one of these stickers. They make parking so much easier."

"I'll wait until I lose a limb."

"Suit yourself."

The receptionist recognizes me and immediately gets up from her seat to escort us inside. "Mr. Holler reserved a conference room for your meeting," she tells us.

The room has a large table and eight chairs. I've been in here before. "Sit over on the far side, Tiffany," I direct my protégée. "You want to be as far away from the germ zone as possible."

We sit. I'm thinking Lloyd reserved a conference room because he has reams of facts and figures that he will use as evidence when he goes after Sheckle with the accountant's equivalent of an AK-47. He'll probably thank me from the bottom of his heartless heart for giving him the joyous opportunity to hoist Sterling on his tax cheating petard and slice and dice his millions into a bag of pocket change.

Lloyd Holler, that's two L's in Lloyd and two L's in Holler, enters a few minutes later with nothing in his hand except a wet, slimy handkerchief.

"Hi, Lloyd."

"Sherlock, you're so stupid you couldn't outthink an amoeba. Why I ever listened to you, I'll never know. You got the brainpower of a dead battery."

Interesting Lloyd would use this analogy in the midst of my current Toyota troubles.

"Nice to see you, too, Lloyd."

"I wasted hours of my precious time cross-checking the figures you gave me against what he filed and you know what I came down with?" he spits at me.

"A cold?"

"I came up short, you idiot."

I should tell Lloyd I come up short every month, but maybe this isn't the time to discuss my problems. "Short on what?" I ask.

"He underreported on almost every gift he made."

"He did?"

"Yes," Lloyd yells back at me. "Do you know what that means?"

"He's bad at math?"

"No, you arithmetical underachiever, it means if he re-files, we could owe him money."

"A rebate?"

"Does this place look like we're selling Chevys, Sherlock?" He screams, shooting phlegm my way like a phalanx of medieval arrows.

"Ah, no."

"This is the IRS; we don't give money back. We take it away, and when we do, we tack on penalties that can break a camel's back in two." Lloyd is on a roll.

I sit in wonder. This revelation is past beyond reason. Sheckle, one of the tightest tightwads on the planet, not only would take a deduction, he'd bump it up so high it would hit the DIRECTV satellite.

"This doesn't make any sense," I tell Lloyd. "The guy squeezes a nickel so tight the buffalo screams."

Lloyd sneezes twice. Then he's right back at me, "I could have been out there putting some tax cheat's fingers in a vise until he screamed, but no, I listen to you and waste hours of my precious time."

I'm still in awe of the revelation. I need more information. "What are we talking, Lloyd, a couple of grand here and there?"

"Millions."

"Millions?"

"Millions of tax write-offs the IRS would have to make good on in the form of cash, which could add up to one less lane on an expressway project." Lloyd is so angry he slams his handkerchief down on the table. It splatters like an exploding water balloon.

That was gross, but the new information is unbelievable.

"Excuse me, Mr. Holler," Tiffany says, "has anyone ever mentioned to you that you may have a teeny-tiny anger management issue?"

"No!" he wails back at her. "You want to be the first?"

"Let me give it some thought," Tiffany tells him.

I get up out of my chair. "I got to have some time to sort it all out, Lloyd. Why don't we just say, 'I'll get back to you on this?'"

"Sherlock, you got the brain of a second grader who's last in his class."

We don't shake hands on the way out. Tiffany puts her silk hankie against her face as she passes by Lloyd. We head for the lobby, where the receptionist remarks as we wait for the elevator, "I heard; that went well."

Inside the elevator, Tiffany says, "Are you okay, Mr. Sherlock, because you don't look okay?"

"Tiffany, I told you not to talk in elevators."

"There's nobody in the elevator with us," she explains.

I look around. She's correct, but I don't answer. I'm whupped, tired, beaten, out of ideas, wrong on all previous counts, and now groveling simultaneously in seas of self-doubt, self-pity, and self-loathing. I wonder which one I'll drown in.

The only person correct, so far, in this whole mess is Lloyd Holler. I am a total idiot.

The elevator doors open on the first floor. We step out. "I can't believe it, Tiffany."

"What?"

"Maybe Mr. Wonderful is wonderful after all."

CHAPTER 19

"So, the money just magically appeared in the petty cash account?"

"Yep." Ling Lew might be speaking to me, but his eyes are on Tiffany.

"How?"

Ling, who has done some remodeling to his new office that consists of taking down the ugly Legends poster and moving one computer screen closer to the other two computer screens, says, "I got the call from accounting the money was deposited back in full."

"They know who put it there?"

"No."

"Do you?"

"No."

"Could you do some computer mumbo jumbo and find out?" I ask.

"I thought you already knew," he says. "Weren't you the one who got it back?"

I cannot tell a lie. "No, I'm as clueless as a caveman with a computer."

Ling Lew stares at Tiffany, who is mesmerized by all the computer screens flashing around her. Ling says, "I'm a Moon Child. What's your sign?"

"Do Not Disturb."

I interrupt, "Wouldn't they have to get into the system to be able to deposit the money?" I ask Ling.

"Yes."

"So has anyone breached the system that you're aware of?"

"Maybe," he says.

"Maybe? Wouldn't you know if someone punched a hole in your firewall?"

"The problem with breaches into any system is that you don't know until they're already in, or already been in and gone."

"You're telling me you have to 'catch the guy in the act'?"

"Yep. And most don't stick around long enough to chat, much less get caught."

This is ridiculous. What am I doing here? I got a snowball's chance in Death Valley of finding who hacked into the system. I feel like an obese camel approaching the eye of a needle.

"Keep me posted, would you please?" I ask Ling.

"How about I report directly to your assistant, Miss Tiffany?" he asks.

"I'm unlisted," Tiffany says.

That went well. My day continues its downward spiral.

Tiffany follows me off the computer floor to the elevator, where I hit the Up arrow.

The second we get into the crowded elevator, Tiffany says, "That guy wasn't just a computer geek, Mr. Sherlock. He was a computer creep."

Her comments elicit a few laughs from our fellow riders.

"What's happened to me, Mr. Sherlock? All of a sudden I feel like a magnet that attracts flies when it comes to men."

"Magnets don't attract flies, Tiffany."

"Whatever."

The doors open on 104. We get out. I approach the receptionist but have to wait behind two guys in security guard uniforms. My immediate thought is they're protection against a rerun attempt on the life of Sterling Sheckle. *If at first you don't succeed....*

The security guys stand aside to be polite and let us go first, or to ogle Tiffany as she passes by.

"Richard Sherlock to see C. Franklin Witherington."

She gives me a funny stare. "You better hurry," she says.

"Is he leaving soon?" I ask.

"That's the word on the street."

I have no idea what she means. *Clueless* has become my mantra of the day.

We're walking down the aisle, cubicles on both sides, and I can't help but notice an impending fear hovering over the floor like sewer gas over a water treatment facility. Employees speak in whispers as they poke their heads above the wall dividers. Sheckle's office door is closed. Witherington's is open. Sheckle's assistant answers phones. Witherington's carries an empty copy paper box into his office. There isn't the usual rushing around as I noticed the last time I was here, although, that visit was marked by an attempted murder. Now, every employee is standing in his or her cubicle peering in the same direction: toward Sheckle's office. It is as if they are all seeing one shoe on the floor and are anxiously waiting for the other one to drop.

"Is he available?" I ask Witherington's assistant's assistant.

"He's in with Mr. Sheckle right now."

"You think he will be long?"

"Not from what I've been hearing."

My phone rings inside my pocket. I pull it out. Al Zazou is calling. I should take the call, but I don't because at that instant the two security guys hurry down the hallway and position themselves like sentries in front of Sheckle's closed door.

My phone keeps ringing. It is the only sound on the floor. Every employee's eyes are fixed on the security men. Nobody speaks.

Tiffany grabs my phone and punches the front. It stops ringing. "Don't you know how to do anything, Mr. Sherlock?"

Sheckle's door opens. Sterling walks out. "Get him out of here," Sheckle orders. Security walks in.

Witherington emerges red-faced and flushed. He looks up at all the employees looking at him and quickly looks down and away. Each guard takes an arm and leads Witherington back to his office, right past us. He resembles a broken, guilty third grader after being caught stealing the milk money.

"Got a minute?" I ask.

"Nope, I'm off the clock," Witherington tells me.

The security guards lead him into his office where I see him pick up his suit coat. One guard pats the coat down for, I guess, corporate contraband. Then he hands it back to C. to put on.

"Here," Witherington's assistant says, handing him the paper box filled with his personal items.

"No stapler?" he asks.

With one guard in front and one behind, C. Franklin Witherington is led down the proverbial corporate green mile of the SSS Financial Corporation.

"Wow, what just happened?" Tiffany asks.

"Sheckle fired him."

"Why?"

I have a good idea why, but I don't mention it to Tiffany; instead, I answer, "They caught him stealing other people's lunches from the employee refrigerator."

"Unbelievable," Tiffany says.

"What?"

"Unbelievable they don't have a private dining room for the big execs," Tiffany explains.

It takes only a few minutes, and the office pretty much gets back to normal. My drop-in appointment is now history, so I decide to drop in on another. "Come on, Tiffany," I say as I lead her down an aisle.

"You know, Mr. Sherlock, I wonder what it's like to get fired?"

"I doubt if you'll ever experience the experience."

"Because you think I'm that good at everything I do?"

"No, because you have to have a job before you can get fired."

"Oh yeah, I didn't think of that."

We reach our destination. The door is again closed. "Can I see him?" I ask Sheckle's assistant.

"He's probably not in the best of moods right now," she warns.

"Is he ever?"

A minute later, we enter the office. Sheckle, wearing the same suit he had on during our last visit, is on the phone, screaming, "Four hundred million, or I walk." He slams the phone down. "You find my money yet, Sherlock?"

"Not yet."

"Then that old man of yours better pay out," he screams at Tiffany.

"Not yet," she says, figuring if the answer worked for me, it will probably work for her.

"If you didn't come in here to give me my money, then what do you want?" he yells at the both of us.

"I heard you have an opening in the finance department."

"Yeah."

"Why?"

Sterling peers at me with his steely, dark eyes. "Nobody plays Sterling Sheckle. Nobody."

"What did he do?"

"He thought he could hook up with a hedge fund and make a run behind my back at some of the companies I've been playing."

"That doesn't sound very sporting," Tiffany says.

"I busted him before he tried to bust me."

"Touché," Tiffany continues.

"How could he do that?" I ask. "He must be indemnified and under non-compete agreements if he left on his own?"

"Yeah, that doesn't mean he can't pass information or squirrel away a few million of his own money to invest."

"Could that be the millions I've been looking for?" I ask, hoping for an end to this whole charade and to giving a big "YES" to the hundred grand offer I received via Clem LaBong.

"No," Sheckle answers, "yours is a different six million."

Darn.

"And if that six mil doesn't get back here in a week," Sterling says, "I'll take Richmond to the state insurance board, and pretty soon he won't be able to insure the driver of a Tonka Toy."

Double darn.

"You know, Mr. Sheckle, the sixty grand from petty cash has been returned." I add a big smile as if to say, "And that was all because of me."

"Yeah, like you had something to do with that."

Three times the darn doesn't fix the sock.

Luckily, my phone rings again. I pull it out of my pocket, look on the screen to see who's calling, and announce, "I've been waiting for this call. It might be the lead I need to break the case."

I punch the receive button on the phone, put it to my ear, and, at the same time, pull Tiffany out of the office with me. "Hello, this is Richard Sherlock..."

As soon as we are out and past the receptionist's desk, the phone comes off my ear without me uttering another syllable. I break the connection.

"Was it the big lead you were looking for, Mr. Sherlock?"

"No, it was some guy trying to sell me faster Internet service."

"I hate those people," Tiffany says.

"How do they get our cell phone numbers?"

"I heard there is a big secret satellite on Mars that picks up the numbers when we buy things on eBay and sells them back to evil telemarketers," she informs me.

She could be right.

Before we are off the floor, I look back and see Max Sheckle moving his box of stuff into the vacated Witherington office. Interesting career move, to say the least.

***

I need a break.

We find a Caribou Coffee, which happens to be across from two Starbucks. Tiffany has a Grandé Sugaré latte and I have a cup of Earl Grey tea. I've always wondered if Earl is a guy or a guy's title. If it's both, I should order a cup of Earl Earl Grey tea.

We sit and start to sip.

"I'm telling you, Mr. Sherlock, if Daddy has to pay Mr. Sheckle six million, he's not going to be a satisfied shopper."

"I realize that, Tiffany."

"Why haven't you figured this out yet? Usually, by this time on a case, it's all wrapped up, and I'm at the Re-New-Me spa rejuvenating any skin tone I've lost."

"If anybody is lost, Tiffany, it's me." I pause and continue. "Nothing fits. There's no connection between any of them. There is no common denominator. Every time something new happens, it throws a different wrench into the works: The missing six million may not have a thing to do with the charities. Chester has no business being Sheckle's accountant. Where did Leslie Ambrose go? The sixty grand gets redeposited. None of it fits with anything; it's all a big jigsaw puzzle designed to make people nuts, especially me." I go on and on like a babbling brook. I look over at Tiffany, and it's obvious she isn't listening to a word I say. Wasn't she the one who started this conversation?

"Oh look, Mr. Sherlock," Tiffany yells, rising half out of her chair. "It's Agent Romo."

Romo and his two flunkies climb out of an illegally parked Ford sedan and head for the Willis Tower. The three are dressed in semi-street action garb, which is a Kevlar vest, FBI hat, and semiautomatic handguns in shoulder holsters. Good cover for a covert mission.

"Yoo-hoo! Agent Romo, over here," Tiffany yells out, waving her hands like an NFL ref signaling a time out.

Romo and friends change their path and head our way.

"Are you here to give me one of those hats?" Tiffany asks, as he gets close.

Romo ignores her question and asks his own, "What are you two doing here?"

I hate it when people answer a question with another question.

"She's drinking a latte and I'm having tea," I answer.

"I love your outfit," Tiffany tells him. "It's so Rambo."

I point to the hardware across his chest. "What are you doing here, protecting the city of Chicago from a caribou stampede?"

"We're going in to arrest Witherington."

"You're too late," I inform him.

"Shoot," he disappointedly says.

"Please don't," I beg him.

"Was it the SEC that beat us to him, or was it the Treasury Department?"

"Neither."

"The Justice Department? Those guys are usually as slow as molasses."

"No, Sheckle got him," I say. "He fired him."

"What for?"

"Trying to stab him in the back."

Romo's mood picks up immediately. "Attempted murder?"

"No, in the corporate sense of the term."

"Shoot."

Romo's two minions exchange their *Look.*

"Now, what am I going to do?" Romo asks.

"Beats me," I answer.

"Darn," he says, "I'll never get to Boise at this pace."

Boise? I decide I'd better not ask for an explanation.

While Romo stews in his own juices, Tiffany asks, "Sure you don't have another of those hats laying around?"

Romo takes off his hat and tosses it on our table. "Here, take mine."

"I don't want a used one," Tiffany says, refusing to touch it. "That's gross."

CHAPTER 20

"Richard... It's Al Zazou calling, but call me Al." Pause. "Richard, Ms. Missy and I have some exciting news for you." Pause. "Are you ready?" Pause. "We want you to be our eyes and ears on the Saturday Broker's Open House Tour." Pause. "Yes Richard, we've picked you for this once in a lifetime opportunity to be first in the door to see what's going on the market next week. You'll be rubbing shoulders with all of the big names in Chicago's North Side real estate market, getting the first glimpse of what's out there, and gaining valuable experience that will propel you over all the other newbie real estaters who will also be getting their test results next week." Pause. "All you got to do is give me a call, and I'll tell you when and where." Pause. "And Richard..." Pause. "Remember, a good salesman never looks back because he's already been there."

After the lady inside my cell phone asks me what I want to do with the message, I hit the #3 key. She immediately tells me, "Your message has been erased. You have one other message."

I listen, and this call, I return.

"Good afternoon, GWWC."

"Richard Sherlock returning Mr. Murtaugh's call."

"One moment, please."

I wait.

"Sherlock..."

"Alf..."

"Stretch told me to call you."

"Why?"

"He said you could help."

"I don't know a lot about global warming, Alf."

"No, he said you'd know who to get hold of if there's a problem."

"So, you don't need me to sound an alarm bell that the earth is melting?"

"No."

"That's a relief."

Alf Murtaugh doesn't hesitate to relay his problem. "Our check bounced from SSS."

"I hate when that happens," I tell him, although this seldom happens to me.

"We have to put a deposit down for our celebrity paintball tournament, and we're coming up a little short."

Join the club.

"I've tried to call, but I can't get through to the guy who writes the checks," he tells me.

"Chester."

"Is that his name?"

"He hasn't been in the office because his wife's been sick," I inform him.

"That's too bad," he says. "What's the matter with her?"

I hesitate. I have to think. "I'm not sure."

"Well, whatever it is, do you think you can get Chester's ass back into his office and make sure our check clears?"

"I'll see what I can do, Alf." There is a very good chance I'm telling a lie, but I can't come up with anything better to say.

I hang up my phone and lay it down in front of me. I sit back with what must be an odd look on my face because Tiffany asks, "What's the matter, Mr. Sherlock?"

"I have a headache."

"Where on your head does it hurt?"

"In my brain, Tiffany."

"Bad spot."

"It's not fun."

"I wouldn't think so," she says. "Describe it for me. I've never had a brain-ache."

"It's like a hundred people are packed into a little room, a loud buzzer goes off, the room begins to shake, and all the folks collide into one another like atoms in a semi-collider."

She stares at me as if I'm speaking Mandarin. "What?"

"It's like having a martini shaken inside your head."

"Oh, yeah," she says with a look of revelation on her face. "I wouldn't like that at all."

I sit back, close my eyes, and try to be absolutely still.

It doesn't work. Tiffany breaks me out of what solace I find with the question, "What's the biggest thing that's bothering you?"

That's easy. "Kelly is going on her first date tomorrow."

"Oh, wow, really? That is so exciting. Is the guy a big stud?"

"Tiffany, don't ask me that."

"Why not?"

"Because that's what I'm worried about."

"Don't. She's almost fifteen."

"Fourteen."

"When I was that age, Mr. Sherlock—"

I cut her off. "Please don't tell me what you were doing at that age. That's the last thing I want to hear."

"You can't stop Kelly from dating, Mr. Sherlock. I bet the boys are on her like Prada on a bag."

"I don't want to stop it. I just want to slow it down," I confess. "Kelly thinks she knows everything, when I know she doesn't know anything. What happens if the guy gets frisky, puts the make on her, and his hand ends up someplace it shouldn't end up."

"She might like it."

"Tiffany!"

"It happens, Mr. Sherlock."

"You're not helping."

"And if it doesn't happen this time, it's gonna happen sooner or later."

"Then how about... later, much later?"

"You have to trust her."

"I do. It's the guy I don't trust."

"Kelly is growing up, and there is nothing you can do to stop it."

Unfortunately, Tiffany is dead-on correct. There is nothing I can do to stop the march of time.

"I'm going home, Tiffany. I need to lie down."

"I'd take you, Mr. Sherlock, but I made a spa appointment since I thought you'd have the case all wrapped up by now."

"Sorry to disappoint you."

"I'll let you make it up to me later."

Lucky me.

***

On Friday afternoons, the 'L' trains start to fill up earlier and quicker, and I have to stand all the way to Belmont. There, I change to the Brown Line, and the same fate awaits me for the rest of my commute. By the time I get off the 'L' and walk the remaining six blocks to my home, I've almost convinced myself to take the hundred grand from the anonymous letter writer and use the money to put Kelly into a convent until she's eighteen.

Thankfully, there are no salesmen at my building when I arrive home. I walk up the three flights, go into my apartment, kick off my shoes, and go right to the front room couch. Instead of plopping down on the couch, I lie on the floor and put my feet up on the cushions because my lower back is sore from all the rocking and rolling on my 'L' ride home. I close my eyes and try to be still, but a new image comes into my brain. This time, instead of people being crowded into a small room, I picture vials of drugs packed together on a bathroom counter. A hand suddenly comes in and knocks the vials around like a bowling ball scoring a strike. As the scattered vials come to a rest, one stands out from the rest. I read the label. It's a label I've read before.

I open my eyes, get up, take a gander at *The Original Carlo*, and begin to move the index cards around. Next, I go to my computer and turn it on. I wait impatiently for the screen to welcome me. I am told most people leave their computers on all the time in something called *Sleep* mode, which seems like a big waste of energy to me. When the Google screen appears, I type in *Nick Klink, Chicago Pharmaceuticals*.

Ten minutes later, I have him on the phone. After pleasantries are exchanged, I ask, "Could you tell me what Avodart is used for?"

He gives me a two-word answer. I thank him, hang up, and call Herman.

"Herman, it's Sherlock; don't hang up."

"Market's closed," he tells me. "I really got to thank you, Sherlock. I've had one hell of a week. I made tons of money."

"Are you still selling short?" I ask even though I'm not sure what it means.

"No. Sheckle's making a play for an almost bankrupt S and L, and their stock is shooting up like third of July fireworks in Grant Park."

"And you're merely going along for the ride?"

"I'm still too big to get on the rides at Disneyland, so I have to take what's available."

"Can't say I blame you."

"And something else you should know, Sherlock."

"What?"

"I lost another two pounds this week. I'm proud to say, I'm now under the 50% marker on the obesity scale."

"Great, in no time at all, you'll be able to get on It's a Small World."

"Can't wait."

I get to the point of why I called. "You ever check out Chester Longtooth, Sheckle's personal accountant?"

"Yeah, he's as pure as snow undriven in."

"He have any money?"

"No."

"Is he in debt?"

"He's got a reverse mortgage on his house."

"How much?"

"I didn't look."

"You belong to Ancestry dot com?"

"No, but I'm on Diet do's and don'ts dot com."

Why does this not surprise me?

"Thanks, Herman, go have a prune."

It costs me twenty-five bucks to use the lowest level of Ancestry.com, but it's worth it. The name I put in to search hits pay dirt. I go back to *The Original Carlo*, add cards, and rearrange others.

I'm finally making connections.

Before the clock hits 5 p.m., I make a number of calls and on each one, ask the recipient for a number where they can be reached over the weekend. Each asks me, "What's up?" and, to be fair, I give no one an answer.

I call my girls.

Care tells me that in art, the teacher told the class to draw anything that came into their minds and then explain it to the entire class. "So, Ernie Bodai draws this weirdo picture, and when he explains it to us, he says, 'It's President Obama doing hip-hop with Lady Gaga on top of the Washington Monument.'"

I give her my best phony laugh, tell her I'll call this weekend, and say, "Get Kelly on the phone, Care."

"She told me to tell you, if you call, she's busy."

"Is she?"

"No, she's painting her toenails."

"Get her on the phone."

I listen as Care yells at Kelly, argues with her, and refuses to take "No" for an answer.

Kelly calls Care a "pathetic loser" and takes the phone. "Dad, I can't talk right now, I'm really busy."

"You're painting your toenails, Kelly."

"I hate my sister."

"Kelly..."

"Please, Dad, don't start. I know what I'm doing, I don't need any advice, and I don't need to learn any ninja tactics to protect myself."

"Kelly..."

"Cameron is really a super guy."

"Kelly..."

"I know what I'm doing. You just have to—"

I cut her off. "Kelly, listen..." I pause to hear her sigh. "I just wanted to say I hope you have a great time on your first date."

Silence.

I can't believe I just said what I just said. "I hope it's a night you'll always remember as being special."

"Really?"

"I can truthfully say that because I've been trying to forget my first date since the night it happened."

"What happened?" she asks.

"I don't want to go into it." I take a breath. "Kelly, I apologize if I've been a little overbearing. You have to know it's hard to be a dad sometimes. I know you don't see that, but it is."

"Okay."

"I'm always here for you, Kelly; please remember that, forever."

"Thanks, Dad."

"I'll talk to you Sunday. I love you."

"I love you, too."

I gently hang up the receiver. These are the times in my life when I wish I were a drinker. It would be so easy to get up, go pour myself a couple of good stiff shots, down 'em in a couple of gulps, sit down, and let the booze ease my unease. But no, not me. If I downed two shots, I'd end up hugging the commode all night. Instead, I sit around staring at *The Original Carlo*. My head hurts, my back aches. I watch the local news and see the same crimes as always, just different names attached. I have a banana for dinner.

It is close to seven o'clock when the phone rings.

"Sherlock?"

"Yes."

"It's Ling Lew."

He's working this late on a Friday; this must be something big. "What's up, Ling?"

"We caught the hacker. We used a reverse version of an illegal spyware program to trace the location of the computer, called the police, and they're getting a warrant to pick him up."

Unbelievable.

"You think this is the guy who lifted the six million?" I ask.

"No doubt about it."

"And how do you know that?"

"I hacked him. I got a trail. He's been living in our account."

"What's his name?"

"I don't know. I only know him by his computer log-in."

I pause. This is all too good to be true. "Congratulations, Ling."

And with that, it's over. My headache disappears.

"Sherlock," Ling says, "since I've been so helpful to you, how about you being helpful to me?"

"Want me to tell Sheckle what a great job you did?"

"No, I want you to fix me up with Tiffany."

CHAPTER 21

I don't sleep well. I'm up before six. And it's a Saturday.

In the kitchen, where I go to start the coffee, I notice I left my cell phone on last night, and now it's as dead as frozen roadkill. I find the charger, plug the little connection into the base of the phone, and put it down. I wait for the coffee to brew enough for me to *sneak a cup*, drink a few sips to improve my alertness, and go into the front room to do my stretching exercises. But before I get on the floor, in the *all fours* position, I look up at *The Original Carlo.* There are quite a few recipe cards tacked up. A lot of them have multiple holes, which denotes the number of times I've moved them around. I peer at the less-than-artful painting from a number of different angles, and all I can see is a number of unanswered questions, lines that don't connect, people left in limbo, and a case far from finished.

Who cares? It's over. Ling Lew caught the guy. Once the six million bucks is labeled as a crime, the insurance settlement transfers into a whole new realm, which usually leaves Mr. Richmond with the money still in his wallet. Lucky him. And that hundred grand waiting for me in some bank account in Bolivia, well bye-bye to those buckos.

I turn over on my back, lift my knees, grab them with my hands, and begin to rock back and forth on the base of my spine. This always makes me feel better, but not today. Why am I not relieved, happy, or at least feeling more positive? Because the movie can't end here, there is at least one more scene to play that ties up all the loose ends, and I can't see it unspooling on the screen.

I give up on the stretching, go back in the kitchen, pick up the cell phone, and notice it's still dead. I shake it, like that's going to help. It doesn't. Then I notice the plug that goes into the wall outlet isn't plugged into the wall. I've been charging a dead phone with an unplugged plug. This mirrors my success thus far on the case and a lot of my life.

I re-plug the plug, check the other smaller plug, and make sure it's beaming energy before I go off to take a shower. When I return, there is just enough energy for me to fumble around and pull up a text from Ling: *They got him at the Belmont station. Any word from Tiffany yet? What do you think we should do on our first date?*

The Toyota turns over like a champ. I put it in gear and I'm off.

***

"Oh my God! What are you doing here?"

Herman grabs the steel bars, comes face to face with me, and screams. "You got to get me out of here. The food they serve in this place is ruining my diet."

Ling caught Herman.

"They busted into my apartment last night like a SWAT team on steroids. They put me on the floor, tied me up like a rodeo bull, and boxed up my hard drive as if they were shipping it UPS."

"Herman, you have to calm down."

"I can't. I've been violated." Herman begins to repeatedly push his entire body into the bars. It looks like Silly Putty being forced through a barbecue grill.

"Stop it. I'll get you out of here, but you have to calm down."

"Help, Sherlock, help."

I tell the jail guard, "You got the wrong guy."

"Yeah, like I haven't heard that before," he tells me.

"You have to let him go."

"If it was up to me, I would. The guy's got enough gas to heat the Hancock Building." The guard holds his nose.

"Herman, just wait."

"What other choice do I have?" Herman screams. "Hurry up. Get me out of here before I get jailhouse rot."

I go outside and call Neula "No-No" Noonan.

The phone rings at least five times before she picks up. "Sherlock, it's Saturday morning."

"Neula, you got to help me out."

"No, no, I don't."

"Please?"

"No," she says. "No."

"Is Jack there?" I am referring to her sometimes-boyfriend, Detective "Wait" Jack Wayt.

"He's asleep."

"I'm glad to see you two are back together."

"Well, don't go thinking its heaven, because it ain't." "No-No" tells me.

"Would you let me speak to him?"

"Sure, I'll get him up. He'll really love hearing from you."

I wait with the phone to my ear until I hear, "Sherlock?"

"Jack—"

"Wait."

"What, Jack?"

"You know anything about jejunitis?" he asks.

"I've never heard of it."

"It's an inflammation of the jejunum."

"Where's your jejunum?"

"Right near my ileum."

"That's good to know."

"Mine is killing me." "Wait" Jack Wayt's major medical problem is probably not jejunum but hypochondria, of which he has a worse than terminal condition.

"Sorry to hear that Jack," I say. "By the way, I got a small problem I need a little help on."

"You always have a problem, Sherlock."

I tell him of the situation and in less than twenty minutes, Herman is released into my custody.

"I was getting flashbacks in the cell, Sherlock. It was horrible," Herman tells me on the way to my car.

"Well, you did hack into the SSS computer system, Herman."

"I was only doing it to help you out."

"And make a killing."

"Don't use that word," he begs me. "I hate that word, especially when it is used near a police station."

Herman squeezes into my Toyota. I have to push on the door to get him *all in*.

Climbing into the front seat, I speak as I insert the key, "I got a couple things you have to do for me today."

"How? They got my computer."

"I know you, Herman. You'll figure out a way."

I turn the key. The car won't start.

"What's the matter?" Herman asks.

"It started up like a champ an hour ago," I explain.

"Come on, get out of this place before I break out in hives."

I leave the key on, get out of the car, push, and the car won't budge. "Get out of the car, Herman."

"Why?"

"Pushing the car is hard enough, but with a load of Herman inside it's impossible."

Herman watches from the walkway as I push. The clutch pop method works. The Toyota kicks over. I drive around the parking lot and return to pick up Herman. I leave the car running, get out, and re-sardine him into the front seat.

"You should get that fixed, Sherlock," Herman says, incredibly relieved to be moving away from the Belmont Police Station.

"The guy wants three hundred to fix it, and I'm not sure if the car is worth that much."

"Sherlock, I couldn't live the way you do."

I drop Herman off at his apartment, give him directions on what I need done, and tell him, "And don't be doing anything illegal, Herman. You go in the joint again, and I'll have to go in with you."

"Misery loves company."

"Goodbye, Herman."

My phone rings. The screen says it's Agent Romo.

"What are you doing? It's Saturday."

"Arresting Sheckle."

"What?"

"We're on our way to his office right now," he tells me.

"On what charge?"

"To be determined," he says. "I got way too much invested in this case to come out with nothing. I'm up for a management position in the Boise office."

"You sure it's a good idea to be arresting Mr. Wonderful?"

"He isn't Mr. Wonderful to me."

"Wait for me, will you? I'm on my way right now."

"Well," Romo says, "I could use a Red Bull before we take him down."

I put the pedal to the metal all the way down the Drive. I enter the underground Willis lot and park the Toyota on a ramp facing downward. If the car doesn't start next time around, all I will have to do is release the brake, put the car in second gear, pick up enough speed, and pop the clutch.

I get to the lobby, flash my PI badge at the weekend guard, and ask, "Did a couple guys in flak jackets already go up?"

"Yep, the riot squad is already on their way."

Luckily, I get an express car. My stomach is a bit queasy by the time the doors open on 104.

The offices and cubicles are empty. I hurry toward Sterling Sheckle's office. The door is closed. They must be inside. When I reach the door, it's locked. I pound. No answer. I listen for voices inside. None.

To my left, I hear a woman's scream coming from Witherington's old office. I rush over. The door is open. Romo is inside cuffing Max Sheckle's hands behind him. "You have the right to remain silent—"

"Max?" I yell out as I enter the room.

"I was just in here showing the new sweetie my office," Max says, hanging over the desk like an overdosed yogi on muscle relaxers, "and these guys attacked me like I was the star on *America's Most Wanted*."

"I didn't do nothing," the overly chunky lady says. "He promised me breakfast."

"Romo, what are you doing?" I ask.

"I uncovered fraudulent accounting practices concerning the Costa Rican project he was in charge of."

"You sure you got the right Sheckle?"

"Yes?"

"Max?"

"He told me he was a big shot," the lady says.

"Are you sure, Romo?"

"Yes."

"Wouldn't Sterling Sheckle be the more logical one to arrest?"

"He's off limits," Romo says.

"What does that mean?"

"The Justice Department put him off limits. We can't touch him."

This is news to me. "Why not?"

"Not ours to reason why, Sherlock," Romo says, sounding as literate as possible. He changes back to his usual tone of voice and says, "Plus, they wouldn't tell me. All they said was he was 'off limits'."

"So, you're arresting his brother, Max?"

"They were shifting money from foreign accounts. My first thought," Romo says confidently, "he was laundering drug money."

"The only laundry I do is at the Fluff and Fold," Max tries to make his case.

"Mr. Big Shot can't afford to send his laundry out?" the lady friend asks. "Oh boy. Can I pick 'em, or what?"

"Romo, I really think you may be jumping the gun here, and it will come back to bite you in the butt," I try to convince the agent.

"He told me he was in charge of this big special project," the lady says. "Some big shot he's turned out to be."

"See, Sherlock," Romo says to me, "I even got a witness."

"Don't arrest him. Wait."

"I can't. I got to take him in," Romo says. "I already read him his rights."

"Don't process him. Let him sit for a few hours. The quicker he lawyers up, the more jeopardy you'll be putting yourself in, and the fewer answers we're all going to get." I'm pleading. "Just wait until you hear from me, please. I'm getting real close on this one."

Romo hesitates, as if to give his few brain cells the chance to make a synapse or two. "Well," he says, "I'll consider it."

Romo's minion straightens Max up and leads him out of the office. Romo follows, then me, and the lady friend. "I tell you, the things people write about themselves on Match dot com," the woman laments.

"You should talk," Max says to her. "You described yourself as a *former model*."

I ride the elevator down to the lobby with the group. Nobody speaks.

As Romo pushes Max into the back of the Ford, I make my final plea, "Agent Romo, I'm this close, just hold off for a couple of hours, please."

"Why should I?"

"Because I know Idaho is particularly pretty this time of year." I do my best to sound truthful, but the closest I've been to Idaho is picking out a potato at the Jewel.

"I'll see what I can do," Romo says.

I stand and watch as the Ford takes off, siren blaring and lights flashing.

I call Chester.

"Mr. Sherlock," he says, "how nice of you to call. Have you apprehended the perpetrator yet?"

"Not yet, Chester, but I'm working on it. How's your wife?"

"A little better."

"I need to see you today," I tell him and add, "in your office."

"I don't know if I should leave Claire alone."

"If I can find someone to come over and stay with her, would you come?"

"I suppose so."

"I'll get right back to you."

I hang up, dial again, get transferred to voicemail, and don't bother to leave a message.

It takes me a few minutes, but I'm able to punch into the Enter Message area: *Need you ASAP, CALL ME.*

It works. A minute later my phone rings.

"Tiffany."

"I'm so proud of you Mr. Sherlock. You sent me a text."

"Wonders never cease."

"And you used A-S-A-P. That is so R-A-D."

"Tiffany, I need you to go over to Chester's house and watch Claire."

"Babysit the old lady?" she asks. "I don't do babysitting, Mr. Sherlock."

"Please?"

"Babysitting is for poor kids who need movie money or don't have parents who pay off their credit cards."

"I'm in a bind here, Tiffany. I need to see Chester in his office, but he won't leave his wife alone."

"You're trying to make me feel guilty, Mr. Sherlock," Tiffany says, "but I don't do guilt either."

"Please. All you have to do is drive over there, sit around for a couple of hours until Chester comes back."

I must have extra emotion in my voice because she relents. "Oh, all right. I'll do what I have to do."

"Thank you."

"What are you going to be doing?"

"I have to go see Witherington, if I can find out where he lives."

"I can do that," she says.

She leaves me hanging for a few minutes and gets back on the phone. "He lives in a corner unit above Saks on Michigan Avenue."

"How'd you know that?"

"We rich people can do a lot of things you people can't do."

I don't doubt it.

I call Chester back, give him the scoop, and arrange to meet him at his office in ninety minutes.

Big decision to make: Do I go back to the car and see if it starts? If it does, do I drive it to North Michigan Avenue and take the chance that it won't start the next time around? Or, do I leave it parked at the Willis Tower on the decline, so at least I'm sure it will start, possibly when I really need it?

Easy decision: I take two buses, one east on Adams to Michigan and one north on Michigan. I get off two stops past Wacker.

The lobby of the building is on Superior, just around the corner from Michigan. I stand at the tenant listing board.

"You want to know what unit he lives in?" the too, too familiar voice asks me.

"Tiffany, what are you doing here? You're supposed to be at Chester's."

"Oh, Mr. Sherlock, I remembered how bad that woman smelled, and I just couldn't do it."

"Then Chester won't leave her. Won't show up at his office. And I can't figure this out until I get with Chester."

"O-M-G, Mr. Sherlock, chill out. I got it handled."

"How?"

"I did what any self-respecting one-percenter would do when they find themselves forced to do something they don't want to do."

"Which was?"

"I hired somebody. I paid extra, and had them put a rush on it."

"Why didn't I think of that?"

"Because you're not a one-percenter."

C. Franklin Witherington lives in a huge corner unit, with views to the north and west.

"Sorry to hear the news about your job."

"It happens," he says. "All part of the game."

"Got anything lined up?" I ask to be nice.

"Phone's been ringing off the hook," he says.

Evidently, experienced, semi-crooked CFOs who know how to play the game are in short supply.

"First, I got to get my parachute money from that tightwad Sheckle."

"I don't follow."

"According to my employment contract, he fires me, he has to pay me off."

"How much?"

"A million or two. I'd have to look it up."

If Mr. Richmond ever fired me, I doubt if I'd get a ham sandwich.

Tiffany is wandering around the spacious apartment. "Why didn't you get a lake view?"

"I enjoy looking down on all the little people out there," he explains.

"So do I," Tiffany agrees, "but a water view is so soothing and stress releasing."

What does she have to release? Tiffany doesn't have any stress.

I get back to Witherington. "What I don't understand is why Sheckle was so concerned about a lousy six million dollars. It's pocket change to him."

"He had good reason."

"He's cheap?" Tiffany asks.

"Yes, but besides that, he needed cash."

"Rent due?"

"No, his foreign companies are not delivering profits."

"Neither are mine," I admit. "So, he just came up short for the month?"

"Not really, he is trying to buy a failed savings and loan in Gary, Indiana."

"And he needed money for the down payment?" I take a stab at being right on a question.

"There's no down payment."

This is making absolutely no sense.

"Since the Dodd-Frank bill passed, the amount needed in reserve at a federal banking institution has increased. I told him he needed cash to prove to the government he could shore up the S and L's reserves." Witherington pauses. "But he didn't listen to me."

Join the club.

"And..."

"He got caught with his pants down."

"I don't think I'd want to see that," Tiffany says.

"A billionaire that's cash-strapped?"

"Something like that," Witherington says. "If you didn't know, Sterling's been on a losing streak the last couple of years. He's made worse investments than the Pentagon."

"Don't tell me he's broke."

"No, guys like him don't go broke. What they go is ego-nuts," C. Franklin tells me.

"Sounds like one of my latest dates," Tiffany interjects.

"Sheckle wouldn't listen to a word I said. I told him to walk away from the S and L deal, but he gets this wild hair, and he refuses to give up."

"Why?"

"Because he needs cash, I thought I already made that clear." Witherington is losing patience with me, and I can't say I blame him.

"So, what does he do?"

"He tries to unload a few of his holdings to raise capital. Remember the stocks taking a dip?"

"Was one of them the Costa Rican Tidelands Project?"

"More like a scam than a project."

"And that's when you made your play with the hedge fund?"

"I'll take the Fifth on that one, Sherlock."

"And...?"

"Sheckle can't get his price."

"So, he doesn't have the cash to buy the failing S and L, which doesn't require a down payment but requires him to have the cash on board if it really goes in the tank?" I'm so confused my head's spinning.

"Exactly."

"But he keeps trying to buy it anyway."

"Precisely."

If someone were to ask me if "Exactly" and "Precisely" were words I would use to describe this conversation, I would have to say "No."

"And..."

Witherington continues, I really think he is enjoying this. "The government comes in and goes through the place with a fine tooth comb."

Tiffany obviously only hears part of the answer and takes out the brush from her purse.

"Because he's buying a federal regulated entity?" I ask.

"Yes."

Hey, I got one right.

"And guess what they found?" Witherington asks me.

"Trouble in River City?"

"Exactly."

Two right answers in a row. Good for me.

"And..."

"During the crash, let's just say Mr. Wonderful was hardly wonderful," he tells us.

"Mortgage for the Masses?"

"Remember, the biggest part of the iceberg is never seen." Witherington sounds a bit like Al Zazou. "There's more accounting irregularities in those files than underwater homeowners in Nevada."

"Let's step back," I say. "Why would he want to buy a savings and loan that's going broke, again?"

"Because he needs cash."

"But he has no cash to pay for it, or cash to shore up the bottom line for the failing S and L?"

"Exactly."

"Does anyone else want to buy the Gary S and L?"

"No, too much cash and too much risk."

"But Sterling does?"

"Now, he has too."

"Because the feds are going through his books."

"Once you're in the soup, you got to eat it," Witherington says.

"And why would the government want him to own the S and L?"

"He agrees to cover all the subsequent losses still to come. Don't forget, he's Mr. Wonderful."

"Of course, that makes all the sense in the world," I say with my tongue stuck in my cheek.

"In exchange for a four hundred million tax write-off this year and a negotiated write-off for the next three years based on actual bank losses."

My write-offs totaled less than eight hundred dollars last year, and Herman had to fudge to get that much.

"Sterling will make a killing," Witherington sums it all up.

"By taking over an almost bankrupt business with millions of dollars and more losses still to come?" Sounds like a great business plan to me.

"Yes, because with the write-off he'll be able to transfer millions of profits he's been holding offshore in foreign businesses he owns, back into the States, paying virtually no taxes to the federal government."

"Something is wrong with this picture," I tell Witherington.

"Apple, Microsoft, Abbott, they all do the same thing. Part of the game, Sherlock."

I wonder if this topic would be good cocktail chatter with Lloyd Holler.

"I don't particularly like Sterling Sheckle," Witherington admits, "but when it comes to making money, there are few who can compete with him. He was way ahead of me on this one."

"Wow," Tiffany says, "that was really a fun story. I love hearing about people making a lot of money."

"You think Sheckle will pay you off?"

"He'll fight me tooth and nail."

"I might be able to help your cause."

He gives me the *Look*.

"But you'd have to make yourself available for a meeting whenever it comes up."

"No problem," he says. "I don't have a job."

"Neither do I," Tiffany says.

In the lobby of the building Tiffany says she doesn't have the right shoes on if we're going to walk all the way into the Loop to Chester's office. She wouldn't mind going home to change since she changes her clothes four or five times a day anyway.

"Why don't we grab a cab?" I suggest.

"Yeah, that'd work."

***

Chester is waiting for us in his office.

"Somebody broke in," he tells us.

"When?" I ask.

"I'm not sure. I haven't been here in a few days."

"What did they get?" I ask.

"I'm not sure," he says.

"Did the cleaning crew discover the break-in?" I ask.

"No," he says. "Unless they see destruction, they are told not to touch or move anything."

This is an interesting revelation.

"Who do you think did it?" Tiffany asks.

"I don't know."

"Do you think it was one person, a group, all guys, or an intergender job?"

"How would Chester know all that, Tiffany?" I ask.

"I want to see if he has any hunches."

"I don't," Chester says.

"And did you find any clues, like carpet footprints made from cheap shoes with gummy soles or strands of perfect, long blond hair?"

"No," he says.

"That's good," Tiffany concludes.

I change the topic before Tiffany asks if anyone saw a guy wearing jeans and a black sweatshirt next to a much younger, gorgeous woman dressed up for a hot date, with the initials TR and RS, hanging around the building that evening?

"Chester, do you remember the GWWC charity being on the recipient list for donations from Mr. Sheckle?"

"Yes."

"Did you stop payment on one of their checks?"

"No," he is quick to say. "Although, it wouldn't be a bad idea."

"Why wouldn't it be a bad idea?"

"I do not consider the organization reputable in character."

I purposely sigh. "Chester, you have to come clean with me on how all this works. First, you tell me you dole out all the money, but Sheckle has a PR firm who tells me they're in charge. And Sheckle writes a few checks himself. What gives?"

"It's not that I have not been forthright with you, Mr. Sherlock. It is just that the situation is complicated."

"Complicated, how?"

"Even when it comes to charitable giving, Mr. Sheckle believes a dollar given is worth a dollar in value received. So, he employs the tall, skinny PR man to advertise his beneficence."

"Stretch."

"Yes."

"A man of questionable reputation and character?" I ask.

"I do not like to speak of anyone in the negative, Mr. Sherlock."

"You don't have to, if you don't want to, anymore," Tiffany tells him. "Now you slam them on Facebook without leaving your real name."

Chester's on the same Facebook page as me: *Page Zero.*

"Stretch gets to pick recipients, doesn't he?" I ask.

"At times."

"Ones you may not approve of?"

"At times."

"Does Sterling ever pick?"

"His are the worst of the choices in my humble estimation."

This is all starting to make sense.

"Chester, do you have copies of Sterling's tax returns here?" I ask.

"No, they are locked in storage."

"How about the backup material?"

"Locked up in different storage."

I should have known.

"How's Claire?" I ask.

"Better."

"What did you think of the babysitter?" Tiffany asks.

"She seemed quite pleasant."

"See what a good job I did, Mr. Sherlock."

"Kudos, Tiffany."

"What does 'kudos' mean? Is that like cooties?"

"No, Tiffany." Back to Chester, "What was the problem with Claire?"

"At first, it was suspected to be a heart attack," he says, "but it turned out to be angina."

"It didn't look like a female problem to me," Tiffany says.

No need to respond to that comment.

"Claire puts herself under an amazing amount of stress, which I believe brought the condition on," Chester says.

"Why?"

"Claire's a worrier."

The topic stays the same, but I change the subject. I ask Chester, "And how are you feeling?"

"Fine." He gives me an odd smile and says, "Thanks for asking."

"When you have your health, you have everything," I conclude.

"I don't know if I'd go that far, Mr. Sherlock."

I start to pull Tiffany towards the door. "Chester, do me a favor and hang around today. I might be calling an informal get-together later on, and I'd hate to have you miss it."

"Anything to help the cause, Mr. Sherlock."

Tiffany and I exit the office with a tinkle from the bell.

Outside the door, Tiffany starts in immediately. "Do you think he suspects us being the burglars?"

"No, Tiffany."

"Whew."

We reach the elevator bank. "What was all that other stuff you were talking about, Mr. Sherlock?"

"I was connecting dots."

"When I was at rich girls camp one summer, we connected the moles on this girl's back with a felt pen, and it came out looking like a smiley face."

The elevator arrives and we get in. "I have things for you to do today."

"I thought you said never talk in elevators, Mr. Sherlock."

Nothing's worse than being caught breaking your own rule. I wait until we are in the lobby before I continue. "Are you busy tonight?"

"I'm busy every night, even when I'm not busy."

"I need you to put a small get-together together."

"Catered?"

"Snack food will be fine."

"Full bar?"

"Not necessary."

"Where?"

"Sheckle's office, 7 p.m."

"Are you sure it's available?"

"I don't think that will be a problem." I take out a pen and start writing. "Here are the people to invite. Call them, and don't take 'No' for an answer."

"Nobody rejects an invitation to one of my parties, Mr. Sherlock."

We are now on the sidewalk in front of the Monadnock Building. "I have one more stop to make, if you'd like to come along, Tiffany."

"Where to?"

"Going to drop in at the IRS and see Lloyd Holler."

"I'll pass."

***

There is no guard on the first floor of the federal building. I get in the elevator and go straight to the audit floor. No receptionist. The space is as empty as a half-completed housing project after the 2008 crash. I position myself in the middle of the cubicles and stand perfectly still. In less than a second, I hear a sneeze and walk in that direction.

Lloyd Holler's office is tucked back into the far corner. The Xerox room to his left and the ladies' room to his right. I can hear him inside clearing phlegm from his throat, hence the reason his office is tucked into the back corner. I poke my head into the door. "Don't you ever go home?"

"This is my home," he says and spits into his wet handkerchief. "What are you doing here?"

"Can't a buddy simply drop by and say, 'Hello'?"

"I don't have any buddies. What do you want?" Lloyd sits behind stacks of files. He's dressed in a similar ill-fitting suit worn the day I saw him last.

I stand in the doorway; hopefully the IRS has installed an invisible germ barrier between Lloyd's office and the rest of the floor. "Did you know the Justice Department is giving Sterling Sheckle a *Get out of Jail, Free* card?"

"It was the SEC, not the Justice Department."

"Want to tell me why?"

"They would rather spend his money than their money bailing out some flunky S and L in Gary, Indiana."

"They pull you off of him?"

"They're trying."

"You're well aware of his foreign holdings?"

"Of course."

"And what's he going to use his tax write-offs for?"

"Nothing, if I can help it," Lloyd says with a sniffle.

"He's too big to fail, or too big to mess with, isn't he?"

"Nobody is too big to mess with, Sherlock."

"I'm not promising, but I might have found a chink in the Sheckle armor."

Lloyd quits sniffling for a few seconds.

"Interested?"

"What do I got to do?" Lloyd asks.

"Let me put you on the guest list for the party tonight in Sheckle's office."

"Address the invitation with two L's in Lloyd, and two L's in Holler."

***

Wouldn't you know it, the one time the car is parked down an incline, it starts up right away. Go figure.

I get halfway to Herman's, and the car stalls at a red light. Now, it won't start. I'm holding up traffic. Car horns are blaring. It's worse than tying up the drop-off line at Care and Kelly's school. I could use some help pushing the car to the curb. Where is Tessie the Terminator when you need her?

Finally, I push my car out of the traffic lanes. The horns cease, but a few travelers one-finger salute me as they pass by. Frustrated and beaten, I look up the street to see the MechanicsRUs auto mechanic's shop where they told me "Three hundred bucks."

I've got eighteen dollars in my wallet and one maxed out credit card. I think of calling Al Zazou and ask for an advance for all the houses I'll soon be selling, but I don't. He'd probably smile and ask me to sit at an open house tomorrow.

I open the hood of the Toyota. There is enough grease and old oil covering the engine to scribble the Preamble to the Constitution with my finger. The battery looks fine to me. The cables are attached without a mound of white stuff covering the connections. The spark plug wires are all on and tight. The container for the windshield wiper fluid is even filled to the brim. And then I notice way in the back, where the cable from the battery leads to the ignition inside the car, there is a slight rip in the black cord. I get to the other side of the car, lean in over the fender, and grab the cable. I stuff the wire back inside where it belongs. Next, I straighten up, go to the back seat of the car, and tear off a piece of the duct tape I'm using to stop a rip in the upholstery from spreading. I take the piece of tape with me back to the front of the car, lean back in, and wrap it around the split, sealing the break with the wire firmly back inside. I climb back in the car, turn the ignition key, and the Toyota kicks over like a bronco coming out of the starting gate.

Three hundred bucks for a bad Lamsky. Yeah, right.

Ten minutes later, I'm at Herman's.

"Are you over your crisis?"

He sits at his table, behind two laptops, eating prunes by the handful, and swigging 5-Hour Energy. "I'll do anything to clear that out of my system," he tells me.

I'm not sticking around to see the expulsion. I ask him two questions. He gives me two answers. "Thanks, Herman."

"Thank you, Sherlock."

I drive home.

Two seconds in the door, I'm at *The Original Carlo.* I fill out a few more cards and remove every card on the artwork. I page through the cards in my hand and find the one I want. I place it in the center of the picture, right over the red roof of the barn. And instead of lining the other cards up in rows, I place the remainder in a circle around the first card. Pretty soon I have another circle around the first circle and another circle around the second. When all the cards are out of my hand, and push-pinned back up, I stand back, take it all in, and smile. It resembles a smiling sun over a too yellow background.

I call my girls. I talk to Care but don't speak to Kelly. I know I'm the last person she needs to hear from. Tough being a dad.

I call Romo. "You still have Max on ice?" I ask.

"He's freezing."

"But you haven't booked him?"

"No."

I tell Romo what he needs to do and where he's got to be, and he complains that he and his wife are competing in the finals of the second annual Chicago FBI's Bocce Ball Tournament this evening.

"You want the Boise job or not?" I ask.

"I'll be there early."

I call Tiffany. "Everybody coming tonight?"

"All in."

"Even Sterling Sheckle?"

"He can't wait to get his six million back."

"Anybody give you a hard time?"

"No," Tiffany says. "Matter of fact, Ling Lew almost jumped through the phone when I invited him."

CHAPTER 22

I'm the last one to enter the office, and one step inside, I have to smile. Positioning oneself, it's so important in corporate America.

Sterling S. Sheckle sits at the head of his conference table. It's Saturday in the early evening, but he's wearing one of his ill-fitting suits as if to say, "In my business, there is no such thing as a weekend."

"Stretch the Truth" De Ruth is seated not far from him, bending his ear with what I will assume are tales of his successes on his behalf. Rosemary Sheckle sits mid table, not too close but not too far from her absent-yet-there husband. C. Franklin Witherington is in the far corner, leaning against the window like a prizefighter waiting for the bell to ring. Chester is on the other side of the room, as far away from any action that may or may not take place. Agent Romo sits Max down across from Rosemary and stands right behind him as if he's guarding his prisoner from attempting to break free. Lloyd Holler sits at the edge of the table, sniffling into a wet hanky; what else in new? Ling Lew follows Tiffany around like a lap dog, asking, "So, what do you like to do for fun?" Tiffany, who is busy passing out canapés and nibbles, sees me come in the room and gives me a look that says, "Help, I got creep on me like béarnaise on a filet."

"Welcome, everyone. I'm sorry if I am disrupting your weekend, but I have good news and bad news for everyone, and I thought you'd like to hear it as soon as possible."

"I was told you had my six million dollars, Sherlock," Sterling speaks first.

"No, you were told I found your money. You'll be first on the list after I get through a few matters of housekeeping."

"Well, hurry up."

"Chester," I ask, "how is Claire doing?"

"Better."

"Hear that Sterling?"

Mr. Wonderful gives me an odd look.

"Ling Lew..." I pause until his eyes come off Tiffany, and he looks my way. "Leslie Ambrose says 'Hello.' He's in Antigua spending some of the money he won last week. Leslie was the one who borrowed the sixty grand from petty cash. He needed seed money for his ante into a private game of Internet *League of Legends*. Evidently, all that unhacking of Chinese threats got his hands in such good shape, and he blew the competition away." I pause. "But you knew that, didn't you?"

"No."

Computer guys are lousy liars.

"Ling, if I were you, and I knew something about computers, I'd refortify your computer system. You got more holes in your firewall fence than the border fence between the US and Mexico."

"Okay," Ling responds, takes his eyes off me, and says to Tiffany, "how about joining me to plug a few holes, Tiffany?"

Tiffany's eyes go skyward. "Oh my God."

Sheckle speaks up again. "Come on, Sherlock, I got people to see, places to go, and things to do. Where's my six million dollars?"

"All over the place," I inform him. "Some I might be able to get back."

"Not good enough. I want my money."

"The money is waiting to become a tax write-off."

"What?" Lloyd Holler yells out. "You told me you'd bring me the bacon so I could fry this tax cheat."

"Wait, Lloyd, you can't start your burners just yet."

"When?"

"Soon."

Lloyd spits into his handkerchief.

I back away from the edge of the table where I stood and start to pace around the room. "You know, I looked at this case from every angle I could and came up with nothing. At first I thought it was a computer hacker who took the money. Then I thought it was Chester keeping two sets of books. Witherington admits to doing financial gymnastics while working for Mr. Sheckle, but that seems to be par for this golf course. Stretch here has been lining up questionable charities that have made him quite wealthy."

"I have not," Stretch yells out.

"Yeah, you have. You've been filling your pockets with donations for years." I pause. "You might want to make a note of that Agent Romo."

"Bingo."

"I even thought it was you, Rosemary."

"Me?"

"Mild-mannered housewife by day but corporate big shot at night."

"Me?"

"I suspected all of you, but I was wrong on all counts."

They all search each other's faces.

"It was you, Sterling. You did it."

Sterling almost levitates out of his chair. "I stole my own six million? Are you out of your mind?"

"It's not that you stole the money; it's what you did to make the money."

"This makes no sense," Sterling snaps at me.

"The only thing I don't understand, Mr. Sheckle, is why do you need any more money. You got so much now, even Tiffany couldn't spend it all in her lifetime."

"I don't know about that, Mr. Sherlock."

"It's not that you're doing any good for the world or helping people in need; you're just accumulating more and more for the simple reason that you can."

"What's the matter with that?" Sheckle asks.

"In my book, plenty. Who needs that much money?" I ask, and hope Tiffany won't answer the question.

"I do."

"Why?"`

"You don't get it, do you, Sherlock?" Sheckle says. "It's not the money, it's the winning."

"You agree with that, Mr. Witherington?" I ask.

"It's a game; that's all it is. And nobody plays the game better than Sterling Sheckle. I have to admit."

"And Sterling, you did win, didn't you?"

"I always win."

"You're too big to be touched. The government has given you a Free Pass to keep your game alive."

"Don't be so sure," Lloyd Holler hollers.

"It's hard to tell you all this, but you've all been set up by Mr. Wonderful here." I make my way over to the idiot brother. "Max, your brother put you in charge of the Costa Rican Tide pools because the oil's run out, and the pool is going to be unfit for swimming real soon."

"What does that mean?"

I point to the next on my list. "Witherington, those accounting moves on Mortgage for the Masses are going to bite you in the butt as soon as Lloyd Holler here gets a hold of them. You could be on the line for some real dastardly doings."

Lloyd quits sniffling long enough to smile. Witherington frowns.

I saunter over to the only woman in the mix. "Rosemary, you didn't know that you're being used as a corporate puppet?"

"Me?"

"You've been voting absentee in your husband's favor on a number of financial transactions."

"I have?"

"Yep."

"My God, where have I been?" she asks incredulously.

"Gardening," I tell her.

"And Stretch," I get to the end of my list, "if you think you made a killing on those charity kickbacks, you have no clue. The insider information Sterling has been able to garner has given his cash register bigger 'ca-chings' than you could ever imagine."

Stretch's Adam's apple bounces faster than a Michael Jordan dribble.

"And by the way, Agent Romo, nothing will shoot your star faster into the FBI sky than busting a few no-gooder charities." I hand over Chester's list with certain organizations highlighted in bright yellow.

"Boise, here I come."

"And what are you going to do about all this, Mr. Sherlock?" a smug Sheckle asks me. "The feds can't touch me, I'm going to make even more money, and now, I even have more write-offs to file."

"What am I going to do?" I pause. "Nothing."

All eyes in the room look my way.

"There's nothing I can do except tell Mr. Richmond not to pay out on your claim."

"Way to go, Mr. Sherlock," Tiffany yells out. "Daddy's gonna love it."

There is a bit of calm or disbelief in the room. I have shot everyone in the foot except the guy who deserved the bullet.

Sheckle laughs. "So, I win."

"Yes, congratulations, Mr. So-called Wonderful."

And, just like that, it's over. "Thank you all for coming. And please thank Tiffany for putting out such a nice spread."

"Thank you, Tiffany," Ling says. "You're wonderful. How about if I return the compliment? Dessert at my place?"

"Oh my God."

The partygoers file out one by one; nobody except Romo and Lloyd seem happy. Chester is last to leave.

"Excuse me, Chester. Did you drive in, or did you take the train?" I ask.

"Train."

"Let me give you a lift."

"I'd appreciate that."

Sterling Sheckle stays in his office. He must have some work to catch up on. No one bids him an "adieu."

Tiffany catches up with me on my way to the elevator. Ling follows her like a bad smell. "Mr. Sherlock, you have to help me get rid of this guy. He's like a pimple I can't reach to squeeze."

CHAPTER 23

It's a sweet sound indeed hearing the Toyota kick over and ignite its 100 or so horsepower.

We're almost on the expressway when Chester says, "You really thought it was me?"

"Yes, Mr. Wonderful, I did."

"Excuse me."

"You don't mind if I call you Mr. Wonderful, do you?"

Chester stares at the traffic.

"You've been giving away Sheckle's money for years, haven't you?"

"Just the money he told me to give away." Chester says hardly convincingly.

"No, you've been adding to the total for years."

Chester's silence is his admission.

"Did you ever add it all up?"

"No."

"Millions, wasn't it?"

Silence.

"How did you do it?"

"It was actually quite simple," Chester admits. "There was so much money floating around and so much accounting fraud, it was easy to move a few million into the charity column each year."

"And you would have never been caught, but something went wrong, didn't it?"

"Yes."

"Do you know what?"

"I suspected it was something Witherington or that awful DeRuth fellow discovered."

I don't comment. Instead, I ask, "Why did you do it?"

"Nobody needs that much money," Chester says. "Millions were piling up in Sterling's pockets. Nothing was being accomplished with it. No good whatsoever was coming out of it. It was a crime. There was no purpose. He was making money from the people who could least afford it. I knew most of Sheckle's charitable donations were for his own good, so I decided to do something right with the money. I didn't hurt anybody; in fact, Sheckle never even noticed." He pauses to add one final point, "Mr. Sherlock, I believe I did a lot of good."

"I'm sure you did, Mr. Wonderful."

He sits quietly for a few seconds and asks, "Why didn't you mention my transgressions in the meeting?"

"I thought about it, but I couldn't come up with a good enough reason to out you, Chester."

"Thank you."

"Don't thank me. Thank this twisted conscience I have."

We reach his home. I park in the driveway. "Mind if I come in and check on Claire?"

"She'd like that."

We enter the house and go right the bedroom where Claire is reading her Bible. She's looking pretty good; the rosiness is back in her cheeks. We chitchat for a few minutes. Then I ask Chester, "You know what I'd really love? A hot cup of that Chester tea."

"Most certainly, Mr. Sherlock."

Chester leaves the two of us alone.

"You're very lucky to have a husband as good as Chester. I bet you're going to miss him."

"What?"

"He's dying, isn't he?"

She doesn't answer.

"Prostate cancer."

Claire's mood changes from the sun dawning to the sun setting on a gloomy night. "I begged him to get checked, but he said he hated doctors and refused to go."

"That's the reason you've been so stressed out?"

She's silent, just like her husband.

"Plus, working all those years for a brother who is such a schmuck doesn't make life easy, does it?"

"No. Big brother thought he was doing us a favor giving us a lifetime job. It turned out to be a curse."

"You knew all about the money Chester was donating in Sterling's name."

"We did it together."

"And you were skimming money off the top by canceling checks to pay for Chester's care, weren't you?"

"We're not on Medicare yet, and Sterling wouldn't put us on the SSS policy. I had no choice."

I hear the whistle blow on the kettle.

"Claire," I say to her with all the sincerity I can muster, "I really did appreciate your offer. If there is one person who could use a hundred grand, it's yours truly."

"I didn't know what else to do."

"I know the feeling."

"Are you going to turn us in?"

"To the police or to Sheckle?" I ask.

"You pick."

I hesitate for a few seconds. "Probably not, I get the feeling you two have suffered enough, but you should find a way to give some of his money back."

Claire sighs a breath of relief and puts on a happier, stress-free face. Chester comes back into the room carrying a steaming hot cup of tea, which he hands to me.

I take two sips and put it down on the nightstand. "I should be going."

"So soon?" Chester says.

"Claire needs her rest," I say and add, "So do you, Chester."

"Thank you, Sherlock," Claire says.

"You're welcome."

***

Just as the Toyota kicks over like a NASCAR car, the weird sound comes out of my phone. I fumble around until I get the phone out of my pocket, see whom the text is from, and read the one word: *Help*.

I quickly text back: *I'm on my way*.

A half hour later I see her sitting barefoot on the steps in front of the mall. Her new shoes lay to her left. Her cheeks are red. The front of her new blouse is soaking wet. I park illegally, run out of the car, reach her side, and put my arm around my oldest daughter. We sit, not speaking for I don't know how long.

"It was awful, Daddy."

"Sorry."

Her tears run down her cheeks. "I knew it was going to be bad when I had to buy my own Twizzlers."

"How bad?"

"We get to the theater and all his friends are there."

"Why?"

"I don't know," she says, sniffling. "But it's not just boys, there's this one girl there, an eighth grader I hardly know who comes right up to Cameron, starts talking, and doesn't stop." She stops to choke back a few tears. "And you know what he does?"

"No."

"He talks to her. Pretty soon, it's like I'm not even there. The two are chatting away like a couple of Elmos, and I'm standing there looking stupid."

I give her my handkerchief to wipe away her tears.

"We go into the movie and she sits on one side of him while I'm on the other. I can't believe it, Dad."

"Then what?"

"When I saw them holding hands, I got up, left, and called you."

"Thanks."

"Why are you thanking me?"

"Someday, you'll understand."

With my arm still around her, I stand her up. "Come on, I'll take you back to your mother's house."

Kelly walks slowly by my side, holding my hand as if she has reverted to a six-year-old. For me it feels nice.

"Can we stop somewhere—I'm hungry," she asks and climbs into the front passenger seat.

"Sure."

I put the car in gear, and we drive out of the mall and into traffic.

"Well, dating can only get better from here, Kelly."

"I hope so."

"It will."

"I can't figure out why it happened, Dad. I was so sure."

"I have a feeling Cameron was a little nervous, so he met up with the troops for moral support. The girl who showed up was probably easier for him to talk to than you, so he took the low road. Guys at fourteen are usually more insecure than girls at fourteen; trust me on this one."

"But it's not fair."

"Get used to it, Kelly. Dating is seldom going to be fair, kinda like life."

"But come Monday, I'll be the laughingstock of the school. I'll have to eat my lunch in a bathroom stall so no one will see me."

"You didn't do anything wrong. Show people it didn't bother you, that you're a big enough person to let stuff like this roll right off your back."

"But I could be scarred for the rest of my middle school life, Dad."

"This I can assure you, Kelly: In two days, it will all be forgotten."

"You sure?"

"Positive."

We travel a little farther. Her tears dry, the redness subsides, and the sniffles cease sniffling. "Can we stop and get a malt?" she asks, pointing to a McDonald's up the road.

"As long as you promise not to tell your sister."

CHAPTER 24

The letter came on Monday morning. It was in a plain, white envelope addressed to Mr. Richard Sherlock. It read:

The Chicago Board of Realtors regrets to inform you that your test scores were not sufficient for securing a real estate seller's license.

Remember, if at first you don't succeed try, try again.

I'll bet Al Zazou is in charge of sending out the reject letters.

I guess it's back to the new career drawing board.

Oh jeesh.

THE END.

Thank you very much for reading The Case of Mr. Wonderful. I certainly hope you enjoyed my novel, and if you did, please let others know of your good reading fortune. The easiest way being through cyberspace via social media networks such as Amazon, Facebook, LinkedIn, Goodreads, and Twitter. Please put in a good review to the above and to your friends, contacts, and fellow readers. It will be greatly appreciated.

About Jim Stevens

Jim Stevens was born in the East, grew up in the West, schooled in the Northwest and spent twenty-three winters in the Midwest. Jim Stevens has been writing for over thirty years. Usually without much success, but for some reason he keeps writing. Jim started writing TV series specs in the 1970s and went hungry. He segued into spec movie scripts and starved. He went into the corporate world for a twenty-five year career in broadcasting and advertising, but just couldn't drop his pencil. He found time to write plays in the Chicago theater scene, wrote, produced, and directed numerous short films, videos, and TV commercials, created TV pilots, and even optioned a few movie scripts that never saw the glare of the Klieg lights.

Jim has been writing novels for the past four years. His Richard Sherlock Whodunit series has ranked him in the top 10% of Amazon authors. He is also the author of WHUPPED, a reverse romantic comedy from many different points of view. His most recent novel, Hell No, We Won't Go, A Novel of Peace, Love, War, and Football is his first writing of a 'serious' nature.

Jim loves to hear from his readers, especially the ones who enjoy his books. He can be reached at JimStevensWriter@gmail.com